KINNEY ROAD
A Novel

Thomas Preiss

KINNEY ROAD

Published independently by Thomas Preiss

Cover design by Thomas Preiss / ChatGPT

ISBN: 978-0-9798620-6-9

LCCN: 2026912772

Printed in the United States of America

Peralta Publishing, LLC

KINNEY ROAD

Foreword

There are novels that tell a story, and there are novels that ask something of the reader. *Kinney Road* does both—and then goes further. It asks us to slow down, to listen, and to consider what remains when the noise of modern life falls away.

At its heart, this is a story about a man in motion. Mitchell Walker walks not simply cross the physical landscape of America's forgotten roads, but across the interior terrain of grief, memory, and redemption. His journey unfolds along the rugged beauty of California's northern coast, where wind, water, and time shape both land and soul. Yet what makes this novel singular is not only where Mitchell travels, but what travels with him: love that has outlived death, questions that refuse easy answers, and a quiet, persistent belief that meaning can still be found in a fractured world.

And yet, for all its scope, this is an intimate book. It is about a man who loved deeply, lost everything, and continues forward anyway. It is about the possibility that love does not end, but changes form. It is about the idea that even in a world that feels increasingly unrecognizable, there are still roads—quiet, unmarked, and waiting—that can lead us back to something true.

A character map can be found on page 483 if needed. Careful, there are spoilers in this list.

*To my dear family and friends who continue to support
me as a writer,*

and

*to all who still listen
for that one beloved voice in the wind.*

"The clearest way into the Universe is through a forest wilderness."

— John Muir

"What lies behind us and what lies before us are tiny matters compared to what lies within us."

— Ralph Waldo Emerson

Kinney Road – M.W. Epigraph Roadmap

A northbound journey along California's Highway 1
through Sonoma and Mendocino counties

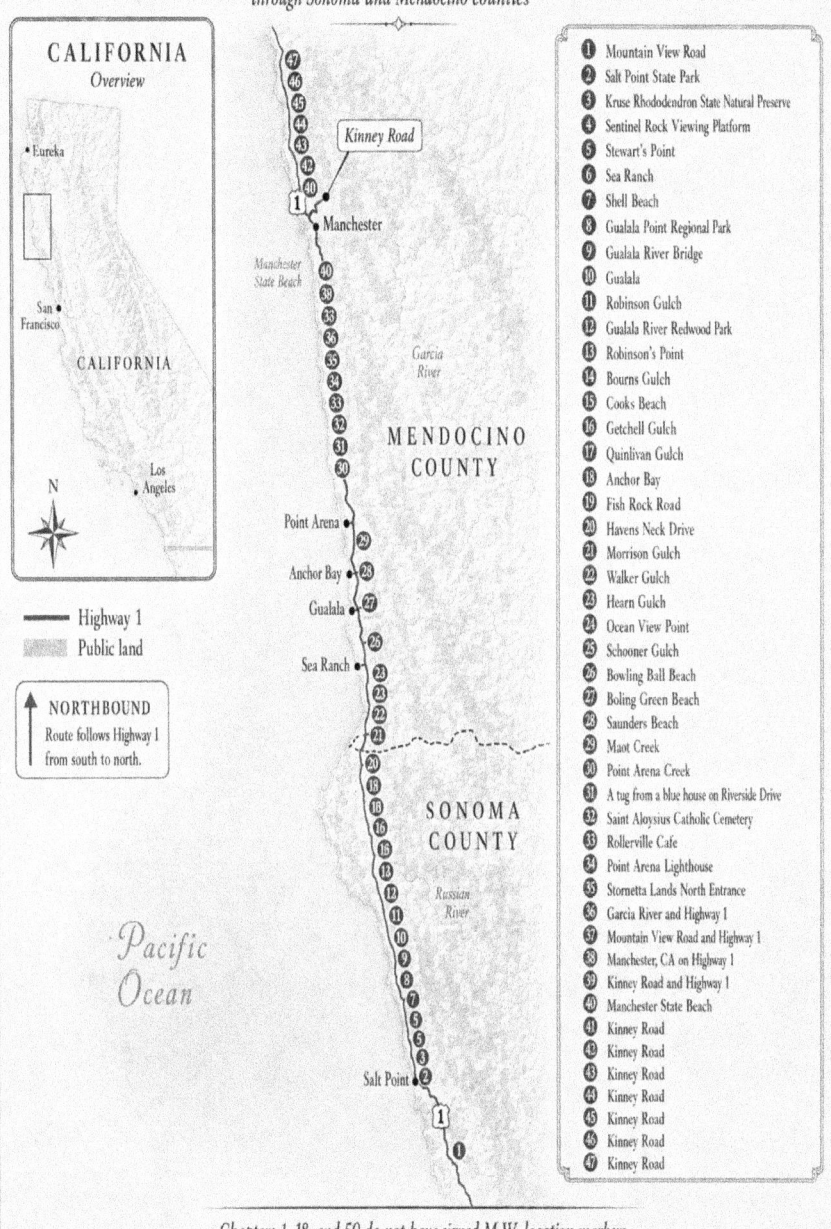

CALIFORNIA
Overview

• Eureka

CALIFORNIA

San •
Francisco

Los
• Angeles

N

Kinney Road

① 1

• Manchester

Manchester
State Beach

Garcia
River

**MENDOCINO
COUNTY**

Point Arena •

Anchor Bay •

Gualala •

Sea Ranch •

**SONOMA
COUNTY**

Russian
River

Salt Point •

Pacific
Ocean

―― Highway 1
▨ Public land

NORTHBOUND
Route follows Highway 1
from south to north.

❶ Mountain View Road
❷ Salt Point State Park
❸ Kruse Rhododendron State Natural Preserve
❹ Sentinel Rock Viewing Platform
❺ Stewart's Point
❻ Sea Ranch
❼ Shell Beach
❽ Gualala Point Regional Park
❾ Gualala River Bridge
❿ Gualala
⓫ Robinson Gulch
⓬ Gualala River Redwood Park
⓭ Robinson's Point
⓮ Bourns Gulch
⓯ Cooks Beach
⓰ Getchell Gulch
⓱ Quinlivan Gulch
⓲ Anchor Bay
⓳ Fish Rock Road
⓴ Havens Neck Drive
㉑ Morrison Gulch
㉒ Walker Gulch
㉓ Hearn Gulch
㉔ Ocean View Point
㉕ Schooner Gulch
㉖ Bowling Ball Beach
㉗ Boling Green Beach
㉘ Saunders Beach
㉙ Maot Creek
㉚ Point Arena Creek
㉛ A tug from a blue house on Riverside Drive
㉜ Saint Aloysius Catholic Cemetery
㉝ Rollerville Cafe
㉞ Point Arena Lighthouse
㉟ Stornetta Lands North Entrance
㊱ Garcia River and Highway 1
㊲ Mountain View Road and Highway 1
㊳ Manchester, CA on Highway 1
㊴ Kinney Road and Highway 1
㊵ Manchester State Beach
㊶ Kinney Road
㊷ Kinney Road
㊸ Kinney Road
㊹ Kinney Road
㊺ Kinney Road
㊻ Kinney Road
㊼ Kinney Road

*Chapters 1, 18, and 50 do not have signed M.W. location markers.
Repeated Kinney Road entries are preserved.*

Prologue: From Red Walker's memorial service in Prescott, Arizona:

Red was a woman who lived out of her time. She sang songs written outside of the era for which she lived, possessing the rare quality and ability to transport the souls of her listeners to the hopeful, joyful planes of life. Her uplifting voice brought heartfelt considerations of a nobler existence. Her voice had, within its lyrical reach, the entrance to heaven intoned within, and made plausible, to all who heard her, the great spiritual stories of the millenniums. Her voice led each of us, past our mind's partition, into our unique Emerald City, and our special understanding of what heaven might be.

-Presley Farmer

ONE

_____

John Doe No. 24 had a straw hat he loved to wear. He carried his collection of rings, glasses, and silverware with him everywhere in a backpack. He danced to the vibrations of the holiday music rumbling off the cement floors and steel rafters in the hospital cafeteria, unable to see or hear the celebration going on all around him.

_____

In Memory Of . . .

A memorial service had started in Point Arena, a small town on the northern California coast. A modern electric sign placed at the entrance of the one-hundred-year-old church said: "All are welcome." Without acknowledging the name on the marquee, Mitchell Walker went in.

Mitchell felt compelled to go into the church, even though he was a stranger to the town and family holding the memorial service. In a distant call from his heart Mitchell felt that this stranger's memorial might make him feel closer to his deceased wife.

The sparsely populated place of worship held a subdued group of friends and family of the deceased. A quiet manner of conversation greeted him.

Songs were heard that helped memories and pain find each other as slow-dancing partners of life passing. A weathered stranger, a man who looked to be in his late fifties or early sixties, Mitchell, took a seat on a chair that was lost in the hall's subdued lighting. He was relieved to be removed from the grief.

His thoughts centered on a chance of finding his beloved Red in a next life. Tender recollection and loss filled him. An image of her appeared before him as brilliant sparkle of color and sound.

Mitchell heard an antiquated male voice whisper: "I'm Charles Hoyt. I haven't seen you around these parts." Hoyt extended his hand to Mitchell in greeting. Mitchell wondered if Hoyt made a habit of conversing with strangers.

Mitchell pulled back from his daydream about Red to suspect Hoyt might be the host of the memorial. The old man found a seat adjacent to Mitchell. He shook Hoyt's hand.

"I watched WWII newsreels from the projection booth in my movie house," Hoyt said gingerly, assessing whether his company was welcomed. "You may have seen it around the corner . . . down the hill . . . as you passed through town on Main Street." He looked at Mitchell expectantly.

Mitchell took note of the old man's profile, a centenarian if he was a day. The grief that registered in the wrinkled skin around the old man's eyes confirmed Mitchell's impression of Hoyt.

There are too many years lived in this cold, hard world, Mitchell thought.

Hoyt's large, ancient hands wrapped themselves around a worn cane handle, and he stared ahead, through a tear, at a fading

4

black and white family photo arranged on a small round table standing in the center of the room, covered by a white, threadbare lace tablecloth. Of those pictured, only the old man remained. The tear suggested to Mitchell that like he, the old man's life had laid claims that were beyond his understanding.

Wiping his eye, Hoyt looked at Mitchell to see if he was listening, and then turned his gaze downward, and rotated his cane slowly in half turns.

"I worked as the projectionist when I couldn't find someone from our local labor pool," he said. "I changed movie reels when the cue mark appeared in the upper right corner of the film. Remember that?" He looked at Mitchell again, to see if he was listening.

Mitchell nodded his head, and then felt his mind shift, as he wondered why the stranger was talking to him.

"It was between reel changes and the many other settings a projectionist must keep a tight grip that I found my chair cocked up against the projection wall, peering through a spare projection window, watching movies. I discovered the silver screen through the blue cigar smoke and artificial darkness of a mid-afternoon matinee. A fantastic world full of adventure, full of humanity, and my imagination. I wrote stories from their inspiration. I have always enjoyed scribbling down short ditties about this or that. I wrote scripts and poems and won the love of my life through my writing.

Mary is still with me," he said, pointing at his heart and the ceiling of the church.

Mitchell's new acquaintance continued, "When I started banking for our family business, when I stopped writing, her happiness diminished. Don't get me wrong, we enjoyed the security my career provided, but on her death bed, she took my hand and stated quietly that she missed the man she fell in love with, the one who wrote her poetry, that set her imagining other worlds and other times."

After a pause, he said: "I miss the man I once was too. I miss connecting to a world of my imagination, and have often wished there was more of him, and less of the banker.

There was one more thing about running my family's projection booth that profoundly changed my life."

He looked Mitchell in the eyes and said, "It was the newsreels. It was the shocking film footage of so many things that were kept quiet during World War II.

"The worldwide suffering, the heartlessness, it sent horror-filled chills up and down my neck every time I watched them, yet I found I could not help but watch. One story saddened me, which, if you give me a minute, I will tell you more about.

"At this same period, at the end of WWII, I would see, almost on a weekly basis, a young woman, Mary, new to town, come in by herself and watch the show. I got to know Mary. I described the world's sorrow using a pencil and paper. I would give her these short stories and poems to read; we kept tabs on one of the people in those newsreel reports. He was a deaf and blind war orphan brought to this country from England. *John Doe No. 24* was the inspiration for my writing, and his situation sharpened my ability to communicate the nature of his world.

"It was *his* story that I wanted Mary to see, it was his story that became the poetry I penned upon her heart, his story that changed our world. And after we were married, we went to Jacksonville, Illinois, to find *John Doe No. 24*.

"We found him. He was well cared for at the orphanage, and by the intake nurse, who cried when we adopted the boy, this child orphaned by the war. The orphanage guessed his age to be about sixteen years old. Because he was unable to tell us what his name was, we decided to call him Louis.

He taught me many things," the old man said, pointing to the casket that Mitchell had assumed held the old man's beloved Mary.

This memorial is for the war orphan, Mitchell realized. He looked at the casket, and then back to the well-worn face of the old man, seeing for the first time Hoyt's timeless sky-blue eyes.

"He taught me how to love, how to be compassionate and patient with the ones I treasure, and how important it was to wait for the things I wanted.

"He taught me about the nature of time and how it pans out in unkind and ungenerous ways if I am not careful with it.

He taught me about people, and how to be wary, but not too judgmental of the lot of them.

He taught me how to hush my mind and let the spirit of nature claim me."

With his eyes closed, Hoyt continued, "most of all though, it was his story on the newsreels that brought Mary and I together as husband and wife. It was his spirit that inspired our long life together. We were married for sixty years."

Wiping his own tear away and feeling a lip quiver in admiration of this old man's life, its simplicity and its greatness, Mitchell wondered how the world could have missed his story.

"And now Louis sees and hears *both* the mother he lost in the war, and the mother, my wife, who raised him, together for the first time.

"I miss them terribly. They were my life: she, and our son."

Charles Hoyt turned toward Mitchell, put his aged hand on Walker's knee, and said, "Life is fickle. Love is the only thing that makes it worthwhile."

Slow but steady, the old man moved away from the quiet corner where Mitchell sat.

Mitchell made his way outside, pulled out the old pocket watch that his friend Presley Farmer had given him, the one that contained Red's ashes within a special compartment, a watch that stopped working the moment it changed hands, marking forever the time when Mitchell first stood upon the ground that held the rest of

Red's ashes. It was a watch never repaired; a watch that kept Mitchell close to his beloved. The watch had moved him further away from the actual passing of time to the fullness of comprehending timeless love.

As the old man's final words moved with Mitchell outside, he imagined the wind carry those same words through the cypress trees along Highway 1, turning into white butterflies in a visual array. Emanating from each was a sequence of harmonic notes, building one upon another, and heard only by Mitchell as the mellifluous and mystic sound of a soprano saxophone, rising into the soft blue sky. As he gazed upward, his thoughts returned to his beloved, to someday, when through chance, he would find her as the winged embodiment of an angel, sparkling with indescribable color and song.

———————

My own true love,

The snow falls past my eyes. The flakes follow the lines of pine, from the sky above to the hair on your head. You move through the trees, clutching tightly your memory of me. The cold shakes you not. You stop. You look up at the snow as it falls toward your face, and I see you, seeing me. You observe my red hair hanging long, and through your experience of my life. Let not the blood dry between us. Let it bind you to me in longing, and in living, as the days begin and the songs end.

You transcend the road. It has become your home, my Mitchell. I want to be your spirit angel. I want you to find me in your hands, and then in your arms, kissing me as this age ends, briefly, as we become again, the day's creation, and the day's dark, humbled end.

Your forever love, your Red

TWO

———

On a mountain road, a winding dangerous pass through the
ranges from here to civilization, a small, one-lane bridge, built
long ago and high above, spans a year-round river far below.
One waits on either end of the bridge before crossing, to ensure
the other side will remain clear once arrived.
One could stop in the middle, view the river far below and take a
moment to understand the imagery found there.

Life is full of signs, full of arrows pointing to the truth. Largely,
we ignore them.

M. W. - Mountain View Road

———

Mitchell thought endlessly about his wife. He lost her years ago. At present, the how and the why mattered not in the living of each day. The white butterflies, the wind in the tall cypress trees, the message heard as the old man left his side at the memorial, and the sound of a sweet saxophone playing in his mind, had all been ushered further down Highway 1, with the passing of cars and motorcycles streaming by, yet the vision of her as an iridescent angel remained. He thought of her in heaven eternally and had banked his soul in the hope that he would see her again there. That is, if he got there.

Mitchell Walker was just that, a walker. After Red's death, and after taking in and raising a troubled boy, a young teenager named Zac, he sold everything he owned and turned his back to the chaos and calamity of living with today's pressures and expectations, which had worsened exponentially with the advent of the Internet. He wondered if the correlation between recent longer life, the duality of living the complex digital life, coupled with ten thousand more ways to die, were feeding the techno–industrial tornado. He answered *yes* and said goodbye.

The walking had begun on the Hassayampa River, in the Bradshaw Mountains of Central Arizona, years ago. He had put thousands of miles under foot since leaving that area, and all that happened there.

He had walked the breadth of his country from coast to coast, on old roads and byways no longer used by the modern world; their slow pace offering no release in society's hurry to get from one place to another. These forgotten roads, and their quiet ways, were Mitchell's home now, bounded by fallen, centuries-old fences that held nothing back, save the ghostly outlines of how life was once lived.

Mitchell having forgotten his age, often saw himself walking on the other side of fences newly erected and painted, moving among the tall grasses, his outline lost on the horizon, strolling toward the one he loved, the one who was taken from him. She would run forward, wrapping her thin arms around his neck, kissing him.

His mind's eye would follow those moments of longing out on the plain, back to his feet, standing on the edge of a byway, realizing that he must turn from the love seen there and begin his walking again.

Emerson had written that walking (or any kind of manual labor) connected humanity to the world. Mitchell felt that connection. He raised the palms of his hands to the sky, and thanked Nature for his byway life. It sustained him. His breath and the horizon were one. Daily, calm resurrected him from his past, a wasteland of death and ash, this death and this ash turned inward, this inwardness his truth. He knew who he was.

Years ago, the world thought it knew him too. Through pictures and stories in newspapers, talk radio, TV shows, network news programs, the spins of the techno–industrial platform that long abandoned the objective journalist Walter Cronkite's character as its guide, and the judge in each listener, laid him out flat, exposing his life and actions that night as bloody, barbaric revenge.

The question remains; asked at his trial to a jury of his peers; *what would you have done if you found her the way he found her?*

Other answers and reactions to his life are not important. He has said he would do it again, he does endlessly in thought, if it would bring her back to him.

He has the old roads now to believe in and to walk upon. He now wanders from town to town, meeting people who have their own pain to express, and he listens as they do. They become his friends in these pages of death and life, and he remembers, when the wind blows against him, what they have shared; their words help him to keep his own heart on a straight and narrow path of simplicity, which now requires him to find a place to bed down for the night.

Highway 1 was quiet this night. A spot under a bank of cypress was his bed. Manchester State Park, home to a five-mile-long stretch of beach, was his bedroom. The pounding surf roared in a muted fashion, throughout the night, its rhythm leading Mitchell into the resting quiet of a tired mind, where thoughts of the old man, his wife, and their war-orphaned son took hold. The stars had shown brightly, even just above the fall of the earth's horizon out to sea. In the dozing moments before sleep, the stars represented life on earth, and the hundreds of billions of souls that have come and gone, in the fashion of the old man and his family.

There has been eternal kindness and generosity in the history of man, he thought. *All of it going unsung as the world marches on, at never-ending, ever-expanding speed, their faces shaded unrecognizable by a growing and caustic cynicism, borne by unprecedented slavery to a new kind of ghost, the Industrial Revolution's bastard child, the techno–digital world. The scramble, the speed and flow of both information and misinformation, mostly useless and/or false, of manufactured color and synthesized sound, of addiction and madness, of cruelty and shock, of darker things that knew only a very limited voice and outline in an analog world.*

We now know too much. The apple tree's roots and leaves have spread to every crack and corner of human existence. We are all Eve. We all know things that have diminished our souls, and left us as splintered, fractured pieces, unable to grasp the elements of our natures, lopping limb from heart, original thought from spirit, faith from the mystical spin of our universe, fashioning so much less than what we fashioned before the simple elements of air, water, earth, and fire were mechanically pressurized into steam, condensing our simple lives into chronic, explosive change . . .

Mitchell shut down his mind's wandering rhetoric, appearing from nowhere, that could ruin the simple observation of stars falling over the horizon.

His last thought before sleep was a question. It was *his* question, **the** question, its terrible truth hidden within it: *Is that the reason why I was not there for her that night? Was I distracted?*

During the night, he awoke to a spirit keeping warm by the glow of leftover light and heat, still emanating from the campfire. She said her name was Rosalie, and she looked to be a woman of many long years, who had kept the length and strength of her life in her extended grey hair. Mitchell understood that Rosalie had every blade of grass, and every heartbeat of every animal within her. Her presence was large in the campfire light.

Rosalie spoke to Mitchell about two others: a young man, no more than twenty-two, and a spirit, who had spent the previous night in the park, under the line of cypress. The first, Leo, came from the corporate world in the south, probably Los Angeles. The other was the spirit of a local man, missing for many years now, named Gunnar.

She described Leo's countenance as being one and the same with his faded business attire, his expensive business suit and shoes out of place in the campfire light. His expression was one of betrayal, and in his eyes, Rosalie found a small, perpendicular dash blinking back at her. His bone-thin face suggested a lack of nourishment, so Rosalie presented to him a plate made of her compassion. She said his countenance then suggested gratitude, but his eyes remained as frames of the pulsing dash, symbolic of what he had recently left behind.

———

My dear Mitchell,

The subtle grain of oak across the table frames my memory of us. Our friendship flourished. Our laughter was the grace that saved me. I will know forever the moment when we first touched. The tips of your fingers came close to mine, and on that oak table was the very instant my heart was to become yours. You were to be my true love, a love awash with tides and winds. Let me know you for all time. My tears now flow. They turn to rain, falling to the ground around your motion in a world I can no longer know. Please feel them on your skin, as you once felt my skin on yours, with the grains of oak framing that which binds us.

Your forever love, your Red.

THREE

_____

How sad it is that we have lost our awe of the world.

Pressed flat against a plastic covering that suspends liquid crystals, forming unfathomably clear pictures in a constant stream of digital color and sound, the Internet renders each of our senses further from their natural place.

No longer needed, our legs and imaginations are suspended by the flatness of the world in front of us.

Nature calls for our return, with our children, without our endless lists and possessions, into the sprays of color and sound found on any outdoor corner of the world around us.

M. W. - Salt Point State Park

_____

"But *Logan's Run* has turned out to miss the mark as a precursor of futuristic society," Amy said emphatically to Linda, her mother, driving down Main Street in Point Arena. They passed a short line of locals waiting to enter the town's only movie theater, enroute to their home from school, where Amy had just won a debate on the effectiveness of texting in social situations. She had argued that hand-held communication devices were helping, not hindering, social interaction among her age group.

The lanky, sixteen-year-old Point Arena High School sophomore had, in recent months, sprouted above her mother's head. Of above average stature herself, Linda's late-thirties attractiveness was apparent in her daughter, though Amy felt the braces she wore cancelled anything her freshly attained tallness would transmit to the boys in her school. They also shared sandy-blond hair and hazel eyes and were referred to often as sisters.

It had been some time since Linda had heard that compliment.

"No one looks at each other anymore," Linda responded. "I could tell if a boy was being sincere, just by looking into his eyes. In *Logan's Run,* it would have been impossible to portray its beauty and truth, using hand-held smart phones. The expressions of actors do more for the storyline than dialogue ever did. Can you imagine a movie with actors emoting by texting? They, and the audience get none of the narrative. The story is lost."

"Yes, but *not* looking people in the eye gives me more freedom to *really* say what's on my mind," Amy argued.

"To speak without immediate consequence or response leads to an incomplete conversation," Linda said. "A wall is built between the spoken word and the listening ear. It's like a voice without its spirit, like an ear listening to echo. Smart phone communication takes away meaning between one soul to another. Somehow, this form of talking is removing the spark, the spontaneity, the emotion of language, which is no longer evolving, only repeating. Smart phones are squelching original instinct, like the first spark of love, or the first awe of inspiration. The spoken word, or the traditional written word, has the rolling effect of life

22

cascading through all existence. Smart phones inhibit truth, and express anger, joy, love, spirituality, and insight with acronyms, or combinations of letters and numbers, in their most basic form."

Amy was amazed by her mother's thought processes. She knew her mother was intelligent, but this conversation surprised her. "Mom, where do you come up with this stuff?"

"I don't know," Linda said. "I feel inspired tonight. I feel like something dramatic is going to change our way of life, something scary."

"What could possibly change?" Amy asked.

"I don't know Amy, but I feel as if I am already immersed in it. Change is wonderful; it usually brings out the best in your mother."

"Immersed in what?" a concerned Amy asked.

"It's an energy I have felt before, but is it rarely this intense," her mom responded. "I'm filled with a sense of adventure and dread and can't seem to let either emotion find a landing in my heart."

At once, both driver and passenger were surprised to find that they had arrived at their house. The orange glow of small-town streetlamps scattered familiar shadows into the cab of their car.

"Well, we're here," Linda said. "Besides, how do you think you won your debate tonight? It sure as heck wasn't because you texted your points. You spoke to them, with face and hand gestures, and by emphasizing your meaning."

"Mom," Amy said. "Wait a minute, what is this talk of change?"

Linda turned off the engine to her dated Honda Accord. She took a deep breath.

"I don't know, Amy. I feel like something is lingering around some corner, something is pending, coming toward us, and it excites me but terrifies me too." She looked at the living room window of her home, a place she had shared with her daughter and third husband, Amy's second stepdad, for many years.

A single tear gathered in Linda's left eye. She wiped it quickly, without attracting her daughter's attention.

"Paul has changed." Linda finally mustered the words she longed to say to her daughter but had always elected not to, letting the statement's shame-filled implications prevent her from speaking it. She considered this an excuse to give up on her marriage.

They sat looking out the windshield of the car. The change in Paul was not lost on Amy. She had seen the man become bitter about his life and could tell that the routine of marriage and fatherhood had hardened him, letting Jack Daniels destroy the only connection he might have had to a meaningful existence.

"I know," Amy said.

Those many long moments, after Linda spoke: *Paul has changed,* and before Amy responded with: *I know,* had now joined with the vehicle's stale air. They had attached to the walls of Amy's memory as paintings that portrayed the cold, hard realities of this small-town girl, the daughter of a small-town mother, paintings illuminated by streetlights, long ago abandoned by the small town's budget deficit, paintings that portrayed her changing life.

"Have you made a decision about him?" Amy asked her mother.

"Not yet," Linda said. "But it *is* coming, and I feel like there is no way to stop it."

An abrupt click of Amy's car door latch stunned them out of their fate-filled conversation. Surprised shouts burst out of the old Honda; the door swung open, a large, flannel covered arm and grease-stained hand groped for something to grab onto.

Linda saw the flannel sleeve and yelled: "You scared the shit out of us, Paul."

"What are you two bitches doin' out here?"

Amy looked up at Paul, as she smelled the stench of his booze and cigarette drenched breath. To her horror, Paul's groping hand first rubbed across her breasts, and up her neck to her hair.

"Don't touch me you filthy pig!" Amy screamed.

"Paul! How dare you touch her!"

Amy pushed at Paul's arm, but Paul had already grabbed a chunk of Amy's hair, yanking it hard, twisting Amy's neck. Amy felt the power in Paul's grip, and heard the ugliness of his words, as he responded to their cries for him to stop: "Come here you little slut. I've been looking at you for a long time."

Pain stabbed Amy's neck, and she felt hair ripping from her head at its roots. Paul succeeded in getting Amy out of the car.

"Mom!" Amy screamed. "Mom, help me! He's hurting me!"

With strength that surprised her, Linda, who was halfway out of the driver's seat and halfway into Amy's, grabbed Paul's arm with one hand and pulled it and Amy, back into the car. Back in the driver's seat and with the other hand, she managed to bend Paul's fingers back, one by one, forcing him to release Amy's hair.

"Let go of her, you bastard!" Linda shouted hoarsely.

Amy continued to scream at the horror of her stepdad's deep-seated ugliness. She had seen hints of it, as he and her mom fought over the things married couples fight about, but never like this.

Hoarse and now coughing, Linda freed Amy from Paul's drunken grasp, and simultaneously pushed him away from her daughter, slamming the car door shut, smashing it hard into Paul's side, tearing his skin, and cracking a rib. He moaned and fell to the ground.

Linda started the Accord. The engine roared to life, and exhaust fumes filtered through a broken window in the back. She jammed the car into drive, released the brake, and pressed hard on the accelerator, making no effort to avoid running over her soon-to-be ex-husband's inebriated body. Luckily, she missed him.

They drove away from the home she had shared with Paul. Her life's destiny roared through her, catching her breath. Old buildings cast black shadows that moved rapidly across the windshield, as Linda rushed through a right turn onto Main Street, up the hill, passing the church marquee announcing her neighbor's memorial service.

She looked at her daughter and remembered the horror of her drunken stepfather in contrast to the astonished destiny that moved through her own mind.

FOUR

The meaning of the word 'destiny' imparts a sense of wonder in each of us. We generally feel its meaning not applicable to our lives; destiny is the fate of a small, select population of humanity; those headed for eminence or infamy in history books.

Nothing could be further from the truth. Each of us carries Providence within, implied by the act of our hands and feet in motion with the day beginning, and in our dreams at night, where our divinity rests. We are, all of us, destined for quality in our lives, inspiration in our thoughts, and that potential is our right under the blaze of heaven.

The Universe reaches out to each of us, asking for our hand in living. The reach, hand-to-hand, fulfills destiny as we move closer to it through our acts of kindness and generosity.

Our lives remain full of unheralded and glorious things yet to do.

M. W. - Kruse Rhododendron State Natural Preserve

Mitchell continued to give Rosalie, the nature spirit, his tired attention, having already listened at length to her descriptions of Leo and Gunnar.

She now spoke of Gunnar in life, or at least what she had known *of* him. He was famous along the Northern California coast for his piano virtuosity. Gunnar shared with Rosalie that his life had been a rewarding one, having known at a young age what his destiny was, and having the courage to follow it. Rosalie said that Gunnar walked along the coast, his great love being the rhythm of the Pacific Ocean, its cyclical tide his inspiration in his composition of music. He had never known a greater heaven than the ability to unify his creative spirit with the themes of nature. It was his blessed existence and remained so even after his exit from life. His hope was to stay on Highway 1, to blend into the sounds of water on rock, of wind in the tall grass, of dew sparking in the morning sun, and in the midnight stillness of thought, when grace floated about the fringes of campfire light. In spirit, he remained, and the music he made in life found him again. In his new ethereal existence, he could feel his musical homecoming of sound sent in life, returning, bolstering his understanding; he knew his ability to offer music could make the world a better place.

Rosalie described Gunnar as continually moving toward the coastal rocks, and their insertion between air and water, becoming sound that filtered through him, onto clean white pages filled with music.

❧

Rosalie watched Mitchell and asked if he had any thoughts or questions for her.

"Do you think I will be able to see Gunnar on Highway 1, as I see you now?" Mitchell asked his host.

"You already see him. If you can watch the surf, and hear music within, then you see Gunnar as spirit."

Mitchell motioned that it was time to fall asleep. He returned his silent gaze to the stars above, while the meaning of destiny followed him into slumber.

The sun had risen from behind the clouds in the east. A low-ceilinged bank of fog extended out beyond the steppes between Mitchell and the shore, plains of grass that ended as cliffs falling into the Pacific Ocean.

Up early, and already on the Highway 1 moving north, Mitchell reviewed the years immediately following Red's death.

He saw how adopting fourteen-year-old Zac twenty-three years earlier was crucial to his contrast of good and evil, but also saw how tough it was on Zac, once the word got out, that he lived with the man who had killed his uncle. The townspeople were merciless, and the 17-year-old Zac left Prescott as soon as he graduated.

Even with all the connections that Mitchell's defense attorney had, Zac's parents were never located, a shadow that permanently scarred the boy.

Mitchell reviewed the devastation of his life; the morning he left Prescott twenty years earlier and how its townspeople ostracized him based on hearsay. He considered the paradox of a jury of those same citizens finding him *not guilty,* achieved by Mitchell's public defender, based on enlarged photographs of that horrifying night.

Post-trial, Mitchell contemplated the dusk of each day. In those changing Arizona sunsets, he imagined the faint outline of a door appearing in the arc of orange and red above the horizon. Each evening as he gazed out, the door became increasingly distinct. He imagined a series of steps that led up to the doorway as it opened.

After Zac left, Mitchell mentally ascended those steps. At the threshold, he turned around and said farewell to the town where fate fell hard and cold, a life further shredded by tabloid news and fanatical news agendas.

As he shut the door, he realized he was no longer exposed, as a sycophant, to Wall Street, Madison Avenue, Washington rhetoric, sex as a selling tool, and mass ideology.

He had made the old, broad highways his home and never looked back. As the weeks, months, and years unfolded, he was aware of his feet kicking out ahead of him, pulling him forward.

The sound of an approaching automobile, heading south on Highway 1, fell oddly silent. The pleasant sound of a lightly fingered piano filled the silence, with pianissimos heard at both ends of the instrument's octave range. Looking toward the open field across the highway, Mitchell beheld an ageless grey-haired figure, sitting upon a stool, playing a rosewood Steinway piano, with thick, rounded legs, suspended in the air, just above the tall, swaying grass.

The music lifted Mitchell from the morning's haunted memories, and he was present again, his eyes and ears assessing the scene before him.

It was Gunnar. Mitchell perceived that Gunnar's music carried the sounds of many instruments with it, as if the blades of tall grass had taken on the task of many Aeolian harps.

Gunnar stopped playing and moved across the highway toward Mitchell. They nodded to one another. Gunnar spoke of Rosalie, the great and kind mother spirit of nature. Mitchell expressed his appreciation for the music flowing across the swaying grass, how it enveloped the air around him with beauty and peace. Gunnar said the composition he played was entitled: *Water on Rock*. Mitchell could hear the inspiration of the crashing waves in Gunnar's melody.

The distant cry of emergency sirens was unexpected on the pristine coastline. The sound traveled over a great expanse of rolling plain. Soon the sirens were piercing Mitchell's eardrums. He and his timeless friend took refuge from that cry, in a cutout along the highway's edge, and watched a line of emergency vehicles stream south. The last two vehicles stopped just beyond where Mitchell and Gunnar stood, they were close enough to hear the police radio:

"Leo Brenamann was last seen standing on Highway 1, north of mile marker 22.42, and south of Alder Creek. Do you copy?"

"Copy," the first officer said. He turned to the second and said, "He must be hiding in these hills because that's mile marker 22.42, and *that* is Alder Creek." He pointed to an impression in the landscape below them that flowed west in a random pattern, blending into the north end of Manchester State Beach and the ocean's surf.

After confirming their exact location and taking photos of the area, the two officers returned to their vehicles and headed south again, their sirens screaming.

Mitchell and Gunnar resumed their walk north. "What's going on?" Mitchell asked.

"Change is coming," Gunnar said matter-of-factly. "The sirens are overwhelming, such a blunt contrast to this beautiful countryside. Stepping into the cut-out was the appropriate thing to do. The world is not what it used to be. If you can create less energy around your presence, you are better off."

Mitchell thought Gunnar's words to be prophetic and disturbing. It brought to light some recent unrest in his heart about the direction in which his culture was moving. "Something about my destiny says that I need to be more present in the world than I have been recently," Mitchell said. "And who is this Leo Brenamann? Is this the same Leo that Rosalie mentioned last night in her visit with me? Is it the same Leo that you and Rosalie sat with at a campfire the night before?"

"I believe this is so," Gunnar said. "Leo is in bad shape. He lost his way in the sheetrock canyon walls of our new scientific world, a world now based on a *reduction* premise that forces creative thought to be constricted to the most popular, the most current, and the most profitable form. These trends that have been implemented by the powerful artificial intelligence search engines of a controlling few and are regionally located south of San Francisco. These search engines have rendered original reflection by the human mind as lost art."

Quietly turning north on the coastal road, Mitchell put one foot in front of the other. His thoughts matched his walking: his ongoing recall of Red. She was his tonic, the unending comfort of his soul, providing the much needed, all-encompassing comfort of what he had known as her husband, what he still knew as her widower. He could still smell her cooking, her scalp, her sleeping garments. He could still hold her perfectly shaped, feminine hands in his, at will. She remained his shelter from a gentle morning rain, continually restoring and renewing him, as he lived out the raw days and nights of his shattered life.

———

My own true love,

My child's delight. My youthful reach in a magical field, as so much of a natural world spins in enchantment around me. I stop. Through my young eyes, I imagine your gleaming blond hair, your determination to imagine me as well. In youth and innocence, we knew the truth. I beheld you in the surface of all things. You saw me as sunlight falling from the sky.

As the child in each of us grew, then slept as the world grew dark, then awoke in the hardness of a tired Earth, when fathers left, and mothers' souls became embittered, we remembered our delight.

Your forever love, your Red

FIVE

Hardship.

It is the precursor to necessity. Out of such necessity is born our faith, our creative force, and our hope. We must have the mettle to face hardship. The act of taking the first step of turning the key to a new life, whether internal or external, transforms us, and for moments in our new days, we feel life soar. The breakthroughs we endure after hardship befalls us are the very reasons we live. Those breakthroughs, too often tragically remembered as the good old days, are kept paradoxically distant, for we live to deny our tears and our calluses. We sidestep the cracks in our souls, and in our communities, in a desperate wish to outlast ...what?

Let me embrace my hardship and allow my divine mind and holy heart to conduct me, time and time again, to those refined moments when I breathe, when I reach for and find the will to be faithful ... to create ... to hope.

M. W. - Sentinel Rock Viewing Platform

Gunnar continued his thoughts: "we need to remember who we are. I have always examined my nature, but now, with the continued expansion of modern technology, this examination becomes essential. Unlike any other time in our human history, this critical examination is paramount to determine what is next for the human species.

Technology is taking us off course. It has grown more in the last five years than in the last five thousand. Technology has separated our bodies from our hearts, hearts from our minds, and minds from our spirits. It is useful to an extent, but it moves from blessing to bane when it removes us from ourselves, when it removes the lessons of hardship and necessity.

Technology has obliterated our experience of hardship. We must remember that calloused skin, hearts, minds, and souls represent our lives moving in harmony with nature. Hardship brings us closer to understanding life. Paradox of mind and spirit reveal our light in the universe, our God within.

Our births force us to grasp the potential and noble purpose of our lives and not pass this quest over to the noise of ones and zeros moving through random-access memory and compiled lines of code. We need to honor our births and plow the fertile, soulful, creative ground that techno-industrial darkness has camouflaged.

We need to plant our hands and feet back into Mother Earth and let the elements and cycles of life rule over us once more. We are now just consumers of goods. We must become the creators of our survival, therein lays the purpose for living."

Mitchell understood every word Gunnar said. Mitchell had already lived through the transition from consumer to a creator of life in Mother Nature's world, a world he had known as a boy, and again as Red's husband. His mind tingled with comprehension that his life had returned to its boyhood state, and the man Red knew.

He resisted the artificial zoning out and mind-numbing conformity of the latest electronic device or Internet mindset.

Overjoyed that Gunnar's words continued to live through him, he understood his actions created their own unique wake. Mitchell stared out over the Pacific Ocean and understood in its rollicking calm his life as sacred. He saw his horizon, and the day coming, as a blessed event, and his wake, his life's energy, rippling out across time as mass impacting liquid; he could see it expand in endless fashion, becoming his addition to God's universal play, and Mother Earth's creation of a new day.

Gunnar smiled, recognizing Mitchell's epiphany, as he remembered his own, at a tender age, when the beauty of understanding his role in the choral arrangement of life brought young Gunnar to his knees, in joy and celebration. Gunnar was happy for Mitchell.

"What shall we do about Leo?" Mitchell asked.

"We should try to find him," Gunnar said. "The pulsating dash Rosalie saw in his eyes is troublesome. I think he might be awash in the industry from which he has come. Perhaps, it is all he has known. Whatever the case, I think he needs help."

"We could begin by walking the length of Alder Creek to the beach, and then back again under Highway 1, into those hills," Mitchell said.

"Maybe the officer is right, maybe Leo has blended himself into the open spaces around us," Gunnar said. "If so, this is a good sign. Perhaps he senses that this landscape might be his refuge."

Leo sat with his fine business shoes near the cold, running water of Alder Creek, staring at his dirt-crusted hands. Many years had passed since he'd last seen them in such a state. Leo had spent his life bound to the sterility of a joystick, headset, and video screen. He was unable to acknowledge these filthy hands as his. He put them in the iced, swift-moving creek water, shaking them about, sliding his feet in next, shoes and all. He rubbed his tired ankles. The chilled water invigorated him, forcing him to gasp for air.

He remained in a disassembled state of frantic thought since leaving Santa Monica several days earlier, with numbers and symbols consuming his mind's eye, as they had always done.

There was also the confounding experience, the horror of treachery by another human being.

Yet, his time on the road was increasing his awareness of other things. There were the unfamiliar observations and mental measures of time. The freezing water passed underneath him, to a cluster of reeds that had grown above the creek's surface. He unwittingly calculated the volume of water in Alder Creek as it quietly flowed by.

One woman had seen Leo coming from a mile away.

Leo was a slender young man, with the familiar look of men in fashion magazines. Oddly, his looks had not served him well in the techno-digital world he had grown up in. He was unable to connect to the opposite sex, much to the chagrin of his fellow female college peers, and later as a programming specialist in the world's leading software companies. He was forever younger than all of them, advancing through his academic career as quickly as any on record. Fellow female students and workers found him distant and sad. Leo's father told him once that communicating through email and text messaging was killing his ability to read the body language and faces of those he was communicating with, but sadly, that advice was an email too.

She had cut through his inexperienced state.

He was unable to reach into the lives of potential friends and companions, having never developed an emotional and spiritual connection to his own life, a development that should have begun as a child in school yards, athletic fields, social clubs, and neighborhood hangouts, growth that would have resulted skinned knees, bloodied nose, and broken heart, critical childhood woes that contrasted with the joys of living in the world.

Sheila was her name.

As the video game culture continued to dictate, Leo bonded with their high scores, the make-believe social construction of Internet gaming, (that included vivid sexual encounters of every imaginable fetish and craving), and the blinking cursor on video screens that hungrily awaited his next input.

She was his boss. Leo had no idea.

With his feet awash in Alder Creek, Leo flashed back to the moment he let go of what was now his old life, sitting in a leased black Porsche, staring at the Ferris wheel that rotated on the Santa Monica Pier. He remembered his head falling to its side as he watched the wheel spinning round and round. His eyebrows creased in downward fashion, as concern for his lackluster life escalated.

She had fed him to her blind ambition; she had ground his creative bones; burned his gullible trust; discarded him; she licked her chops and had finished him.

It was a life much like the rotating Ferris wheel, with the same repeated highs and lows, the same views above and below, and from one side of his life to the other, all moderated by a central hub that tumbled repeatedly, whirling out streams of code that increased the numbing speed that was now human living.

Leo met her in a social Internet gaming room. They had become friends, as one might become friends with a voice emanating through a hole in a wall. He had assumed her intentions were honorable.

He noted that the wheel was a metaphor for the society in which he lived. Experience, material, and transcendental, extended to each member, much the same way the massive and all-encompassing Internet had become the hub of his society. Each aspect of living was reduced to sought Internet pages that tracked the input of every viewer in the world. He noted how the Ferris wheel, in design, matched the foundation of his Haltronics programming project, which he dubbed Code as God. This new code reached out beyond the bounds of Earth, through a special satellite-based portal, into the expanding universe, claiming the world much the way white matter becomes the nerve superhighways in the human spine.

They had become fighting partners in their war-crafted digital world, standing side-by-side, battling great evil, making everything right in the world.

Nothing was private. Nothing was sacred. Everything, even the simplicity of a beating heart, was prompted, monitored and recorded, executed, filed, and archived.

Falling in love through word and digital deed, the two consummated their love under a bridge while above them a siege roared, hammered out by all manner of hero and demon. The act of making digital love with the beautiful Sheila had become Leo's world, and he gave her everything he knew to give, including his genius in the industry he served.

All creative output, all love, all hope, was filtered through templates of marketability and profitability and became the property of neural networks that learned and reached out to the masses, from dark and unknown corners of the Earth.

Repeatedly they had made love. Often it was spontaneous and depraved, Sheila pulled Leo through every corner of such wantonness, shredding his undeveloped sense of propriety, and blackening his sensibilities.

At that very moment, when he recalled Sheila's depravity, Leo got out of his Porsche, grabbed a backpack filled with provisions that included, two sets of two-way radios, all set to send and receive on channel eleven, though such a detail was meaningless to him now, and a sleeping bag his father had given him many years ago. He pulled the car key fob off his key ring, threw it on the driver's seat, and slammed the car door. He turned his back on his past life, the symbolic Ferris wheel spinning on and on, stepped up to Highway 1 and began walking north.

After one particularly long and grueling session of sword-swinging and complicated, mind-numbing battle maneuvers, Leo found Sheila under the same bridge where they had first made love. She was with another. The knight, one of Leo's clan, had turned and smiled at him while he and Sheila had sex. Leo turned from the scene, and his character in the game moved out into no man's land, absorbing unimaginable shame and embarrassment into the game's electronic server farm, not to be seen again in the war-crafted digital world.

fh

Leo let the thoughts of the Ferris wheel go and noticed his mind's eye following the water's flow downstream, taking note of its bend and blend in and around rocks and branches. Somewhere in this small scene his life, with his mind mathematically calculating how water interacted with rock, he noticed time standing still.

Leo left the game without knowing the facts of his own undoing: that Sheila was a man, and that this man was the owner of Haltronics.

SIX

Free will.

If I think long enough, and read widely enough, I will find the answers to the questions of free will's sharp-edged sword slicing through my life at every turn. How does free will evolve in my life? That is what I want to know, what can free will determine? Emerson connects to nature. I too, calmly lay upon the ground with the cycles of life. I exercise free will yet how do I continue to become God's intention for my life? Let me imagine it. Let me continue my story. Let me know in my heart what action a human being with an evolved free will takes.

Will humanity return to the sea, return to a migratory hunting/gathering way of life, where hardship, at the expense of comfort, dictates a well-lived life, a life filled with simple survival?

What about riches and treasure? Symbolically, free will came with the grasp of an apple from a tree. That grasp brought avarice into the world, and the grasping continues. Has free will turned humanity into a barely acceptable life form, as determined by own observation of it?

How does free will evolve? Let me find the courage to seek what I don't know.

M. W. - Stewart's Point

Linda and Amy were awakened by the sun's rays burning through the Accord's windshield, and by aching joints and muscles.

Memories of the previous night tunneled through Linda. She felt anxious remembering the confrontation with Paul, the need for a painful heart-to-heart with Amy, and a visit with a divorce attorney in Fort Bragg.

Do I need to get a restraining order? Linda considered.

Her thoughts returned to the discussion with Amy. Leaving Paul would lead to her second divorce; two failed marriages after becoming a widow. She lost her beloved husband, Nathan, Amy's father, to a storm-related work accident aboard a fishing vessel that operated off the Point Arena Pier.

She thought of how easy divorce had become. Thankfully, it would be relatively simple to terminate this bad marriage, but she worried about the example she was setting for her daughter. Amy's generation viewed marriage as negligible in a person's life, like choosing a car or a pair of shoes.

She knew that she was chasing what she had with her first husband. She looked at her failed marriages as chances to rekindle a special place for someone she loved. Linda now knew that it would never happen for her again. Nathan was her destiny; a rogue wave ended that destiny.

She thought through it all, knowing the consequence of every move she had made except for one, her pending conversation with Amy.

≺≼੬≽≻

Linda looked deeply into Amy's eyes and saw hope in them.

Amy sat up and stretched, glancing around their surroundings. They had pulled into an empty campsite at Manchester State Park and were surprised to find the campground nearly vacant.

Smoke from a dying campfire rose from a nearby fire ring but was absent of human activity.

They saw a small tent staked against low shrubs. They spotted early morning wildlife ambling through the campground and were surprised by how tranquil it was. By their estimates, over one hundred deer grazed on the grasses.

Birds of prey hunted, soaring up and down with the rise and fall of wind currents. They felt the cycle of life moving through the morning and found grace in this.

"What will we do today?" Amy asked.

"Well, let's get you to school," Linda responded. "We'll go home first; I'm sure Paul has left for work. He's a good man for the most part but grabbing your hair last night can't be forgiven. He has always worked hard yet struggles to understand how to act as part of a loving relationship."

They opened the car doors, letting cold beach air wash the staleness out of the car. Stretching hard, Linda looked down Kinney

51

Road, toward the ocean. The tall lighthouse emerged from the sea mist produced by pounding surf, tinted orange by the early morning sunrise. The lighthouse made Linda think of a compass needle. She recalled that the beach acted as a large catch basin for driftwood, and remembered seeing the beachfront covered with driftwood, and at times empty.

Amy listened to the quiet, muffled sounds of the campground. Moisture had collected on her mother's car. She listened to the crash of waves that rolled down the five-mile-long beachfront. Amy watched a large flock of starlings murmurate around the lighthouse, like they were texting one another. *How else could they coordinate such a magnificent display of aerobatics?*

"Are we leaving Point Arena?" Amy asked her mother.

"I don't want to. I would like to stay and keep the friends we have, our daily routines; all the things that make this feel like home."

Linda took a deep breath of ocean air. She felt invigorated and hopeful. She was saddened by last night's events, but also felt challenged to rise above them, which inspired her to confront the changes.

"Let's stay, Amy," Linda said after a moment's thought. "Let's stay here in Point Arena."

"I'd like that, Mom, very much."

Shivers claimed mother and daughter. They slid back into the car and shut the doors. Linda started the car and looked at the temperature gauge, waiting for precious heat to pour out of the dashboard vents.

She looked around the camp one more time, backed up, then out onto Highway 1 via Kinney Road. They passed a man on foot who looked cold but content in the morning sunshine. There was something strangely familiar about the man. A fresh beard and the bill of a baseball cap made it difficult to view his face.

She saw Haltronics in her rearview mirror, where she worked; the massive quasi-governmental business that managed a significant part of the Internet infrastructure. The nondescript building at the end of Kinney Road was surrounded by a two-story chain-link fence, topped with circular barbed wire and video cameras. The property contained a water tower, which Linda knew contained no water, but highly technical satellite antennae and radar equipment. She sighed at the thought of where she worked, and what went on in that weather-beaten building. She was grateful for days off when she could focus on her daughter's needs.

Now she spotted the Haltronics building in her rearview mirror, Linda hit a sharp metal object, a piece of barbed wire, that pierced the balding right front tire, blowing a hole in the tire that sounded like a handgun discharging.

Linda swerved, flattening a highway warning; Amy yelled in alarm.

Linda found the wire still lodged in the tire. She pulled hard on it, successfully dislodging and throwing it into the grassy meadow that lined Kinney Road.

"You probably shouldn't do that," the bearded man said. He had quickly turned back at the sound of the blowout. "Are you two, okay?"

With dismay, Linda responded to the stranger, shaking her head, wanting neither his help nor his input on where to discard the barbed wire.

"Deer graze through here, it could cut one, perhaps more," the man said, gesturing toward the meadows. "Can I give you a hand changing that tire?"

Amy got out of her mother's car. She stood with her mom, and they stared at the strange man.

"I think we've got it," Linda said, walking toward the back of the Accord, hitting the top of the trunk, causing it to fly open. Linda stared at the contents of her trunk. A quick inventory revealed an upturned carton of laundry detergent, and a spare tire, a jack, and a tire iron. Linda grabbed the iron and turned back toward the strange man.

"Mom, he's only trying to help," Amy said.

Linda looked at the man warily, a strange combination of disheveled youth, and his ragged but expensive business suit, leaving mother and daughter conflicted. Linda thought he looked familiar.

The stranger looked around, trying to decide if he should keep moving down Kinney Road, toward the state park, where he was going to rest up for a while.

He started out and then heard the woman speak. "Well, if you'd care to try, we'd be grateful."

He walked slowly toward the Accord. The pair moved off the road, about ten feet from where the car rested. Amy went a little further out, picked up the short length of wire, and brought it back to the roadside.

Moments passed. The stranger went to work. Linda and Amy watched as he pushed tools here and parts there, observing the man's hands get progressively dirtier. A small band of sweat broke across his brow. In quick order, the job was finished, and the stranger was organizing a flat tire and the assorted tools into the trunk, ignoring the spilled laundry detergent.

Linda noticed his reserve, his gaunt expression, and wanted to express gratitude and concern for his welfare.

"Are you hungry? When was the last time you ate?"

The stranger closed the trunk. "I guess I am hungry."

"Well, where are you headed? If you want, we could go to town and pick up some groceries and bring them back to you."

"I think I'm going to take a day out of traveling and stay at the state park," he said, gesturing toward the entrance.

"Okay, we will be back in about an hour. We'll look for you there."

The man hesitated, staring hard into faces of care and concern, then said, "Okay."

⋘⋙

Turning right onto Main Street, and then left, Linda saw that both the curb in front of her house and the driveway were vacant. Paul had left for work. Both mother and daughter got out of the car and looked together across the street to the big blue house that sat on the corner of Riverside Drive and Main Street. They thought about the old man that lived there and his recent losses, a wife, and a son, in two short months.

Life is a sad thing, Linda thought, as she and Amy entered their home. They retrieved a pillow and two blankets, returned to the car, headed further down the hill to a general store thinking about the stranger, speculating why the man was in the state he was in.

———

My own true love, my Red,

You are the hand that holds my heart on a hard night. You remain the transcendent sea, the comforting wind, the warmth of every fire at my feet, and each blade of grass that makes room for my head when I finally let go of the day. I still wonder how I have put one foot in front of the other without you. I see you in clouds, I hear you in the pounding surf, each note a memory of your place in the history of all things. My Red, if pain is a sign of living life, my heart lives fully for you. I love and miss you forever.

Your

Mitchell

SEVEN

The video game culture has robbed an entire generation of its childhood. Strong sentiment I know, but each of you know this to be true.

Digital dark rooms have replaced blue sky, scraped knees, and blistered palms. Jumping, hiding, discovering, climbing, and kicking a rock, are now done inside computer memory programmed by human robots in their own windowless hells. Children need to play outside. They need to come home for dinner at dusk when the streetlights come on, and not come home because of a scrape on their elbow, that is what scabs are for. Each needs to experience running into the back of a parked car on their bike. The shock and pain of that event gave me everything I needed to know about overcoming adversity.

M. W. - Sea Ranch

Leo was an important individual in the techno industrial world, and was known everywhere, especially in Cupertino, California, where his employer stored the server networks that accelerated the infinite and boundless Internet traffic. He had created key algorithms for Haltronics, enabling the reach of the military/industrial/intelligence complex. His algorithms monitored the IP address of every electronic device used by the world's urban sprawl save one item, the simple two-way radio.

Leo knew about this. Two-way radios were hard to track; their weak signal strength was barely able to bend around the corner of a building. Often sold as having the ability to travel many miles, Leo knew otherwise; the radio was good for, at best, a half mile.

The knowledge that a two-way radio emitted a weak signal was not Leo's only connection to them; when he was younger, he had used walkie-talkies with his father during camping trips. His father prioritized getting Leo out of the *dark room,* Leo's bedroom, and into nature, away from the Internet video game culture, especially on weekends.

Internet video gaming was a bad sign to Leo's dad. He often tried to tell stories to Leo about his glorious times spent outdoors, to stave off his son's assimilation into the Internet and companion isolation.

But the gaming lifestyle prevailed. To his father's dismay, Leo did not venture outside, but chose to stay inside a curtained off, cut-off room. He wanted, and needed, to pursue the pulsating cursor into the latest and greatest digital metaverse and inhabit that fantasy world.

Leo's father decided to let this dark culture become a part of his son's life, rather than lose him to his increasing anger and resentment. Leo became enraged when Internet access was limited. Leo lost himself in digital worlds, attempting to assuage his hunger by manipulation and immersion.

Leo regretted his teen years, when he shut his father out in favor of the intensely colored, artificial, nature-deficient world. When not sleeping from exhaustion, close to 24 hours a day, seven days a week, he lived there. He first learned, then worked and played simultaneously. His never-ending appetite for the generation of complicated information grew like an addiction through his creation of increasingly complex code.

His was an addiction akin to a black hole that sucked the life from him and could never be filled, constantly increasing in depth and circumference. His was an insatiable appetite for the hum of hard drives, for zeroes and ones, for the possibility that his intellect could connect to God, however diminutive his understanding of God was, *and that God would answer.*

Leo obtained two doctorates in computer science by his early twenties from prestigious, world-renowned universities. He naively signed contracts with the government funded Haltronics, that covertly converted his brilliant creations into their sole intellectual property. His mind became obsessed by small-minded men and women who grew obscenely rich on his talents. They capitalized on his inability to connect socially, and on his broken common sense and intuition. This created the corporate deception that did him in.

Haltronics ended Leo's contract when he stated in a company-wide email that he found proof of a pending cataclysmic change. Late one evening, Leo completed what he dubbed the God Code. It revealed a collision course between the ancient, chaotic, unpredictable, analog world, and the controlled, manufactured, digital universe. His calculations revealed that the natural world would soon re-assert its evolutionary mastery over humankind, forcing the species to supplant its race to Armageddon with Armageddon. Leo refused to yield the code to Haltronics, keeping it locked in his mind. Haltronics fired him.

As Leo sat on the side of Alder Creek, he fumbled through his backpack and found one of the four two-way radios he packed before departing his Santa Monica life. He pulled it out and looked at its hand-worn condition. The talk push button was losing its click.

He longed for the sound and texture of his father's voice coming through the speaker. He wanted to go back to those few and far between places as a teenager with his father.

He took the radio, already set to channel eleven, to his mouth, pressed the talk button and softly said, "Dad, can you read me?" He recalled how he had used the radio this way when they camped. He let go of the talk button; there was no response.

He let his mind wander through the years remembering their camping trips; his father playing music on the truck stereo: compilations of songs from the music groups and singers from his father's youth. Suddenly, Leo recalled one of the songs. He looked at the speaker of the two-way as if the song was emanating from it. He knew it came from his own memory but channeling it through the speaker in his mind's eye made the memory more real. "Getting in Tune," by *The Who,* was one of his father's favorites. He played make-believe drums with his thumbs on the truck's steering wheel, as they drove north on US-101, heading for coastal campgrounds in the California State Park system. This included the one he had left earlier in the day: Manchester State Park, off Kinney Road.

In memory, Leo looked past his father's profile to the horizon outside the truck's cab. He remembered the Pacific Ocean looming large, behind his view of his father, and the blue-green coastal waves turning white and misty, as winds created the frothing white caps on the mighty, churning, body of water. He vividly remembered his father's ability to melt into their surroundings and to become a different man on the weekends they camped.

Leo remembered his own feet planted next to his father's. He longed for another hour doing nothing but watching the tide roar in and then recede.

The sound of two men walking above him on the Alder Creek Bridge pulled him back to the present. He turned off the radio and placed it in the backpack with the others. Quietly, he removed his feet from Alder Creek and hiked up the bank toward the hills to the east. He looked through the brush to see if he could get a better look at the men, and saw that they were in uniform, California Highway Patrol. One spoke into a police band radio while another took pictures of the surrounding area.

———

My dearest love,

*I thank you for remembering me. I love you,
Mitchell. My heart falls back in time, and my death haunts
my new existence. I know peace, yet I long for the days
before I was defenseless, cut by an evil blade.*

*It was the steel that took me, cut my life out of me. I
thank you for remembering me that day. I thank you for
coming, and for holding my memory in your lonely walk on
the open road.*

Your own true love, your Red

EIGHT

The ground moves, the gears turn, the great land masses and oceans that make the Earth unique in this solar system, and possibly our galaxy, have always given man markers which we can use to measure our lives and our histories. These gears, the greatest of which is the Pacific Ocean, fill the collective spirit of man with a sense of insignificance, so overwhelming, so unfathomable, that only the most insightful writers (Emerson and Whitman) can reach into the dark hardwood of their souls, to bring forth meaning in our lack.

I rely on their poems and essays for markers in my life.

As the Earth turns in its orbit, a process so much more important than any inconsequential life, She offers a place for all to plant a foot firmly, and to place a hand securely on Her constant upheaval and change.

For every question, there is an answer; for every desperate moment, there is faith to carry us through. Such is the profundity of Nature.

M. W. - Shell Beach

Leo had slowly ascended the bank of Alder Creek as it washed down from the mountains east of its intersection with Highway 1. Alder Creek Bridge was lost in the thickets of trees at creek's edge. He was not visible to the patrol officers, who had returned to their cars and sped south. Leo was not so sure about another pair of men, who, as soon as the CHP officers left, abruptly turned around and headed back toward Alder Creek Bridge. Leo rested behind a centuries-old cypress tree, watching their progress. Arriving at the bridge, each took a side and searched the creek bed below. One man seemed to float above the surface of the bridge, his feet gliding along, first surprising, then reminding Leo of video game characters that this an ability: a superpower.

They made their way to the south side of the bridge, turned toward one another, and coordinated their next move. They both hiked along the line of the creek, west, as it cut through farmland and emptied into the Pacific. They did an about-face and headed up-creek toward Leo.

Not waiting to run into them, Leo turned toward the lower hills and mountain range behind him. He spotted a V-shaped indentation higher up in the ridge. The creek's flow had cut the wedge, and he determined that it would be the best place to put distance between he and his pursuers. He looked back to check on the pair's progress, and saw the Pacific Ocean grow on the horizon.

Mitchell thought he heard steps breaking twigs and moving earth up-stream from where he and Gunnar hiked.

Gunnar remembered something disturbing about Alder Creek that he once experienced, yet it remained beyond his grasp. Mitchell noticed Gunnar's perplexed expression.

"There is something about this creek that is important, but I can't quite place it," Gunnar said.

"Now I remember."

"What?" Mitchell said, alarmed at Gunnar's tone.

"Look! Right there," Gunnar said, pointing to a subtle formation under the surface of the water.

Mitchell saw tan and gold sedimentary striations, layered rock, on one side of the creek, which tucked under granite-colored stone running with Alder Creek, on the other side. He noticed this second rock layer covered the first like a blanket.

"Mitchell," Gunnar asked apprehensively, "do you feel it?"

Mitchell looked at Gunnar, not sure what to say. He may have felt something but could not put his finger on it. Mitchell felt nauseated.

Up creek from them, Leo listened to the pair, as they discussed the shapes and shades of rock in and around Alder Creek. He became uneasy.

Apprehension gripped all three men. For long moments, each remained entranced by the intense energy waves emanating from beneath Alder Creek.

Leo too became nauseated, and their coughs alerted each to the other. Gunnar looked up at Leo, as he ran upstream. Gunnar tried to speak but could not. The energy, pouring out of Alder Creek, shook every tree, rock, and living creature. The San Andreas Fault, which had created Alder Creek, was shifting.

The stone over which Gunnar moved began to slip beneath the rock under Mitchell. Leo stopped running uphill and turned toward the ocean. A reverberation amazed and terrified him. His thoughts could not conceive of what creased the surface of the ocean. A trough had formed, arcing out from Alder Creek, in the shape of a giant rain-gutter, one hundred yards wide, turning along the coast, out of sight.

"Run!" Gunnar warned. "Run! Run for your lives!"

Leo and Mitchell, overcome with fear from the shock waves, began to run from Alder Creek. Every time their feet hit the ground, it felt as if the ground hit back. They looked up at the ridge where the V-shaped landmark had been. It disappeared in a heartbeat, crumbling into a dust storm that soared above, dispersing into the blue and yellow sky. Giant Redwoods began to rock, and then crack, sounding like shotguns discharging repeatedly.

Anguished and dizzy, both men grabbed their heads. Each struggled to move away from the aggressively shifting San Andreas Fault line.

The men rose and fell, bouncing like rubber balls, consumed by the mixed messages of their senses as they tried to grasp the unreality of their surroundings.

Mitchell had nearly caught up to Leo. Leo's face reflected the chaos around him. Mitchell guessed that Leo was on the verge of a mental break as his eyes darted wildly about, he flailed his arms, and produced feral, incoherent sounds. To Mitchell's horror, Leo was sinking into the ground, up to his knees in churning earth. He then sunk neck deep into the pulverized ground, whipped about like he was in water.

Leo cried out for Mitchell's help; Walker struggled to reach him. Leo watched in terror as Mitchell was knocked to his knees by the shaking ground, and then sprang up only to be thrown down again on his side. Ten feet from Leo, Mitchell started crawling on all fours. He could see Leo's head and hands waving frantically above the shifting ground.

Trembling, Mitchell reached out to Leo, desperate to grab his hands.

Seconds seemed like an eternity. Inches separated them. Nausea and dust continued to wreak havoc. Mitchell saw pockets of earth rotate like whirlpools in a hot tub. Leo, trapped, began to spin in the vortex of mud.

The whirlpool's centrifugal force moved Leo's hand closer to Mitchell, and he wrap his hands around the young man as he circled by, using his body weight to pull Leo from the grip of quicksand.

Leo lay on top of Mitchell, who held him, as a parent might hold a child. Dust spun around them; a brown fog coated them.

They lay side by side, unsure about how much time had passed. Everything was different.

Mitchell and Leo thought they were looking back toward Alder Creek, but nothing looked as they remembered. Alder Creek had boiled. Its vegetation, the rock profile, all of it had totally changed in shape and color.

Both men saw the spirit of Gunnar. He was floating above the earth, above the once serene and beautiful creek, his arms spread out, his hands turned upward to the sky. Colors of every hue emanated from him as he rose. The choral and orchestral sounds he had known in life followed him above the earth. Gunnar beheld the planet creating another age within itself. The Pacific Ocean churned in complete turmoil. Great waves pounded the beaches. Landscapes changed right before Gunnar's eyes. Vast tracts of farmland disappeared. New earth rose from millions, if not billions of years, dark, unknown, dormant.

Like a great tiller, the quake forced all living things to find a new way to survive. True north changed. What was once dear was gone. Belief had snapped. Experience had been erased.

Gunnar, Mitchell, and Leo, spirit and man, shook uncomprehendingly. The Earth's gears churned. A new compass emerged.

———————

Wait!

No!

Mitchell, help me, oh my Mitchell, my own true love, I cannot see you upon the road. I know not where you look, or how you feel, your fears, your joy. Oh, please come back to me, my love.

I have lost my way. Pulled by my memories of our life, I have fallen through color and sound, to death, and can feel nothing of your love. Where is the beat of your heart, like a bell sounding in mine. I have lost my way. I have ceased to be.

Your forever love, your Red

NINE

I wonder about the short-sighted leadership of the desert
communities of Las Vegas, Phoenix, Tucson, and others; the
unabated growth of every conurbation in the southwestern United
States; why this growth has been allowed to continue, despite the
lack inherent to a desert climate: water.
Water. It is not for everyone. The reservoirs are filling with silt.
There is now not enough to go around. One tiny disruption to this
fragile infrastructure will be the ruin of all who live there.

M. W. - Gualala Point Regional Park

The western coastline from San Diego to the Aleutian Islands, succumbed to a 10.5 Richter Scale 'megathrust' earthquake, a seismic movement of tectonic plates along the Cascadia Subduction Zone, which triggered massive releases of pressure along the San Andreas Fault resulting in more killer earthquakes and deadly tsunamis. At one hundred feet, they swept every low-lying city and town, from the Alaskan island chain to Cape Mendocino. From Vancouver, Seattle, to Portland, and down the northwestern coast. Nearly every manmade structure was decimated. High rises, surrounded by the aftermath of destruction, rose from the wet ashen debris like tombstones. From them hung signs made from bedsheets and curtains, words from desperate human beings unable to fathom the Earth reclaiming itself.

All food sources, all utilities, all available water sources were gone. An epoch of man had ended. A new one had begun. Those not killed in the shifting land and water masses would die a longer death: one of starvation, thirst, or fear.

Mass hysteria played itself out in the adjacent arid states of Arizona, Nevada, Idaho, and Montana. From north of the 49th Parallel, to south of the U.S./Mexico border, where seventy million people resided, a colossal and collective epiphany of stupidity and chaos arose, followed by wave after wave of terror, from extortion to torture, all designed to identify and horde sources of water. It was available for one out of every one thousand lives. Millions were trapped with no way out, panicked to see immense U.S. military build-ups closing off every interstate and highway leading into and out of frantic stricken communities. Most were left to an anguished death by dehydration.

On the western coast, the irony of living next to an ocean while dying of thirst started heated exchanges. In downtown Los Angeles, power brokers and political stooges gathered in makeshift tents, to keep themselves watered and fed, and to find someone able to restore the crumbled digital infrastructure upon which their existence depended.

Around one table, a frenzied debate took place. The participants were top executives of the major digital infrastructure companies; the conglomerates and individuals that stood to lose the most if order was not restored.

The discussion revealed that the crucial Internet backup located in Cupertino, south of San Francisco, one of the hardest hit areas, had been reduced to dust by the seismic waves of tectonic energy. The catastrophic events of the preceding day vaporized the entire area's electronic campuses.

"Have you seen our Cupertino facilities first-hand, General?" John Jespa, CEO of Haltronics, asked.

"I have," replied General Jim Orth, the Joint Chief of Staff, and Commander of the Armed Services. "I flew over it this morning, by helicopter. There is nothing left except the severed underground cables that served those facilities. The backup centers have been obliterated, leaving no trace, as if they never existed."

John Jespa gasped. "Goddamn it to hell, I can't believe this shit," he said, glowering at the general, then toward the ground shaking his head, wondering how the safeguards he had installed had failed.

"We could not have anticipated an earthquake of this magnitude," General Orth, said. "The energy released yesterday, by the Cascadia Subduction Zone, and by the San Andreas Fault, and other similar fault lines, vibrated everything within a one-thousand-mile-wide circumference from the epicenter into dust. Every telephone pole, every road, house, every structure is gone, washed away by tsunamis no one could ever imagine. Every tree was snapped at its roots. Water is pouring out of water mains in a hundred thousand different places. Reservoirs are emptying, some fast, some slowly, all of them revealing decades of silt buildup that will never be cleaned up. Trucking supply lines have all but vanished, leaving stores of food and bottled water in grocery chains and warehouses to last those who are still living and are able get to them, for ten days.

I have received reports that gangs have already formed, taking control, and implementing rule over their territory, from as small as an isolated high rise, to large tracks of wilderness, rule that benefits those few. Armed and vicious. These tyrants have started to enslave those they have overrun. Soon, factions from one town will be attacking their neighbors for food, water, gas, for anything required for survival, comfort, and barter.

We have long known how all of this would unfold in the face of such a catastrophe. We have issued a 'stand down' order to allow the local fighting over goods and services to play itself out. We will then deal with the leaders of those factions when necessary. We estimate the local fighting will end in approximately two weeks, when food and water have run out, even for the victors.

I have paper phone logs from the California Highway Patrol in Fort Bragg. They describe the numerous phone calls that came in claiming that a massive earthquake was coming, and that the area had less than an hour to prepare. Every one of the callers said they felt sick to their stomachs for no good reason. One caller stated that the source of his illness was compression waves from tectonic plate pressure. Like everywhere else, electronic records of these phone calls were wiped out by the tsunamis.

78

We are continuing our search for Leo Brenamann, per your instructions, Mr. Jespa. Do you still believe he could be the man we are looking for to restore the Cupertino infrastructure?"

"I do," Jespa barked, "which, if not restored soon, will set us back seventy years in our ability to control the western coast of the United States."

"By 'control,' you mean 'protect,' right J.J.?" General Orth asked, revealing his weary regard for the greedy, power-hungry politico sitting at the head of the table. "None of this takes into consideration what is happening to the rest of the country and the domino effect this quake is having on the rest of the world. The entire Western Hemisphere felt this quake. It stimulated hot spots. Every volcanic site, active or dormant, has shown signs of renewed life. Currents of magma flowing just below the surface of the earth's crust, have shifted. Volcanic ash is filling the atmosphere. Life is changing, and not for the better, save maybe for Mother Nature herself, who seems to be saying to all of us that it is time for transformation and renewal."

General Jim Orth stood up, closed his situation report, looked around the table, and realized that there was more fear on the faces of these supposed leaders of industry than he ever saw in the field of battle. Orth's last gaze was upon the face of Jespa. *There is the worst of it*, Orth thought. *Jespa's fear has become desperation.*

TEN

————

Patience, allowing things to come to you, that is the magic in living.

Avarice obstructs this glorious and simple way of life. The American Dream has been striped clean of the prevailing notion that hard work is the perfect way to live an enlightened life. Now the dream has become the nightmare, the indentured servitude of every newly educated student, who, upon graduation, owes their creative energy and lives to the U.S. Government, effectively enslaving the first one third of their working lives to repayment of student loans. The nightmare continues each year as sixty percent of graduating students will not find work in their chosen fields, and if they do, at greatly reduced wages and benefits. All of society retreats toward servitude, where comfort and success belong to the few, while the many experience toil and disillusion.

Life on that plane is folly. Life on a small scale, where simple actions play large, move a mind and heart to a good night's rest, minus the debilitating worry of nightmares driven by greed and selfish extant.

Let go. Walk through the door of change, to the unknown magic of a small life, where patience plays the music of grace.

M. W. - Gualala River Bridge

————

The Lennon McCartney song, *Eleanor Rigby,* transfixed Amy. The lyrics seemed out of sync with the cadence of the music, which would elevate her heart rate, making her tense, as she looked out her upstairs window toward the big, blue Victorian home she'd grown so accustomed to staring at in the recent years of her young life.

Her mother's music intrigued her. Although not a musician herself, she worked to find the intent in music, as well as her own interpretation, in lyric and in musical mood.

While the words mirrored her sorrow and emptiness, Amy was tied to the beat of *Rigby.* The terse, stringed instrumentation pulled her into the present moment, her life colored by the actions and apathy of the adults in her life.

≼ઝ∽

Sitting on a cushioned seat, at the base of the bedroom bay window, Amy recalled the countless conversations she had had with the man across the street. He was a boy really, in a man's body. Deaf and blind, his unusual reflections moved her into other worlds.

Saddened by his death, she had believed that the man-child would live forever, simply because he was genuinely happy.

He did not. During the long days of her youth, the man-child was ushered into the cosmic beyond. He was gone, buried in the side yard of the large blue Victorian home.

She recalled the small group standing around the hole in the ground, which had accepted the ornate wooden box that held Louis.

Eleanor Rigby ended. Amy found the complete quiet of her room soothing. She lifted her chin and face toward the blue sky outside her window and felt the presence of life. She saw red hair and smiles outlined in the blue sky. She felt a younger self reach out into the sky for the smile and red hair, realizing she was reaching for a distant memory of her father, who was taken from her much the same Louis. She knew well beyond her years, that life could not exist without death. She knew that balance eventually occurred in all things; in color, in sound, in love, in touch; all of this came to her with understanding and paradox.

Quietly, she stated to the smile and red hair; "Hello dad. Where are you today?" She beheld her tiny hand in his, giving way to the fine memory of his whirling her through the air in joyful surrender to the moment. She remembered him that way. She looked down again, through the bay window, to the burial plot on the side yard of the old Victorian home. She remembered the white-capped sea moving toward cypress trees. In the Odd Fellows Cemetery, north of town she stood, cars passing on Highway 1. A fresh hole filled with a box held the effects of what was still precious to her, inside it the memories that carried her from one childhood moment to the next.

Her thoughts returned to Louis, and his descriptions of daydreams, and of his life.

He would tell her about the overwhelming need to feel joy, while sitting in the home's parlor windowpane, the one that framed the daily life of the town.

She remembered his description of joy, and how he could sit anywhere in his home and find that same joy. He imagined other worlds in other universes coming together in threes, as three winds, and three moons, and three sunrises that passed every thirty-three hours.

To Amy, it was a mysterious and beautiful world where Louis lived. The color and sounds so breathtaking, so kind, and so generous in their offerings of what could be.

She looked up again to find her red-headed, smiling father in the blue sky.

While she looked, she noticed her father looking down on the spot where Louis was laid to rest. She watched his gaze move from the burial site to Louis' bedroom window.

Amy stared. She lost her father's face, replaced by Louis' profile appearing in joyful anticipation. She remembered it was his appearance in his bedroom window that was his invitation to visit.

There he is, she thought. She imagined that Louis' face was in the window. She could see him. The window was opened, and she saw him wave her over to the white picket fence where they spent all their time talking.

She recalled going downstairs and walking across Riverside Drive to meet her friend.

"Are you really there?" Amy daydreamed.

I am here, Louis said.

"Why?"

I did not want to leave you, Louis responded.

Amy thought about this for a moment. She thought about her father's red hair and smile, and his gazing down from the blue sky toward Louis' bedroom window.

"You can see me?" Amy asked.

I can hear you too. Death has brought my dead senses to life.

"Do you know my father?" she asked, the dream-state continuing.

I do. He misses you.

Amy began to cry, her heart unable to contain her joy and grief.

"Would you tell him I love him, and miss him so much," Amy said.

You just did.

Amy smiled at the thought of her ability to talk to her father, through Louis' spirit.

I know that the world I came from is ending, Louis said sadly.

I felt like the captain of a sinking ship, floundering in an ocean of time, swelling, and slamming against the confines of its past. As I lived my life inside this Grand Old Lady, *I noticed the outside* world was out of sync with the routine I found inside her," he said, pointing to the old blue house.

Amy noticed Louis was made of the same outlined bend of light that she saw her father drenched in, moments before. "What was out of sync?" Amy asked Louis with interest.

I know that as soon as I stepped out, through the front gate of my home, I was confronted with an anxiety that created fear and awe in me. I no longer heard the orchestral joy of the home's heart. It was this home that brought to me a greater understanding of the world outside. This understanding transcended my existence as a deaf and blind orphan boy. It raised the intensity of joy between the hearts of my adopted family and me. There is a co-existence in this home, of energies long comprehended by the aboriginal tribes as the creative force of Mother Nature, as the freeing will of God. Non-aboriginal man can only grasp the movement of time and the deep richness of space through what can be touched. The anesthetized sense of man today is made more brutal by reaching for further indulgence and laziness, by considering only money with each action that is taken. In my home I can transcend into the flawless existence of the moment, into unknown color and sound, with hues and harmonies steps resulting from endless years of becoming.

We, and I mean you Amy, can connect to these old worlds. You, Amy, can become a blessed being, by faithfully walking through a door of change. This door is not of your making or your world and is a pathway to a thought process that is alive with possibility. So many in this possessions-driven world have mistaken an attachment to people, places, and things as the meaning of life. They have nothing to do with it. The young ones know, for they are a part of the tides, the cycles of not just this world, but of all worlds. Amy, there are so many worlds out there, so many universes, that contain limitless joy and inspiration, unbridled effort, and comprehension. It is said that humans use barely one tenth of their minds. Where do you suppose that ninety percent of comprehension and limitless joy come from? It is there for you to connect to: inspiration, joy, effort, creation and most of all, love.

Our minds, in that ninety percent, are found: our doors, windows, and portals to the God in each of us. God is there, as universal love and creation, in our minds. We once knew where the entrances were, but the base existence of our societies has moved us away from the creative God-force within, to the repeating failure of measuring time with money.

There can be no connecting between a soul and its creator if the volume of coins and bills, stuffed in shirt pockets and floorboards, is the measure. There is no motivation to drive understanding to a higher plane of existence.

You must ask yourself what might be found in that unused portion of your mind. Knock on it. Say hello. HELLO! LET ME IN! What do you know? What can you comprehend? What can you create in the remaining days of your life. What has meaning to you? What makes you look up? What takes your life into the multiples of your senses?

I know love does. I know creative thought does. I know I can find these human emotions to be very God-like.

In its simplicity, is found the truth of this unused mind. Much has been written about what is found there. All I know is that it is truly there, in the confines of your human brain, inside the bone mass, as part of the blood in your heart. Your breathing and eating, your survival, keeps this partitioned mind alive, and through it, heaven is found. It is already yours.

Love certainly puts you at its threshold and can elicit mighty notions of what life can be.

I know now. I knew then," Louis said, pointing to the window of his room in life.

"I knew what life could be, and knew, as I breathed the air found in this house, that I was living such a life. I found all light and color within it and felt all manner of vibrations from the universe within its walls.

I thank you for being my friend, Amy. I have benefited from your young heart and your yearning for the truth. Please, make your way into my room, upstairs, and find a gift. It is a gift too important to bestow to you, until now. It sits upon the bed. My father may be surprised by your knowledge of it, but both of you will understand why I have given it to you."

Amy stared up at the front door. The big blue house towered over her, as if it was leaning forward. Standing in front of the white picket fence and the locked gate, she gazed at the entrance's decorative stained-glass artisanship that gave the home its local name: *OZ.*

The stained glass above the height of the broad door was a beautiful representation of a sunrise, with the sun coming up behind the letters "O" and "Z."

Local stories of why the home's builder installed the stained glass ranged from spiritual to conspiratorial, but Amy knew that the inspiration for the stained glass needed no further explanation than the one Louis gave Amy long before his death:

His grandfather, Scott Hoyt, installed it at the turn of the twentieth century, in 1901, just after reading L. Frank Baum's, *The Wonderful Wizard of OZ.* The book's theme, a quest for intelligence, courage, heart, and home, impressed Scott Hoyt so much that he decided to name this home—his home—*OZ.*

She remembered what Louis said about a gift and Amy knocked on one of the front gate's white fence posts, loudly saying "hello." She wanted to be sure that Charles Hoyt heard her. She waited at the gate; the yellow and blue stained-glass window calmed her. It pulled her into the possibility that there really was a place like OZ, where everyone gets cleaned up and ready to go down a great hall to meet the master.

She observed the pathway from the white gate up the stairs and found him standing in the doorway. The master of the Oz House, Charles Hoyt, looked back at her.

"Hello back," Hoyt said.

"Hi Mr. Hoyt, I'm Amy . . ."

"I know who you are."

"Can I talk to you?" Amy said hesitantly.

Hoyt looked at Amy. His illuminating light blue eyes startled the young girl. The old man felt for a belt loop, upon which hung a set of keys. He fiddled with the hook, placed the keys in the palm of his hand, and descended the stairs, never taking his gaze from his son's friend.

Amy backed away from the gate to allow a respectable space between them, and to give the gate room to swing open.

Amy followed the old man to the freshly painted wooden stairway. He sat quietly on the bottom step, inviting Amy to sit with him.

For a moment, they watched the world go by. It was a small town, with a very small census population, but it seemed at times to Amy and Hoyt, that the intersection of Riverside Drive into Highway 1, was as noisy as any intersection in California. The roads intersected on a hill. Vehicle engines revved up the steep inclines while over-worked brakes screeched going downhill to the stop sign.

"It's noisy today," Amy said.

Hoyt surveyed the horizon. A herd of white cattle grazed on distant hillsides. Bands of clouds drifted across the sky. Amy was unsure of how to say what she wanted to say to Louis' dad.

"What's on your mind, young lady?" Hoyt asked.

"I'm not sure how to start this conversation, Mr. Hoyt."

Hoyt knew what she had come to say. It was the sign Louis told him to look for, the one that would initiate a seemingly insignificant series of events spanning ten minutes. Hoyt took a deep breath, connected to his departed son, and stated what he had longed to say:

"You are the one my boy said to keep an eye out for."

Amy turned toward the man's weathered face. He smiled broadly. Tears rose in his pale blue eyes.

"I am? What do you mean Mr. Hoyt?" Amy shifted away from Hoyt. She felt unsure. *How did he know I was coming over to give him a message from Louis, about a gift that he wants me to have?*

Hoyt looked hard at Amy. He accepted his son's assessment that Amy was the one who would receive what belonged to his boy.

Then Amy answered her own questions.

"In a daydream, he talked to me for quite a long time today, Mr. Hoyt."

"What did he say?"

"He talked about his hope for our world, that change was coming, and that it would come from, or be the product of, what lies up there, in his room," she said.

∽⑥〆

Hoyt pushed himself up. Using the blue wooden handrail, he steadied himself and turned to see if Amy was following him. She was behind him watching. He was fine, he could still get around, with the aid of his cane while he walked.

Hoyt opened the door. Amy could feel it instantly, what Louis described to her about the home he had lived in all his adult life. She felt light.

A steep, ornate set of stairs rose before her. To her left, a fine wooden doorway led into a large parlor-type room, to her right, the dining room, and in front of her, down a hallway that paralleled the stairs, was a long and narrow old-world kitchen.

"This way," Hoyt said, grasping the hand-hewed guardrail that rose to the second story, disappearing around a corner at the top.

Amy followed as the old man slowly moved ahead and up the stairs. She was surrounded by one hundred and forty plus years of photographs, starting at the bottom with ancient photos of the many businesses that the Hoyts still owned, and ending at the top, with the latest photos of Charles, Mary, and Louis.

Amy lost sight of Hoyt. From Louis' room, she heard him call her. She entered the light blue room, a color that perfectly reflected Hoyt's eyes.

Hoyt stood next to his son's bed, looking down at the object Louis had spoken of. Amy noted that it was the size and shape of one of her large Point Arena High School reference books. The room was filled with workbenches, desks, and bookshelves. One dim, incandescent light revealed everything to be in exacting order. The unusual dark work surfaces contained watch making tools, oils and lubricants, precision cutting instruments, jeweler's implements, and small tap and die sets. Amy looked questioningly at Hoyt. He invited her to touch the illuminated areas. She approached one of the dark surfaces, peering at it from above. She felt as if she were looking down into a well. Slowly extending a finger, Amy touched the surface and gasped as her finger sunk into it like water. She spun her finger around, inside the black water-like substance, and found that it was without temperature or weight, like air, having a dreamlike characteristic that made her smile at Hoyt. Removing her finger from the work surface, Amy inspected it and found it was dry, and odorless.

She walked to where Hoyt stood. He picked up a book-shaped object and lovingly handed it to Amy.

It was surprisingly light in her hands, and this surprised her. Her fingers began to appear as silhouettes, as the book began to radiate light. Through her fingers, holographic-like shapes appeared. They took on the outlines of figurines moving softly about the six sides of the book. The figurines displayed richly colored skin tones and brilliant garments, *costumes*, she thought.

As she turned the book over, closely examining each side, she distinguished the characters who were acting out a familiar literary scene: *it is Dorothy, the Scarecrow, the Tin Woodman, and the Cowardly Lion, walking along the yellow brick road!*

"Open it," Hoyt said.

Amy hesitated. Her eyes watered. The brilliantly displayed scenes astounded her. She lifted the top cover, and a bright green iridescent light poured from its interior.

"Touch it," Hoyt said.

Amy lightly touched the book. Vivid images appeared to her.

"Read it, like you have seen Louis read his Braille books."

She began to run her fingers over the surface, starting at the top, left-hand corner of the interior surface. She closed her eyes as her mind filled with images and sounds that she had never experienced before. The images organized in sequence, and the familiar story began to unfold: *The Wonderful Wizard of Oz.*

She pulled her fingertips away from Louis' creation, and asked, "What is this?"

"It's what Louis left for you, Amy. It is his creation. As simply as I can state it, this is a roadmap connecting your brain to that part of his mind that Louis' called *Oz*.

Forty years ago, he created a new kind of technology for the imprinted Braille world, based on colored liquids - specialized inks that somehow transferred information through his fingertips, into his mind. He began to read and to perceive, through his fingertips, an entire spectrum of colors and sounds. They traveled across his receptor nerve endings, as he tried to explain to me countless times, into the previously unused portion of his mind. Louis said that he had found a pathway beyond our existing memory, into what he wanted to call heaven, but chose instead to name after this home, and L. Frank Baum's story."

"You mean that as I read this . . . new kind of Braille . . . through the Baum story, I will be lead, as Dorothy was, line by line, paragraph by paragraph, page by page, and chapter by chapter, to the Emerald City . . . to Oz . . . to heaven . . . in my own mind?" Amy asked.

"That, in a nutshell, is correct," Hoyt said.

Amy sat on the bed, with Louis' telling of Baum's story in her hands. She looked back up at the old man. "And he wants me to have this?"

"Yes."

"Why? What will I do with it?

"Amy," Hoyt said. "There is a stream of consciousness disregarded in this world that carries great significance. This stream says that the message must get through. Louis was very direct about this. He told me that someone will appear at the front gate, a most unlikely person, who will tell me that he or she was sent by him to ask for this precious tool. That person is you. What you do with it is now up to you. You are obviously Louis' messenger."

Amy stared out the window of Louis' bedroom, across the street, to her own bedroom window. She sat with Louis' weightless invention on her lap, holding it carefully. She saw her mother pulling into the driveway, home from work.

"Mr. Hoyt, I must go. My mother is home."

Hoyt gestured toward the bedroom door. Amy got up and began to leave when Hoyt asked if he could hold it one more time. She gave it to him and watched his tears stream down his face. She put her hand on his. He looked into her eyes and gave the box to the young girl.

"You go," Hoyt said.

Staying behind in his son's room, listening to the familiar footfall of steps down the staircase, and out the front door, Hoyt remembered Louis bouncing down the stairs in like fashion. From the window, he watched Amy enter her home holding the book. He stayed there, staring. For how long he was not sure.

❧❧

"Hello," Linda said from the front door entrance, tossing her keys and purse onto a side table. A printed email fell out of her purse and floated to the floor. "Amy, are you home?" At first, Linda did not notice Amy's lack of a response. The day's thoughts consumed her. She was anxious to tell her daughter about work, about the email from company headquarters, and more importantly, about the talk she had with Paul on the phone.

"Mom! I'm home"

"Where were you honey?"

"Across the street, Mom. I was visiting with Mr. Hoyt. I have so much I need to tell you."

"Hold on Amy, I've got a couple of things I need to share with you first."

"But Mom . . .!"

"Amy, hold on, did you go into his house? Wait a minute, we'll come back to that. I need to talk to you. I spoke to Paul this afternoon . . . he's not coming back."

With that, Linda broke. She flew into her daughter's arms and sobbed. "I'm sorry, Amy. I'm sorry to put you through this again. Please, forgive me. I don't know why this keeps happening."

Amy gently pushed her mother away, cupped her face with her hands, and gave her a long kiss on her forehead.

"Mom, it's okay. Paul was Paul. You did your best, but I've seen it coming for some time now. He just wasn't happy."

Linda looked at Amy's scalp, for signs of healing. Scabs had formed where hair once was. Her daughter seemed to be unfazed by Paul's assault.

"I'm going to miss him, Amy."

"I know Mom, but you keep looking for someone like my father, and though there is no shortage, I doubt you'll ever find someone like him again."

Linda gave Amy a sigh of resignation.

"To try and change the subject, I have a bit of odd news for you Amy."

"Mom, I've got some strange news too."

Linda finally noticed the object in her daughter's hands.

"What is that?"

"When I was sitting upstairs this afternoon, I had a visit from Dad, just like the ones before, only this time Dad's face turned into Louis'."

Linda sighed. She had always been concerned about Amy's visualizations of her father but had grown accustomed to them. But to have these visualizations now include Louis upset Linda.

"Amy, how do you know it was Louis, and not your imagination, or inspired by you missing him?"

Linda looked questioningly at Amy.

"Wait a minute, did you tell me you went into his house today?"

Linda remembered the odd stories, thoughts of the strange long life every Hoyt enjoyed, and of the superstition that a Native American medicine man was buried at the foot of the house's tall, century-and-a-half-old American Elm.

"How many times have I told you not to go in there? Why do you disobey me, Amy? Before I forget, I need to tell you something that happened this morning at work. I received a company-wide email that asked whether anyone had seen a man whose photo was attached. The photo was our buddy from Kinney Road. He is quite the looker when he's cleaned up."

Linda looked for the email finding it under her foot.

Amy suddenly felt protective of Louis' book. Without understanding why, she slid it behind her, to hide it from her mother, who was lost in her description of the young man, and the strange coincidence of him helping them with a flat tire earlier in the week. Amy could tell that Linda was stressed. She decided not to mention the details of her afternoon. She went upstairs to clean up for dinner.

Suddenly she and her mother were thrown to the floor, their bodies heaving repeatedly. Debris and dust were everywhere. Windows burst. Books flew. Shelves toppled. Walls began to crumble. Death felt near.

ELEVEN

Foreboding.

A powerful word, its definition conveying doom and fear.

Debilitating in its worst form, foreboding links to a sense of warning, then trepidation.

There have been repeated cries over decades that our use of the earth's resources is unconscionable.

We justify using a full tank of gas, in one day, as our right in the pursuit of our American Dream. We justify eating more than we need for much needed comfort. We alter the natural state of our minds with alcohol and drugs, desperate to fill the emptiness in our hearts.

We have become, a people who consume. We take more than we give. Most of us have a sense of foreboding about this. We know that shortages will catch up to us or our children.

M. W. - Gualala

Dust settled. Though emotionally and spiritually shaken beyond understanding, by the magnitude of the earthquake, Mitchell Walker, and Leo Brenamann, were physically fine.

"Are you okay, son?" Mitchell shouted, his ears ringing from the noise of the quake.

"I think so." Leo looked around, dulled, and frightened by the enormity of their present situation. He recalled the quicksand as he tried to sit up, touching the clay drying on his neck, and the heaviness in his mud-soaked clothes.

"You saved me . . . from the quicksand! How did you pull me out? Where is it?"

Terror seized them, with the realization that Leo would have lost his life had Mitchell not been able to pull him out.

"I don't know how I did it, I just knew I had to." Mitchell pointed to a discolored patch of ground next to their feet. "I think that's the quicksand. It's resumed its natural state. The vibrating has stopped."

Suddenly, Gunnar appeared, wrapped in a ragged garment made of striped, multi-colored cloth. The coat made him look like a vagabond. Its rainbow of colors changed shades between each hue.

"Who is this?" Leo quietly asked Mitchell. "How does he float above the ground? I saw him walking along the top of the bridge earlier without moving his legs. He rose into the sky when the ground around us started to move. Is he God? Why is he here? And for that matter, who the hell are you?"

Leo regained his short-term memory, remembering everything that happened since they stood near the now dead Alder Creek.

"I'm Mitchell Walker. This is Gunnar, and he is exactly what he appears to be, a spirit. You must be Leo Brenamann. You know, the police are looking for you. Are you in trouble?"

Leo answered, "Yea, I'm Leo Brenamann. Thank you for saving my life."

He looked into Mitchell's eyes, assessing his trustworthiness. He wanted to tell the man who saved his life exactly what he was running from, and why the police were after him.

Mitchell turned toward Gunnar. "Are you okay?"

"I am finer than that," Gunnar said, in a trance like state. "I experienced Mother Nature yawning and stretching. She has awoken from a long rest and beheld the skin of Her body, the surface and soil of the earth, and is shocked by its treatment. She is outraged at the condition of Her space, the air that She, too, breathes to stay alive, and of the water She drinks, and has decided, with full agreement from the Great One, to alter man's imprint upon Her. She is washing her hands of twenty-first century man."

"Just like that?" Mitchell asked. "We're through. No more chances to make amends?"

"She is only altering those who have taken more than they give, those who over-consume, those who are changing Her natural order by creating chaos and altering life in ways She never imagined. She is angry."

Gunnar put his arms around himself, turning his face to the sun, then towards the four winds, knowing he was an extension of Mother Nature, his music a wave of Her hands over his life. The air he breathed brought with it Her inspiration.

"This is why we live," Gunnar continued. "Not for the consumption of goods, but for our individual connection to God's Mother Earth."

Leo and Mitchell stared at Gunnar. He rose above the ground, slowly turning again to the four winds, his profile blending into each horizon.

"I want this," Leo said, his eyes upon Gunnar, and his heart filled with Gunnar's words. His eyes teared up, remembering his father's face in long-ago camping and fishing memories. Gunnar's expressions reminded Leo of the sound and smell of meals prepared in a camp frying pan, his father smiling and talking to him about the nature of things.

"I've had this," Mitchell said, his eyes fixed on Gunnar. "I often lose it, but then find it again when I stop looking for justice to the madness and cruelty I've known in my life. I knew this connection as a younger man, with my son, walking along the banks of a river in Arizona."

"To go back to what I have done," Leo said, "to become a part of the digital-techno culture again, would kill me. I want to be a part of the simple rotation of Mother Nature. I want only what I've been given and wait in peace for the rest. I want to know patience, and heart-felt connections to life. I want all things to exist in moderation, and to feel some want in my living. How can I expect to know what Gunnar knows by staring a computer monitor, filled with scrolling code? How can I know my heart, when my senses are consumed by artificial color and synthesized sound? I've known that something like this was going to happen. I tried to warn my managers. Code that I was developing revealed unexpected results that suggested change was pending. My boss wrote it off as a product of my over-active imagination, and to all the years, I spent playing Internet games. This is why the police are after me. The code I wrote proved true. I deleted all of it from the company's servers. It's locked in my head. The science that serves as its foundation proves the spiritual existence of paradox, which I believe proves the existence of God. I don't want to go back to that windowless room, filled with blinking cursors and complex algorithms."

"I understand Leo," Mitchell said. The deeper meanings in Leo's words spoke to him; he felt akin to this young man's thoughts, based on his own memories and experiences.

"I want to know the reason for my life, to understand the makeup of my soul, to know why paradox exists, and to understand free will. There is so much amiss in today's world. Humanity has lost its instinct for living, its innate connection to nature. Humankind has lost its understanding of the paradox, the self-contradiction that life presents every day. Life has been reduced to common automatic responses with no dimension or color, on innovation or creativity. We work too hard and too long in prolonging our lives, all in a self-absorbed effort to deny death as the natural, unavoidable end of life. As rabid consumers, we give little thought to the consequences of our actions: excessive debt, deteriorating health, exhausting natural resources. Yet when death appears, we expect these same behaviors to save us – the definition of insanity."

"What can we do?" Leo asked, in response to Mitchell's comments.

"I think there is much to be done," Gunnar said. "There are many souls that long for the insights you two have expressed. There is a world out there that is lost, now more than ever. Self-serving pundits have long exploited this, known as the *End of Days*. Now, as technology has taken over the collective soul, humanity has lost its grip on what is critically important and why we are here.

The actions you take will greatly affect the world. Your hearts will change the course of humanity. You will bring the principled 'well-lived' life back to the fore-front; a life filled with courage, compassion, and faith in the Great One, loyalty to Mother Earth, and kindness, respect, and fine fellowship for one another."

―――

My dearest Mitchell,

I lie awake in the darkness of my soul. Murky water still drains about me, trickling like dead blood into the broken past. You are not here with me. Everything with color is gone, every nuance of feeling has decayed. I wither. I have lost my way, and I cannot find my way back to you.

Your lost and true Red

TWELVE

On the horizon, a vision appeared, translucent outlines of concrete,
steel, glass, and paper. These symbolic elements of our culture
slipped under the surf, disappearing with the double yellow line.

It was a road to the end, a return to the sea. I watched as the
mighty Pacific claimed the march of man's materialism for Her
own. Her clawing waves of water and salt grabbed those things
that gave nothing back.

I saw my car submerged, triggering an old, overwhelming fear that
I would not be able to make its monthly payment. I saw my old
friends, Peter and
Paul, walking together along the double yellow line. With their left
hands in front of them, one paid the other, and behind them with
their right hands,
payment was returned. I realized the ghostly images had been part
of my life for years. It was not my hard work, or my character, that
carried me through my life: it was Peter and Paul.

I cried as I realized I had created nothing but debt in my life. I was
drawn toward Peter and Paul, and for a moment wanted to walk
with them along the double yellow, into the sea, and end my
misspent life, but the vision of Mother Nature reclaiming all things
man-made stopped me.

M.W. - Robinson Gulch

———————

Mitchell pulled out a pen and journal from his backpack. It had been a while since he last wrote to his beloved, his Red. Upon a rock, facing the Pacific Ocean, Mitchell put pen to paper, and wrote another letter to the memory of his wife. Although never mailed, he believed these letters still got through to her.

Dear Red,

In my last letter, I was writing about clearing out my soul. Through no effort of my own, it seems an earthquake has accomplished this.

I do not know where to begin. Maybe just right here, fifty feet south of the San Andreas Fault, where I endured the great quake. The field where I sit is lined with ancient fences and open spaces of tall grass, tips pressed like paintbrushes against blue sky, ocean borne breezes as hands that move them. At eye level, fields become Pacific Ocean white caps. My soul is pulled as waves recede. Ancient lives move through me: fence builders in simpler times.

Simplicity is the gift. My soul longs for the natural world, where present moments are paramount. On near hills I see ancient Redwoods; surviving two thousand years, nothing when compared to the Pacific Ocean: a great gear turning Earth's evolution forward. Passing histories of time puts my short life into perspective. It appears that Mother Nature spared the lives of the old Redwoods, my Red-love.

My life, as fleeting as the shadows of ravens flying overhead. My life, once filled with toxic Wall Street and Madison Avenue priorities. My life, consuming mass quantities of resources to heat, cool, feed, and protect it. My life, defined by credit scores and debt. My life, stained by blood and revenge of your death. I am sorry, Red. Memories overwhelm me at times.

I continue to live frugally, paying as I go. I look across inactive farms of former times, across white water, to a lighthouse that, oddly, like old Redwoods, still stands. I look at curving horizon. I live without walls yet feel more at home than any other place I have known. In walking away from mass consumption, my soul remembers boyhood beliefs, something you gave me. Here on this rock, I feel as I once did during our life together. On this road, I have come home to you and our life. I feel free. I remember what a deep, unencumbered breath meant to us, in our cabin, south of Prescott. I am dancing with you in the tall grass, while you whisper your truth in my ear, that the great value in living is known only in this here and now.

I walk up and down this California coast, rediscovering Mother Nature's great art and magic. Not a single traffic light flashes for forty miles going north on

Highway 1, and for seventy-five miles in either direction east or south of where I sit. It is as rural a land as I have ever known, far more beautiful than expected.

I am amazed at the turn of events. I struggle to understand grace and serendipity. I survived this earthquake. I know that my effort, and your wings upon my shoulders, will deliver me with the few clothes and supplies I carry.

I am safe, fed, and am fortunate to have the company of two new friends, one old, and one young. Red, I am quite blessed and quite lucky to find my soul here, safe after this great quake, among the Redwoods, and Pacific Ocean, owing nothing to no one, except what effort my life calls from me at this moment. I have become, without trying to be, Longfellow's village blacksmith.

With all my love,

Mitchell

———

Leo did his best to settle himself following his brush with death: the earthquake, its breathtaking movement through land and sea, and quicksand's boa constrictor swallow. He felt snatched from the slimy gullet of sand in the nick of time.

Out to the sea's horizon, Leo saw the road he used to access Manchester State Park, its end covered by shallow ocean water. The non-descript buildings at the end of the road still stood, but their foundations were under water. The water tower's support legs were submerged by surf.

He remembered the spirit Rosalie, her goodness, her warmth. Rosalie had renewed him, had given him hope. Staring down Kinney Road, Leo followed two bright, narrow yellow lines flowing into the shallow water at its end. He saw Rosalie. She moved toward him as Gunnar had, effortlessly over the fields of grass. Her endless grey hair cascaded around her face, and Leo felt the old ways of the world within it. Natural cycles: survival, change, and hardship, moved through her hair like orbiting planets around a sun. Her eyes filled with the deep blue of the universe. As her hands reached out across the distance for Leo's, he heard her say:

> *From the Saints Peter and Paul, I bring to you a message of hope. Your sin of debt is forgiven. Today you will live differently. Now you will live within a day's effort and nothing more. Now you will live without scores, cleansed of their evil hold on your life. They have marked you, but today you can reject them; today you can purge their crushing control over you, and live without them, come what may. Soon you will know exactly where and how you stand on this earth renewed. Known you shall be, by your actions, each day that you have left to live.*

Leo watched as the familiar saints of biblical tales, Peter, and Paul, herding man-made insanity into the all-consuming energy of the earth's great gear. The Pacific Ocean gladly consumed the debris of comfort and convenience, of material madness, of debt-

113

filled living, the soul-robbing detritus, of a world gone mad. There was no escape from the hard, simple, true rule of living as Mother Nature intended.

———

My dearest Mitchell,

But I remember you. I remember our home, our love, our days in the sun, our nights under the moon. I feel those flashes of our life. Sudden and sharp are my visions of you.

Now I feel the dark water remove more of me. How can this be? Please, my love, reach for me, and pull me through, into your warmth, into the spirit of breath, into our time as husband and wife. Please, lift me up, and away from here.

Your own Red

THIRTEEN

---

*They have been called the Greatest Generation. I believe it.
History books and first-person accounts of those days are real and
direct.*

*Yet their greatness was saddled with horror and
depravation.*

*This terror was the Greatest Generation's inspiration to
overcome.*

*The world had demonstrated that good comes with evil. It is
the law of paradox. Whatever presents as benevolent and truthful
co-exists with wickedness.*

*The courage and kindness in this generation were matched
by the moral turpitude and iniquity of the times: endless acts of
heroism during WWII in stark contrast to the scoundrel of our
epoch, who methodically murdered six and a half million Jews, and
was directly responsible for the deaths of another fifty million
people between 1931 and 1945.*

*As a nation, the character of this generation raised the bar
in the face of unspeakable horror. Both are necessary if we are to
learn from the experience of war.*

M. W. - Gualala River Redwood Park

Lois put her hands on the fabric of her dress, which covered
a full, pregnant belly, and let the tenderness of the thin, dry, cotton

soften the guilt over her circumstance. Disgrace overwhelmed her. When she touched growing stretch marks on her hips, shame tunneled its way in. She was humiliated, and cried as if she were cursed, mortified by the baby she carried, embarrassed that she brought dishonor as an unmarried, pregnant woman.

Her dress, one of three that she washed and pressed each week, was also her uniform. She looked in the woman's washroom mirror, and adjusted her nurse's bonnet, getting herself ready to face the persecuting judgement of her fellow nurses. They shunned her, and had lobbied, unsuccessfully, to have her fired. Fortunately, they knew only that she was *not* married. Who the father was had remained a secret.

Had Lois been aware, she would have been heartened by a kind reprieve: that at no time in history were illegitimate births more prevalent. The war brought fear, want, sacrifice, and loneliness. All these human emotions drove men and women to seek one another, forgetting for a few moments, seeking comfort in skin touching skin.

The world was burdened with illegitimate babies born by the millions, during these fighting years. A man and a woman wrapped themselves tight in the call of life, longing for safety. Physical love was a momentary heaven in the hell they were living.

Lois traveled from Illinois to Maine to an institution for women in similar conditions shunned by their communities. Her hospital administrator made all the arrangements in Cloudless, Maine, through a childhood friend: Homer.

The train ride was long. She saw other pregnant women at train stations imagining they were waiting for their husbands. She was sure she was the only one who had succumbed to temptation; especially the depraved kind of temptation while she watched the father of her unborn child masturbating under his bed covers.

She sighed remembering those confusing moments when she made the decision each night to start her rounds ordering *lights out*. She would quietly walk down a particular hall in the old orphanage building, to a particular door. It had no knob, no latch. It was often silently left ajar. Timing was important. She had to wait long enough for the boy to feel alone.

Discovering him, and his activity, was purely by accident. She was securing doors and checking lights when she found his door open. The light of a softly glowing new moon revealed bed covers over a boy that moved rapidly up and down. She knew instantly what he was doing and could not look elsewhere. She stared at the boy stroking himself and listened with wonder as imperceptible moans emanated beneath sheet covers. She waited and watched each time he removed the bed covers, exposing himself to her, getting ready for the climax and his ejaculation. Each time it happened, she felt dizzy and short of breath, instantly removing herself, walking briskly to the woman's restroom, where, in a private stall, she would relieve herself of the overwhelming desire to put the boy inside her.

This happened often. For weeks, then months, as one full moon followed another, she would soundlessly open the door just enough to watch the covers come off. She would wait, with great anticipation, for the blissful satisfaction that he would emit when he was done.

Again, Lois hurried to the bathroom stall, putting her fingers between her thighs, sliding them up and down, watching with wonder as her white skirt moved in rhythm with her building ecstasy. It was the memory of his moving blankets that pushed her over the edge, lust bubbling forth. She keenly longed to know what his erection felt like.

Finally, after feeling the self-induced joy of her fantasy, and the guilt that always followed, she discovered what haunted her so intensely.

Lois walked silently down the sanitized hallway, feeling the wall for balance, as blood rushed through her, as the anticipation of what she was about to do excited her. She found herself at his door, and with a pale new moon visible through the room's window, she opened the door and slipped in.

She stood breathlessly, as she watched the boy's hand move under the sheets. She marveled at his ability to pleasure himself with delicate movements of his fingertips, gently caressing his organ, as it grew. She caught her breath when he put his hand around it and began slowly to stroke it. Her sudden intake of air stopped the boy for moment, but he began again to move toward the joy he wanted to feel.

Lois moved closer to him, sitting on the side of his bed, startling the boy. She put her hand gently on top of the mound under his sheet. She put her other hand on his face. He could smell the aroma of soap and indentified her instantly. The boy knew who was with him and pulled his covers back fully erect.

Without delay, Lois positioned herself above him and sank over John Doe No. 24, taking him in, and with a lustful reach, made herself and the deaf and blind orphan boy orgasm together.

As she stared down upon his angelic features, she fell in love with him.

She touched his face, running her fingers along his cheekbone, across his nose, then lips. He smiled, putting his hand on her hand, lifting it up and resting it on his forehead. She felt his forehead's warmth, thinking it might be a fever, but it was not. The warmth was more than just a rise in body heat. It calmed her and led her into feeling love again. She put both hands upon No. 24's face, and kissed him, loving him.

This silent, moonlit dance by Lois and No. 24 occurred on several more occasions, on consecutive nights, as the moon traveled from wax to wane.

Her love and lust for the boy grew and then dissipated, following the pattern of the earth's orbiting satellite. Soon the risk of being caught with him outweighed her desire to answer his swelling nighttime habit, and she stopped.

It became enough to just watch his nightly exercise lull him into a peaceful sleep. She would come in, wipe his hands and penis clean of the semen's scent and stickiness, and wrap his sheets and blankets tightly around him as a mother would her child.

The quiet, emotional acknowledgment of her loneliness in the world came from her love for John Doe No. 24

On the train to Cloudless, she opened a book of Longfellow poetry and cried for the blacksmith who had lost his wife.

FOURTEEN

Got to get past negative
thinking.
Got to get past fear, ever-
growing.

A door of amends that has
been long arranged,
becomes a familiar part of
our lives now changed.
So, we walk up and cross
the threshold,

and find only trust, as
our friend of old.

There is nothing of an old life to hang on to; all of it has
transcended. Nothing can touch us now, gone is the long arm of old
habit, invisibility has given relief to secrets now dead. We are in
tune to a new way, a new world way, where chaos holds no quarter
while the sun is setting.

We know our talisman, we hold it close to our hearts, and before a
full moon rising, we thank our new and everlasting God for it.

M. W. - Robinson's Point

Poama was the child's name. She flowed over the broken landmasses in elevated and playful motions. She would stop along her way to comprehend the new earth revealed by the quake, and sadly, beheld the fallen, especially the younglings. They were just babies, Poama's youthful spirit thought, like me. They had just started their long reach of the blue heavens, they had just begun their grasp of Earth's angels, falling free form from the clouds above, to feel their presence on their skin and bark.

Poama looked upon the upturned earth and beheld a group of beings gathered around a fire, two spirits and two humans, conversing with one another.

Slowly she made her way to the group. Initially, they did not register her presence.

Mitchell saw her first. He noted the peace found in her eyes; a peace through acceptance of her old life.

Poama moved closer to the group. Each welcomed her. Smiling, she approached the light of the fire, grateful for the symbolism found there: quiet comfort and warmth. She said she was daughter and descendant of a great Pomo Indian family that had lived in the area for a millennium.

She recalled her death. Mitchell, Leo, Gunnar, and Rosalie all steadied her as she remembered landmasses shifting and a great wave of seawater covering her, filling her lungs then crushing them. Ocean water filled with floating boulders, trees, wooden framing, and farm equipment. She saw members of her family looking at her.

124

Her soul longed for gravity to force the water to recede. She remembered her body convulsing, and her mind reeling, as the cold salt water burned her lungs. She felt the pain lessen.

The beauty of the evolving earth replaced her fear; it fascinated her soul. As she rose through the water, her earthly body, in its simple dress, floated in peace among the fractured pieces of her familiar life. Her spirit looked toward the sea and saw time shred all human life. Untold millions of human souls were claimed by the mighty Pacific Ocean, each accounted for, each honored for breathing the earth's air, for drinking its water. Poama claimed this vision as reference for the future.

She knew what was and what would be. Rosalie and Gunnar smiled at her. Mitchell looked through Poama's vision, to a time when he would again hold his Red.

Leo realized his time with this human and these spirits allowed him to understand that life was more than code, a tumbling of numbers that dictated who he was for as long as he could remember.

The humans, in search of rest, placed their worn bodies next to fallen redwoods; the spirits in trinity around fading campfire light. Mitchell smiled at them. The world had changed by hands of a dual God, part mother and part father, in raging change of the world.

≈๑๑≈

The morning sun light was obscured by a thickening fog bank, rolling up steppes around Manchester, California. Quiet ruled this moment. The trinity was gone. Mitchell looked at Leo, who looked like a young boy, sleeping.

Mitchell rebuilt the fire. He rummaged through his pack to find two food bars, opening one and putting the other in his breast pocket for Leo.

Light and heat filled the campsite. One by one, Gunnar, Rosalie, and Poama followed the light from the redwood tree line and returned to their appearances in life.

"I suggest today is the day we act," Gunnar said, as Leo stirred. Mitchell gave Leo the food bar with a smile. Leo sighed, *Life has changed*, he thought. Rosalie looked at Leo and noticed that the flashing cursor in his eyes was blurring.

"Act on what, Gunnar?" Leo asked.

"I think it is time for the two of you to move back into society, with information describing how it is changing," Gunnar said, speaking not only to Mitchell and Leo, but to the entire area around them.

"What information?" Leo asked, in alarmed tone.

Mitchell looked at the trinity. Had he finally arrived at the moment when all that he had lived through would manifest into a greater good? He understood Gunnar's call to action. Leo noticed Mitchell's comprehension.

"What information?" Leo asked again in increasing concern.

"I passed through Point Arena, a stone's throw from here," Mitchell Walker stated. "Into an old church to rest, I met an old man who spoke to me. Perhaps we relocate there, see how we can help, and seek shelter from this cold and fog. Do you three feel the weather?" Mitchell asked, looking at Gunnar, Poama, and Rosalie.

"We sense color and sound in all things, including weather, but not its temperature or force," Gunnar said. "I think shelter would be a good thing for you two. We have spoken; you two are the catalysts, the interpreters of change, our collective voice in this volatile age. We are your guides. We are the way, the truth, and the light, as it was once said in your religions gone wrong. We have among us, youth, age, and contributions, to finding your path in this new, imaginative time. Youth will give you energy and dreams, age will give you reason and understanding, and our contributions will reveal your gifts, as they are needed in this new world."

Looking directly at Leo, Gunnar finished: "You will find the meanings of your lives in the days to come. Soon you will understand why you are, who you are."

———

My Dearest Mitchell,

I watch. The sun sets upon you this evening. I put my hand upon your shoulder, my face mirrors the orange blaze of God's child, of Helios and Clymene, of endless reflection, of day's end, and with you, through your stars of tears, I too cry.

I weep. I long for my earth-bound love. In the cobalt blue grey of dusk, as the blaze succumbed, as the ocean's white tips curl into darkness, as the horizon blends ocean and sky, I remember you.

I sing. Among the cypress, I hear long departed music, cascading back to our life, from unimagined places. My lips open, I voice my heart to you, and as the quivering of the world resonates its change, your sense of the night unfolding trembles through me.

I love. You are my return road. My open road. My soul's longing for its time beside you. Your pain and your hunger keep me by your side, though you know not that I am here.

Your own true love, your Red

FIFTEEN

Statements of fact from the pundits of Internet forums are never to be trusted.

Long ago, the political and religious blades of power-hungry minds sliced the truth away from the democratic process. The vision of young men two hundred and fifty years ago, who knew how to comprehend heaven on earth, did so through passionate, inspirational thought and deed. That comprehension included to live and let live, recognizing each life as precious.

Yet now, such inspired living, the pouring out of heaven on earth, is cut by the few at the expense of many.

M. W. - Bourns Gulch

Amy clawed her way toward Linda during the quake. An exhausted part of her mind could barely comprehend how walls, ceilings, and broken glass had not cut her and crushed her body to dust. Her only desire was to reach her mother.

Mother and daughter finally were able to find each other, entwining their fingers together.

Silence followed the sounds of massive destruction. Water and gas bubbled noiselessly from pipes; electricity sparked gently to the ground. Man's industry and development lay useless.

In her imagination:

Amy ascended a long, wooden, beautifully hand-crafted staircase. She stopped and looked over the edge of the handrail. Glowing softly below, rainbow colors blended and rotated, merging, and creating an endless spectrum.

Resuming her climb, above she observed the opposite: filtered light, grey in all its shades . . . gloomy . . . dusty . . .

Amy, and her mother, fainted.

∼ঔ৩∽

Amy woke first. She sensed simultaneously pain, weight, and the horror of mangled collapse around her. She coughed and heaved. Dust and debris flew about, settling on her face and in her eyes. Flashes of her recent life skimmed by – *my mother, Paul's rage, Louis' spirit, his invention.* A changing blue sky appeared through the roof joists and fragmented walls, streaked with colored smoke.

Linda stirred and coughed. She began to gag, as mold, mixed with dust, entered her lungs. Her eyes widened as she took in the scene above her. *Pixie sticks*, she thought. She tried to move her legs, pinned motionless by rubble.

Her diaphragm convulsed. Liquid rose in her throat, pushing dirt with it. She inhaled too quickly, sucking gastric acid and mildew into her lungs. The sensation of drowning added to the weight of being crushed. Each time she coughed, she tasted more stomach acid.

Linda was dying. The sensation of life passing calmed her enough to recognize the clutching fingertips of her daughter's hand. *My Amy, beautiful, beloved daughter, still alive enough to reach out for me.*

Linda was now inside her daughter's heart. She could feel Amy's love and fear.

⊰⊱

In fading consciousness, Amy's vision continued:

She turned around, running down the ornate staircase, toward what was rainbow color but a moment ago, now turned blood red. As she looked down at her feet, the stairs dropped into the earth. Sweat formed across her brow, her heart beat like a bass drum. She missed a step and stumbled forward, landing hard on a corner platform, where the staircase turned left at a ninety-degree angle. Grey and gloom swirled above her. Always turning inside . . . always inside . . . always sinking down . . . always down.

Amy crawled to the platform's edge and peered into the abyss, glowing red.

She frantically turned back, climbing upward, faster, harder, wanting desperately to get back to where her mother lay prone and pinned down.

Tears lined Amy's face. She feared her mother was gone. She could feel and hear her life end. She did not let go of her mother's fingers. She squeezed them with all her might, thinking that the pain of doing so might wake her.

As she clutched her hand, Amy remembered her mother's nose. In her mind, as she leaned in, she saw her tears drop onto her mother's face. Linda's eyes were open, staring. She put her mother's head in her hands, lifting her forehead close to her lips. Amy kissed her mother's nose endlessly, deeply inhaling her scent. Remembering: *her laughter, her broken hearts, her harsh words, her spontaneous opinions.*

"Mom, wake up!" she said loudly, not hearing her own words, which made her think she was dreaming, or that her mother was sleeping.

"Wake up! Please wake up!"

With no response, Amy thought, *she is sleeping. Yes, I am certain, she is sleeping.*

⊷⊶

Amy was unable to measure the amount of time she laid with her arm outstretched, her mother's fingers laced in her own. She was unable to gauge shadow as day or night. Linda's fingers grew cold in her own and then stiffened.

When she was no longer able to bend her mother's fingers, Amy reluctantly let go. She felt her mom's hand curl away from her.

Slowly, she recognized her mother's head falling to one side, the position found between gravity and the weight of dead things.

Amy wailed.

She dragged her hand across the floor, bumping into Louis' book, pulling it close to her side. It emanated gentle warmth, like a puppy's tummy. She slipped back again into the immediate past, and the nightmare made of wooden stairs, unable to comprehend the vision's meaning.

She had found a place on the staircase, closer to the world above, where she was less anxious. She wanted to know why her mother was gone and why everything in her life had changed.

No answers came, just the haunting redness of walls revealing jagged shadows of evil, brighter and clearer, as time passed.

She remembered her mother. She no longer had to contend with living; her struggle was over.

The scorching redness on walls diminished, and grey covered the grey shadows above.

She could not see whose voices came through the rubble. Earlier there was shouting and cries for help. Rescuers stopped entering the many debris mounds that now were the town of Point Arena, fearing further collapse.

Now Amy was ready to shout for assistance but heard shooting. Someone pulled a gun, killing another, ordering others to fall into line with him as boss, or face the same fate. She heard footsteps move down Riverside Drive and then south on Main Street. Fear crushed her, and she slipped into further nightmares of life, crushed by nature's reverse on man's greed.

Instinctively, she moved her feet. Surprised, she felt each toe move, registering a response. She could move her legs, she was not pinned, as her mother was.

Amy pulled up into a sitting position, turned toward her mother and saw her mother's lifeless body, covered by shards of glass and wood. Amy could feel every cut on her mother's body in her own skin.

She shook her hair loose of debris and dust, spitting heavily onto the floor between her legs. She wanted to wipe away the muddy tears on her face but chose not to grind more dirt into her eyes, ears, and skin.

Columns of smoke were streaming through the moonlit sky, and reminded Amy of clouds that traversed the blue sky earlier in the day . . . *or was it the day before?*

The memory of clouds made her think of Mr. Hoyt, his son, and then Louis' invention, which remained by her side, providing some warmth and comfort.

Daylight returned. More voices woke Amy. Their quality was much different from what she had heard the night before; these voices had an uplifting tone. Her spirit reached upward, through the rubble, as a hand might find its way from hell toward heaven. She summoned the strength to cry out to those reassuring voices.

Help me please! She thought, reciting the phrase repeatedly.

Help! Help me!

Amy could not get the words out. She sat up, saw the group's heads, and saw three Louis-like embodiments floating about Mr. Hoyt and two others. She looked down at Louis' invention, which had increased in its light and warmth.

Amy thought she saw a furrowed brow grow across Mr. Hoyt's face as he viewed her shattered home.

I'm here Mr. Hoyt. Please come across the street! Look for me! Mr. Hoyt! I'm here! I'm here!

To Amy's surprise, the trinity of spirits each looked in Amy's direction. To her dismay, each turned back to the conversation taking place between Louis' dad and his visitors. The entire group began climbing Mr. Hoyt's stairs, making their way into the Oz House.

◈◈

Amy fell back, defeated.

In her continuing vision, she turned around and walked down the enchanted staircase, toward the diminished red embers that glowed from the bottom of the abyss.

SIXTEEN

Someday, the Promise *says, we will find everything we are looking for. If paradox remains on both sides of the same road, "everything we are looking for," is found within us.*

"Everything we are looking for," is now driven by the madness of "keeping up with the

Jones," which more than our neighbor next door, extends to everyone's ceaseless desire for everything advertising has instructed us to purchase.

M. W. – Cooks Beach

Scott Hoyt watched the calm, blue-green waters of the Pacific lap around his feet. He looked again at the date on the banner of the local newspaper: July 1st, 1874.

With a nervous but keen eye on the ocean's horizon, he awaited the arrival of an important consignment barge from San Francisco.

He heard no word of the barge's progress. He was there on a hunch; that the arrival of his precious freight was imminent.

Many obstacles had been overcome to put his plan, his dream, into place. He was to build a house on a hill, about a mile inland from where he stood. Crowning pieces to his home were aboard the barge: a three-paneled front door with overhead lead crystal glass windows and the railing and newel posts for the staircase, all made of Manchester poplar, found only in northwest England. The stylish and grand Victorian home, made of local redwood and oak, stood on a lot over-looking the small coastal town of Point Arena.

As a prominent dairy farmer and merchant, Hoyt felt it was time to build a home that reflected his success in life. His theatrical wife of ten years and his precocious nine-year-old daughter loved its ostentation. His seven-year-old son appreciated having his own room. The home provided all the utility that could be afforded in late nineteenth-century America. Hoyt wanted the house to stand out, and it did. It contained inch-thick tongue and groove oak flooring, hand-turned porch posts, Steeply pitched roofs, colorfully painted brick, ornate gables, painted iron railings, churchlike rooftop finials, sliding sash and canted bay windows, octagonal towers to draw the eye upward, two stories, a generous wraparound porch, and a large rectangle-shaped kitchen, with one wall devoted to classroom activities for his children.

His intuition was rewarded. The smoke from the barge's engines could be seen on the far horizon.

He relaxed. The fine poplar pieces would be safely unloaded by Point Arena Pier workers and delivered in short order to 10 Riverside Drive. He walked up Port Road to town and alerted the moving crew to ready their cart and horse. This day had finally arrived.

≈≈

It took Scott Hoyt eleven months to build his home. The final touch was hand-painted map of the world. It was the center of attention during the home's opening party, held the weekend after the Hoyts moved in.

The mural was an eight by thirteen-foot map that revealed an imperceptible 'X' on the coast of northern California, where Point Arena was taking shape.

The Hoyt's children, Murella and Charles, who spotted the hidden 'X' on a sunny afternoon.

They considered many reasons why their father would paint this symbol on their map. When he arrived home that night, Murella and Charles pulled him into the "Map Room," walked up to the fresco, pointed, and respectfully demanded an explanation.

Scott was nervous, like how he felt on the day he stood on Point Arena Pier, waiting to catch sight of the barge. He told his children of the local Native American tribe, the Pomos. The 'X' revealed the location of a sacred burial ground for the tribe—a group of people he had befriended during the many long years before he married Ava, their mother.

They were entranced. Scott told of his friendship with the great Indian, Aqurar, chief of the Pomo tribe. Aqurar was also the tribe's medicine man, and had once saved Scott from a slow and painful poisoning death, after inadvertently eating mushrooms he thought were safe.

"Luckily," Scott told his children, "Aqurar had come across my fields looking for me and saw that I was doubled over with pain and sweating. He could see by the look in my eyes that I was suffering from mushroom poisoning and showed me mushrooms he thought I had eaten. I weakly nodded in agreement.

Aqurar carried me across the fields, moving aside tall grass to reveal a small hole in the ground big enough for a grown man to pass through. He dropped me into darkness below the fields—fields that I had worked for many a year but never knew concealed such a place.

I was so surprised," Scott continued. "Aqurar helped me to inch down into a crawl space, where we rested and while our eyes adjusted. I felt the coolness rushing air. I cocked my head to better hear sound coming from deeper within. It was the sound of water. I learned that it was a running, underground stream." Murella and Charles were wide-eyed.

"Aqurar lifted me to my feet and told me that we were to follow the underground creek for a short distance, to a place where his ancestors had come in the beginning of their reckoning of time. He said it was the tribe's sacred place of healing. On the floor, in the center, was a small hole just larger than a man's head.

I saw light emanating from the hole. As I entered the cave, I found myself feeling better. Suddenly, the sound of pounding surf, like wind ripping through the tops of redwoods, filled the underground room. The light and sound were intense. I noticed the cave was richly painted by Aqurar's ancestors.

Aqurar laid me next to the hole and told me to breathe quietly, to let the air escaping from the hole take away the poisoned mushroom's effect.

He began to hum a forceful *'pah-pah'* of surf and a harmonic *'whuz'* of wind, charging through treetops.

He asked me to mimic the sound he made. I followed his instructions, and after a time noticed all the pain leaving my body and a kind of peace taking hold in my heart. At that moment, the medicine man pulled the colors and sounds from the hole and wrapped me in them with his hands. Through the night, I feverishly dreamed of many new worlds and new ways and the experience changed who I was as a man."

Murella and Charles listened to their father with wonder. Murella's love of the theater revealed many stories of great men but none had captivated her as this story had.

When Scott finished telling his story, his wife, Ava, joined them, smiling at her children with a knowing gaze. A secret had been passed to the next generation of Hoyts—about the healing power of their father's friend, the great Chief of the Pomo Tribe. The 'X' their father said, marked the general location of where the great chief, dying at the age of one-hundred-and-fifty-one years, was buried.

∽ॐ∾

Scott, at Aqurar's request, did not reveal the location of the healing cave's entrance to his children, stating instead that he entered the cave under the spell of poison and then exited it in a dream-like state, unable to recall where the entrance of the cave was located.

Aqurar had told Scott that the next great healing agent would be led to the cave through a series of events that even Aqurar could not guess. He knew that this agent would be a product of Scott's heart, of Scott's love, and that this person would be able to translate a series of marks found on a parchment that Aqurar had given to Scott for safekeeping.

He said the cipher on the parchment was of an ancient Native American text and disclosed, through the study of angles projected from sky-bound talismans, the exact location of the cave's entrance and its source of power.

At Aqurar's request, Scott put the parchment in an elm strongbox, along with a note about the meaning of Aqurar's coded message.

In 1906, on their way to Fort Bragg for supplies, Scott, Ava, and Murella, were killed by an enormous redwood upon crashing down on their horse-drawn coach during the great earthquake that set San Francisco ablaze, and also destroyed most of the small port town of Point Arena. The strongbox, which Scott was transporting to a bank vault, was thrown from the coach by the force of the falling tree, which pushed the box deep into the ground.

The Hoyt home in Point Arena, and young Charles Hoyt, withstood the earthquake. It became a landmark and symbol for the town to rebuild.

Charles Hoyt inherited his father's estate, and when old enough, assumed control of his father's business interests, including a movie theater. He could not have known when he inherited the movie house that one day his son, also named Charles, would spend his young summers in the projection booth, wooing his girlfriend.

SEVENTEEN

Our society seduces us to want more of the latest and greatest.
You can repel this temptation by buying used: a CD for fifty
cents, an old, repainted chair for three bucks, the latest book
for a song, five movies for four bits at garage sales that work
fine. So, you have to rewind them!
Never buy retail, never buy new. It is amazing what our society
throws away.

The American rat race: unparalleled deception, corporate
greed, lying, double-dealing, political tyranny, and heartless
grasping cannot last much longer.

We must see our world in a new light. Herman Wouk writes in
War and
Remembrance: *"The thousand-year night of technological*
barbarianism descends." We are distancing ourselves from life
sources, hoping to insulate our lives from hardship and nature's
elements. These two sources of inspiration are the basis of
individual purpose. If we remove the experience of hardship to
shape us, we are becoming nothing but the sheep of those who
sell the insulation.

M.W. – Getchell Gulch

The humans, with the help of their spiritual counterparts,
gathered in a circle around a campfire, deciding unanimously to

disperse in hunt and gather mood for survival, seeking signs of others that survived the quake.

Mitchell with Gunnar, and Leo with Rosalie and Poama, who had found in one another a special mother/daughter connection.

The two groups headed south of Alder Creek and east of the now jig-sawed road previously known as California Highway 1.

They roamed into the foothills gaining elevation. The day was clear. The Pacific Ocean expanded, blending into sky.

Mitchell found a comfortable perch facing the ocean. He rummaged through his backpack and found his old copy of Ralph Waldo Emerson's *Poems and Essays,* opening it to where he last read.

"Emerson says here," Mitchell said to Gunnar, breaking the quiet, "that we have a responsibility to act on our abilities while at the same time making no apologies for them."

"His mind captured the essence of living," Gunnar added. "It seems odd that we find ourselves above joining tectonic plates, where force meets force, past meets future, and must find our place in this newly created world. We have no way of knowing how this great quake has shaken the rest of the world. Logic states that the quake was of a magnitude beyond any possible measure or experience. It has laid waste to most of what Man created, intended to protect itself from just such a catastrophe.

"Now, more than ever, Emerson's natural world, where innate abilities foster survival and justice in a simple community, must be called upon. Such communities once thrived among the natives of this great land. They flourished spiritually while finding harmony in the physical world. During my life, I read about the local Pomo Indians and of their great chief Aqurar, who befriended the white man, and who tried throughout his life to bring the secret of living well to his white friends. It is serendipitous that our conversation includes Emerson, as we rest here on this hill. It is my understanding that Aqurar travelled east, in 1848, to meet Emerson, who was so impressed by Aqurar's mind and life that he wrote one of his most memorable essays: *Representative Men.* Aqurar shared with Emerson his knowledge of a life well lived. Aqurar said that this geographic fault here on Alder Creek, also known as the San Andreas Fault, was the center of great natural energy flowing through the Earth's mantle, from far below the surface, spreading in all directions. He understood what Emerson's essays spoke of so eloquently: our natural place in the movement of the world's rhythms, and our ability to live out our physical lives and the many spiritual incarnations thereafter. Aqurar confirmed Emerson's insight that organized religion had systematically shredded the natural covenants between man and nature; the Church buried the truth as Aqurar knew it to be. – relevance to story?

Aqurar was able to harness this natural energy. He delivered to Emerson and to others his understanding of mystical talismans—

talismans that once appeared over the San Andreas Fault where it entered the ocean at Alder Creek, seen in the sky after sunset."

Mitchell looked up at the inspired Gunnar, who had risen off the surface of the rock he was sitting on, and asked: "What talismans?"

"They appeared in stunning clarity, in all manner of color, and in multiple dimensions," Gunnar said. "They filled the sky. They were like great lenses into other worlds in the universe, where one could see many moons circling great green and blue planets. Aqurar painted the talismans as he saw them—in three equal parts, ranging in shape, from clover, to sphere, to needle. The trinity of shapes was each matched in color as reversed reflections—the object of each talisman held in it the combined reflections of the other two. The talismans strangely disappeared the same day Aqurar died, never to reappear again."

Mitchell was amazed Gunnar's descriptions. His vision of a connection to the universe rising from between the tectonic plates above the beach stunned him into silence.

Beholding the vision, Mitchell was spiritually lifted into the blue California sky; shades of azure, from the darkest to the most brilliant. He knew that life as he had known it was evolving. Gunnar's description of three-part talismans became palaces of spirit that above the setting sun. Mitchell looked to each side, then down the hill. Leo, with Rosalie and Poama had been moved by Gunnar's words, anticipating unknown moments to come.

The group's collective vision moved like wheat in the wind. It rose in three parts from the water, a world not seen before, of possibility not considered, of the magical play of chaos and order in the color and sound of all things, and within the universe's spiritual abundance.

Mitchell looked back to the earth with sadness. It had suffered at the hands of man's will and man's greed.

———

Dear Red,

I dreamed of you last night. My dream has troubled me. I have always believed that where you are now is a place known by most as Heaven.

Am I wrong? If you are not there, if you are among us here on earth and not in heaven, safe, loved, then why can I not see you, as I did the day you followed the Hassayampa downstream?

I no longer feel your presence. I have always been able to imagine you with me but in my dream I could not. I reached out to that place in my heart where you have always been but you were not there. I feel now that you may be in another dark hell that is beyond my reach. Am I again too late? Do I know the way to where you are? Why do I not hear you sing?

Stay with me, my love. Return to me. I have always been able to feel you. In my dream and right now I cannot.

Your own true love, your Mitchell

EIGHTEEN

———

First, there was a cabin, with an adjacent winter storage room
built into the ground.

Next, a church was erected, and then a school, and the one who
had built the cabin looked around and longed for what was.

Then there were dirt roads and railways, accompanied by a
peculiar line of redwood posts strung high overhead
with metal wires.

Referred to as progress, the one who had built the cabin looked
sadly upon his grave, as all he knew was consumed by the
advancement of the age, upon it.

Then came twelve lanes of freeway traffic and the acceleration
of time, and the one who built the cabin in the woods turned
away, never to look back on the folly of man again.

———

A surprised Mitchell spied a fabricated shape in the quake-tilled ground at his feet, where he was sitting with Gunnar.

Gunnar saw it too. The corner of a wooden box, made of Manchester poplar, protruded from the ground. It showed the ravages of time and the pressure of soil.

With great care Mitchell removed the box using his fingers, coaxing it from the moist, clay ground.

The dove-tailed corners holding together the cigar-boxed sized wooden container revealed its age.

He brushed it off, looking for marks that would help determine its purpose. He placed the box on his lap and played with what was left of the clasp. Fingering the line along the front of the box, Mitchell made a gap between the bottom and its lid, lifting it open.

The contents of the box were intact. Two discolored sheets of parchment were rolled next to one another. Mitchell picked one up and carefully unrolled the document revealing a note written in English on one side and an unknown set of symbols appearing on the other. The symbols lined up at different angles, extending out from the center, around a perfect circular hole was found. The second document was a rudimentary map.

Gunnar remarked that the map and English text were written by the same hand; the symbols were written by someone else.

Mitchell positioned the first document to maximize the reflected sunlight. It read:

My name is Scott Hoyt.

As he read the name *Scott Hoyt*, Mitchell's memory flashed.

It is August 19th, 1899.

I am recording the name, deeds, and location of my friend and great Pomo Indian Chief and Medicine Man, Aqurar, who recently passed from old age. This document records the location of Aqurar's final resting place, which is next to the American elm in my front yard.

He has told me about many things over these last years and has demonstrated his knowledge of Mother Earth and energies that are fading into the ground with him as the white man takes over this area of the world known as the Northern California coast.

Aqurar has saved countless lives—his own people and we, the white man—using his ability to manipulate the great energies that emanate from earthquake faults in this area. He saved my life many years ago, after I consumed poisonous mushrooms. He did so by taking me into the ground to a secret cave where the energy billows up through a hole in the cave floor.

Leo, Rosalie and Poama joined Mitchell and Gunnar, and listened intently.

Mitchell continued:

I built my home in 1875 for my wife and children. 10 Riverside Drive is its address. It is a blue house with a tall roof and windows facing each of the four winds. A white picket fence surrounds it and sits on a hill, front door facing south looking down Main Street, in Point Arena, California. A mural of the world is in the great room. On this wall map, by using Aqurar's cartography on the reverse side of this document, one can find the location of the healing cave.

Access into the cave comes with a price—self-discovery. And great responsibility. It will grant one power over illness and give long life. It will bring healing on many levels. It will provide information that was lost when the natives of this great land called America were wiped out by the white man's ways and diseases.

It is Aqurar's hope and mine that the cave's energy be used for the betterment of humankind.

Scott Hoyt.

Silence wisped with the breezes.

"I recognize the last name," Mitchell said as a haunting afterthought.

"In these parts, it is somewhat well-known. If the home still stands, it survived three earthquakes; in 1906, in 1928, and now ours."

"Finding this box indicates what we do next," Mitchell said. "It is not by chance that an earthquake revealed this box for us to find."

Enchanted, Leo spoke: "I feel we should try to find our way to this man's home. I feel drawn there."

Gunnar, Rosalie, and Poama looked upon their human friends with compassion that comes with observing a fork in the road of life. Foreboding and freedom haunt such a moment. *What might have been* hangs in the air as decisions are made. The choice to go back to Point Arena was no different. *Choices change lives,* they thought, *and not always for the better.* "Let's go then," Mitchell said, "and follow the map. My guess is that the authorities are still looking for you Leo. And we should get a handle on what is happening in the world before the world finds us."

The group stowed the box and its messages safely away, then began their search for the hidden path to what would become known to them as the Oz House.

———

Dearest Red,

The world is different. It has quaked. It has convolved and covered its past. I cannot see my way clear to where you are. All the mechanisms of change have begun to churn.

But there are cracks in the horizon. I hear you, your brilliance. I hear us, our many years in sweet living, in sweet loving, in this transparent, changing world I remember you.

Your own true love, your Mitchell

NINETEEN

———

*Is it true that there are more unwanted children born than
wanted and planned children?*

*Is it fifty-fifty? For every son or daughter born in anticipation,
are there sons and daughters borne silently in loneliness
and despair?*

*I think it might be so. Who among you does not know of such a
situation?*

*I think that in the dark history of man there is an even
percentage of such births, but out of this bleakness is the
unconstrained hope of each. Grace finds
every child worthy of respect. All are of the creative universe.*

Born into hardship; these are the souls that overcome.

Blessed are unwanted children.

M. W. – Quinliven Gulch

———

The Talisman Trinity, as they were now known to one
another, moved south with their human companions amid the
atmosphere of an oddly placed time gone by; there was nothing on
the old path back to town that reminded them of the recent past.
Determining date and time was easy enough, but civilization's
avariciousness was missing. Gone was yesterday's greedy
consumption of time and energy, of money and things via Internet

outlets. No automobiles, no contrails, no wires, no synthetic waves of any kind. Quiet prevailed as diurnal unfolded in the rolling hills. Trees swayed. Ocean churned. After the ground roiled, existence was their experience in Eden Garden anew.

Flowers appeared along their footpath. Rosalie called out names and at once before them and as far as they could see came evening primrose, balsamroot, goldenrod, hawksbeard, and fourteen-foot-tall daisies and sunflowers, marking their way back to Point Arena, lifting spirits and sparking conversation about colors Rosalie canvased before her.

With conversation came other notions: hate and war being unknown, love of man reigning, compassion answering hardship, courage in the face of loss and pain, all needed to manage a quake-ravaged realm.

From their starting point along Alder Creek, they hiked all day along Highway 1, staying in wilderness shadow until night fell. They decided for Leo's sake to sleep in Point Arena's outskirts.

In front of a long-setting sun, Mitchell walked into the church he had stopped at days earlier. It had not fared well. Its steeple had fallen forward, and its roof had caved in, out of sight from where the group assembled.

Night came clear and cold. Leo and Mitchell stopped behind the church, while Gunnar searched Highway 1 for signs of life. He gave the 'all-clear' signal. Through tall cypress trees, a view of decimated Point Arena shocked everyone.

The church's bell tower lay across Highway 1. It narrowly missed the downed marque that still listed a recently deceased name, his interment earlier in the week being the last sacred event held inside its four walls.

Leo and Mitchell stopped and stared at the name. It rang familiar to them in ways that defied logic. The name pulled at them like a lost memory.

৩৩৯৯

Leo sat next to an air grill near the floor in the hallway of his childhood home. His mother, Carmen, was working. He recalled intense arguments between his mother's parents, hearing the name he'd seen on the church marquee:

"She never knew his name," his grandmother said. "It was as sick as people remembered. She basically raped him."

"It's impossible to rape a male that way," his grandfather said in a tired voice, not happy to repeat such words.

"Yes, but they say he was not right in the head."

His grandfather sighed. Repeating himself again, he stated: "Because *he* couldn't see or hear didn't automatically make *him* mentally disabled."

"His name was John Doe No. 24. Why do you always try to make this black sheep in your family tree something more than he was?"

"Louis!" he screamed. "My father's name was Louis. I don't ever want to hear you call him *No. 24* again. My mother swore by this, and I have always believed it."

"Well, believe what you will. I've always thought Lois was mentally disturbed too. This argument is over!" Leo's grandmother stormed out the kitchen door without either grandparent ever knowing that their grandson was listening.

∽৩৩৯

His grandparent's argument faded but not before Leo recalled *John Doe No. 24's* full name. He stared at the church marquee, reading the name of *Louis Hoyt* while remembering the tone in his grandfather's voice as he said that same name.

". . . Louis Hoyt?" Leo questioned out loud, surprising Mitchell with the alarm in his voice.

"According to my grandparents, Louis Hoyt was the name of my long-lost great-grandfather. This couldn't be the same man!"

Mitchell was now alarmed as well, remembering that the old man at the service had introduced himself as a Hoyt. Mitchell remembered the old man's story of his war-orphaned son—an older boy—that he named Louis.

"Leo, do you know this, Louis?" Mitchell asked.

"Only by name if I do," Leo responded.

"Is this the same Louis Hoyt?" Mitchell asked. "It would make the man I talked to in the church much older than he already appeared to be."

166

"Leo, are you somehow related to the Hoyts?" Mitchell asked incredulously.

Leo's answer hung in the air. The symbolic shaking of his recent life continued. A response was a source of shame to all in his ancestral tree. He inhaled deeply, looked at Mitchell, and the Earth Mother trinity, and said calmly: "I doubt it and there's no proof. But it *feels* true and my gut, as of late, has been serving me well."

Mitchell looked at him with the compassion felt only to those who knew how the quakes of time shatter and remake lives. He walked over to Leo, and put his hand kindly on Leo's shoulder, feeling reserve melt away.

From the grass in front of the church, both Leo and Mitchell saw a house, still erect, made visible by the catastrophic leveling of every other house around it. It was a beautifully preserved, blue Victorian home.

With wise air in his voice, Gunnar stated to both Mitchell and Leo: "That may be our *10 Riverside Drive*."

———

My Dearest Red,

In my mind, I see iridescent lamplight flow downstairs, over balcony railing through our blessed home. I look up. I hear your bath water. I look forward to that moment when you crawl into our bed beside me, warming me with your heat, now this memory's heat.

I told you that very night of a vision I had on the Hassayampa; one that I recorded in my journal:

Fifteen thousand years ago, a great trinity of sky-bound talismans gifted the blue and green planet, and its eight winds, with the ability to multiply a finite body of souls into time. The river said that each soul would live a life that turned into two, followed by two that turned to four and then to eight, etcetera. This was reflected throughout the universe.

The river said that each soul would be stored in the universe as a singular, polished, perfect shape of mirrored glass. Living, as in anything that evolves, would crack each. Shards would form, where once there was perfection, but only those souls who regarded themselves and others as flawlessly shattered would find their eternal place in the ever-forward moving of time and light in the world.

Do you remember that night? We promised to push the shards of our lives back together, so that we could see one another in the forward motion of time and light in the universe?

Tonight, I could use your re-assembling of my fractured life. Tonight, I could use the reflection in your eyes of my broken soul as perfect in the luminance and instance of yours.

Are you, my love, perfect again?

Your own true love, your Mitchell

TWENTY

Grief—the decay of my heart.

M. W. Anchor Bay

Mitchell and Leo stared. Every structure around the blue Victorian home was leveled. It stood untouched.

"Could that pristine structure be nearly one hundred and fifty years old?" Leo asked.

The Talisman group continued east on Highway 1, then turned right toward Point Arena's down town confines.

They were astonished to see Point Arena in rubble. Piles of colored, pyramid-shaped debris lined both sides of the highway.

Walking down the middle of the ruptured road, Leo and Mitchell watched for signs of life and for clues of what used to stand in each debris heap. One held a movie house marquee, another a bank sign. Serrated chunks of cement containing words like *Fraternity*, *Druids*, and *Mercantile* were scattered about, protruding skyward. Documents, papers, file cabinets, office equipment, desks, chairs, shattered glass, broken mirrors, and shredded paintings were strewn everywhere. Misshapen stacks of books mixed with brick looked like remains of Point Arena's library.

Evidence of a massive tsunami was evident. It had roared up a ravine from the west, dropping portions of the pier and the hulls and pilothouses of fishing boats everywhere. The high watermark

173

of the wave provided reason enough why so much of the town had vanished.

Small groups of locals appeared from behind debris mounds, huddling about oil drum fires. They directed menacing stares toward Mitchell and Leo.

They turned back to avoid confrontation, to the blue Victorian home and its white picket fence.

The fence stretched east on Riverside Drive for a quarter mile. The crisp white fence seemed to define a boundary between good and evil. The fence exuded a force that protected all that lived within from a wicked world, a wickedness no longer isolated by mountain ranges or great bodies of water, a wickedness that moved along hidden, transparent, electronic highways. The white picket was now symbolic for Mitchell. Each stake represented high character: the willingness to lend shirts off backs, to give staples of bread and peanut butter freely, to help and encourage. The goodness of man existed opposite his position on a ravaged Riverside Drive.

As Mitchell moved closer to the old home, he felt its one hundred and fifty years of grace. Leo noticed the trinity moving through the gables and windows and in and through the patio posts, up and down the wide stairway that led to its entrance, and around branches and leaves of a giant elm. They weaved across unmarked graves of beloved pets and played with infrequently remembered spirits of dogs that once lived there.

Mitchell's heart brought him great grief as he comprehended a scene found at the end of the picket fence.

He saw the old man who had talked to him at the church. Mitchell saw him lying between long fresh mounds of dirt and heard him sobbing on the ground. Each arm embraced a grave, one around his wife and the other holding Louis.

Mitchell yielded to his own memories. Fresh, cooling pools of his Red's blood collecting in the soft depressions of their bed manifested.

The old man tried in vain to keep his loved ones warm in the cold ground, protecting them from cruelty found outside white picket fences. His sobs and his prone position as he cradled his loved ones stabbed Mitchell's heart. He covered his face. Losing Red tore at the flesh of his soul.

Leo walked over to where Mitchell knelt and gently lifted him back on his feet, holding the older man with a kindred kindness he had not felt before. Mitchell noted a familiar stirring within his heart for the young man. They turned toward a gate in the picket fence and walked through it together. They felt odd warmth, comfort and strength emanating from the wide front door of the home. When they looked up, they saw a beautifully crafted stained-glass window that pictured the yellow sun rising into the world, and in a blue foreground the name 'OZ'.

Mitchell turned his gaze again to the old man, who still lay upon the graves of his loved ones.

As he moved toward the old man, the horrid, vivid memories of the night he found Red filled him . . .

> *. . . a shadow moving across the ceiling of their tall A-framed cabin in the woods south of Prescott, Arizona.*

Mitchell stumbled over a thick root that protruded from the ground, powerless to catch himself. He landed hard, his mind unable to let go of the night his wife died:

> *A door ajar and the crack of floor joists above his head seared fear into his heart. He quietly ascended the basement steps, the rush of insanity pushing his body up the loft stairway.*

Mitchell slowly sat up, trying to move as his mind and body passed the hellish, evil night that had consumed and changed his life. Another reddened slash of memory consumed all of his senses:

> *The unfocused vision of shadow, flying, landing on the sofa below. Disbelief in watching that shadow jumping again to the hard ground from the front patio and wailing from a man whose femur fractured through muscle and skin.*

"God. No!" Mitchell yelled. "Do not let me go back. I've come so far. I have pleaded my case and have asked for forgiveness. I beg you God—stop this . . . this.
. . memory:"

> *The slow turn of his head toward the soft light of the bedroom—of their precious bedroom—of the bed*

holding the glistening naked body of his beloved—of the soft movement of blood flowing from her neck and thighs in the soft lamp light—her frosted hands upon his frozen cheeks.

Mitchell knelt in prayer. He asked God to take these memories of death and dying away—to free to know the gentle ways of the world where he had found his God, and where God found him. He sighed as the familiar door of evil within flew open— his despair reawakened, changing what the Talisman group had come to know as a good man:

And now his descent into madness begins—his killing the killer—by tearing free from that devil a broken femur bone—pushed from its socket by crushing impact—cutting away tendons and meat while the killer stared helplessly up in utter terror upon the blank eyes of Mitchell Walker.

———

My Dearest Red, I
am quieted.

A deep breath swells within and I smell the still mist that engulfs me. A fog, unbroken by any movement, not even a whisper's hush, or a sigh of shadow life beyond a veil, just out of sight, is watching me.

I hold a canoe's paddle on my leg and let the lapping of this tear-filled pond lull me where it will.

Distant memory and drumming pull me into mystic pasts when I held in my hand, just like this paddle, the life of my beloved; her hand warm, her breath soothing to my neck, her presence my joy, her character my compass.

Yet a compass still, as now her rich memory moves me through the still, fog-filled waters of my grief.

Your own true love, your Mitchell

TWENTY-ONE

We have become complacent about grace and accept sin as commonplace.

Jon, age 11, rode his bike home from a city park wearing black and white hand-me-down Converse high tops, wishing he had his brother's new ones, bitter that his brother had tattooed his current pair with ink. Melted ice cream on the sidewalk forced Jon into the street to avert it. The rear end a passing 1972 Buick Riviera, a Jack Daniels-pickled driver at the wheel, narrowly missed hitting him. The driver threw a Jack bottle from the Riviera's passenger side window hitting Jon's front tire, its contents splashing across Jon's shin.

Less than one block later, a woman skidded to a stop to avoid hitting him. She was in a hurry to beat her husband home. She had just had sex with her husband's friend and was so guilt-ridden she did not notice Jon until it was almost too late.

Jon knew both drivers; his parents.

He sat with his thoughts at a local gas station. He recalled the profiles of his parents. Wild-eyed and unfocused, his parents were consumed by their sins, but Jon understood only that he was not seen. He noticed an alarming gash on his shin where the bottle hit him and suddenly felt the warmth of trickling blood. He picked small glass shards from the wound and knew it needed stitching.

He reluctantly headed home to a house in an uproar.

Still not seen by either parent, Jon's older sister took him to the
emergency room.

The ER doctor, who sported a pair of heavily tattooed
Converse All

Stars used seven stitches to seal both the wound on his shin and
the hole in his heart, looked Jon in his eyes and said, "grace is
sin not claiming you."

M. W. – Fish Rock Road

———

HELLO VIEWERS, DON Johnson here. We interrupt this broadcast for a special live report covering the Mitchell Walker murder trial in Prescott, Arizona . . . I believe we are going to go live right now to our own Arimie Weld . . . Arimie . . . are you there?

HELLO DON, YES, I AM HERE, REPORTING TO YOU LIVE FROM PRESCOTT.

NORMALLY PRESCOTT IS EVERYONE'S HOMETOWN, AND ARIZONA IS USUALLY QUITE PROUD OF ITS OFFICIAL CHRISTMAS CITY. NOT TODAY.

MANY ARE FAMILIAR WITH THIS COURT HOUSE AND ITS AWESOME DISPLAY OF CHRISTMAS CHEER, BUT NOW, IT IS HOME TO AN ALL TOGETHER DIFFERENT AND GRIZZLY STORY, DON.

Is the jury close to a verdict, Arimie?

182

I THINK SO. TODAY THE CITY OF PRESCOTT IS FACING THE CONSEQUENCES OF ITS PENDING JURY DECISION IN THE MITCHELL WALKER TRIAL. IT IS EXPECTED TO CONCLUDE TODAY WITH A VERDICT THAT MOST HERE HOPE IS A VINDICATION FOR THE MAN WHOSE LIFE WALKER TOOK IN A SENSATIONALLY BRUTAL, REVENGE KILLING.

Arimie smiles into the camera, giving the shot her white, perfect teeth. She turns away from the camera, which then focuses on her form-fitted hunter green dress. Her breasts and hips draw the viewer's eyes away from her fresh, cascading blonde hair. Most of the local television news audience remembers how their local celebrity made the big time, embarking on a career that started when she was selected as queen of the local annual rodeo.

From the shot of Arimie, the camera pans the courthouse square. Exploiting Walker's national trial exposure, local merchants and politicians advertise the highly anticipated event. Populated with hundreds of American elms, the square boasts a beautiful canopy of green against Prescott's mile-high blue sky. On the horizon, the camera reveals a seasonal afternoon build-up of monsoon clouds, laden with summer rain.

LOCAL OFFICIALS ARE EXPECTING THE TOWN SQUARE TO FILL WITH SPECTATORS, ALL HOPING TO WITNESS HISTORY.

TO RECAP, MITCHELL WALKER'S TRIAL HAS BEEN VERY SHORT-LIVED. BOTH THE YAVAPAI COUNTY PROSECUTOR AND WALKER'S DEFENSE ATTORNEY SUBMITTED THE SAME GRUESOME EVIDENCE: HORRIFIC, DETAILED, POSTER-SIZED COLOR PHOTOGRAPHS.

THE PROSECUTION PRESENTED PHOTOS OF THE MAN WALKER KILLED.

THE PUBLIC DEFENDER LAURIE WESSON SHOWED THE JURY PICTURES OF WALKER'S WIFE: RED.

LOCAL TOWNSPEOPLE I INTERVIEWED HERE WERE VISIBLY SHAKEN BY THE TESTIMONY AND PHOTOGRAPHS. THEY WERE IN SHOCK AND MANY OF MY INTERVIEWS WERE CENSORED BECAUSE OF JUDGE JACOBSON'S GAG ORDER.

Another shot pans the immediate surroundings of the county courthouse, showing the wide cement stairways leading up to the north-facing entrance where jury members were expected to exit. The doors were surrounded by newspaper reporters, magazine columnists, and television news teams.

DON, PANDEMONIUM HAS BROKEN OUT HERE IN PRESCOTT. MITCHELL WALKER HAS BEEN EXONERATED OF ANY WRONG DOING IN THE MURDER OF THE MAN WHO MURDERED HIS WIFE.

184

IN WHAT THE COUNTRY UNDERSTANDS WAS THE EXECUTION OF PATRICK JOHNS, RED WALKER'S MURDERER, BY HER HUSBAND MITCHELL WALKER, A MESSAGE IS BEING SENT TO THE WORLD THAT *HERE*, IN THIS COUNTY, THE LAWLESS IDEAL OF AN EYE FOR AN EYE WILL BE EXCUSED IF YOU CAN PROVIDE ENOUGH GRUESOME EVIDENCE TO SHOCK A JURY INTO AN ACQUITTAL.

LEAKS IN THE PRECEDING MONTHS LEADING UP TO THIS TRIAL INDICATED THAT JOHNS WAS TORTURED TO DEATH BY WALKER, WHO SURPRISED JOHNS WHEN RETURNING FROM A WALK. JOHNS JUMPED FROM THE PORCH OF THE WALKER HOME ATTEMPTING TO ESCAPE THE ENRAGED WALKER, BREAKING HIS LEG. AFTER VIEWING THE BODY OF HIS MURDERED WIFE, WALKER USED A HUNTING KNIFE ON JOHNS, REMOVING HIS BROKEN FEMUR. JOHNS SCREAMED FOR MERCY WHILE HE WATCHED WALKER IN UTTER HORROR AND DESPAIR. JOHNS BLED TO DEATH WHILE WALKER WATCHED.

Arimie surprised her camera operator instructing him to follow her through a growing circle of media forming at the north entrance of the courthouse. Elbowing her way through, she learned that Judge Jacobson excused the jury and that some were now talking to the press. She accosted Ann Fry, juror number six.

ANN FRY, ARIMIE WELD HERE, CHANNEL FIVE NEWS. I AM REPORTING LIVE ACROSS THE COUNTRY. CAN YOU ANSWER A FEW QUESTIONS FOR ME?

Fry looked at Ms. Weld, then her camera crew. A look of distain and then revulsion filled her eyes. Fry couldn't believe the circus outside the courtroom doors. She was frightened by the hysteria and sickened by the trial details. She turned away from Arimie Weld, trying to escape down the stairs where her husband and children waited anxiously for her.

As she turned away, Ann Fry was nearly struck in the face with a large, silver microphone. Weld asked her for specific details of the crimes committed on that fateful night.

ANN, WHAT WAS IT LIKE FOR YOU TO VIEW THE EVIDENCE PRESENTED AT THIS TRIAL?

Ann did not reply.

WE WERE TOLD THAT SEVERAL OF THE FEMALE JURORS WERE REMOVED, DUE TO ILLNESS, AFTER VIEWING THE PHOTOS. WERE YOU ONE OF THOSE JURORS?

No response from Ann.

DO YOU FEEL IT WAS A FAIR TRIAL?

Ann tried to maneuver further from Weld.

MANY PEOPLE FEEL THAT WALKER SHOULD BE EXECUTED FOR TAKING THE LAW INTO HIS OWN HANDS. DO YOU FEEL THAT WALKER ACTED JUSTLY?

Ann Fry disappeared into the crowd. Her family whisked her away.

With no cooperation from Fry, Arimie was frustrated. She and Fry knew each other in school. A twinge of regret surfaced, as Arimie remembered taking Ann's boyfriend to a dance as freshman at Prescott's junior high school, and wonders if Ann ever forgave her.

Weld is distracted by more commotion at the courthouse entrance; Mitchell Walker emerged.

GET OUT OF MY WAY! Arimie shouted.

The crowd barely registered her demand. The sight of Walker overwhelmed everyone.

Arimie watched despairingly as Walker, protected by a man and a woman, ran to a waiting vehicle. Walker and the man got in, while the woman rushed to her own vehicle, just beyond range of Weld's shrill voice calling her.

Weld noticed a non-descript man exiting stealthily from the courthouse's north door.

YOU, CAN I TALK TO YOU SIR! ARIMIE WELD OF CHANNEL FIVE NEWS SIR! WERE YOU IN THE COURTROOM WHEN THE VERDICT WAS READ!? SIR, PLEASE, SIR!

The man stopped short and turned around. He placed his hand out to stop her advance.

BUT, SIR, PLEASE! JUST ANSWER ONE QUESTION FOR ME!

The man observed her beauty and smelled her ambitious and self-serving heart from ten feet away.

"One question."

WHAT DID YOU OBSERVE IN THE COURTROOM, WHEN THE VERDICT WAS READ?

"What strikes me when the verdict was read, was Mitchell Walker's apparent disinterest. He stared out the high windows of the courtroom, not looking at the judge or any member of the jury. He just stared out at the blue sky. I would swear that he saw something, and whatever it was he saw drew tears of joy. He was smiling. He was happy *before* 'not guilty,' was stated by the foreman."

WHAT DO YOU THINK THAT MEANS?

"Lady, you stink of self-serving ruthlessness. Get away from me."

Arimie Weld dropped her hands to her side, the microphone brushing her hunter green dress. She pictured Walker lost in genuine happiness, wondering why his understanding of life was not important to her.

———

To my own true love:

It is after midnight. A half-moon glides past dark sky's apex. My emptiness becomes night knells that rise reluctantly into my senses; they know how their end shall be heard.

In my sleeping bag, my body shudders, causing dust to fly into fire light. Harsh contrasts of fire and night sky chill me layer by layer, from skin to marrow, bones frozen.

I roll over. Removing cold and gray from my view makes room in my heart for what I know now as home: the memory of rolling into you, into your night breath, your face warm with love. Through such a veil, the softness of your heart gives me what living tried to end: I love you still.

Your own true love, your Mitchell

TWENTY-TWO

_____

Some questions are harder to answer than others.

As I have lived my life, I find the result of it, the condition of it, too influenced by the actions of others. Monitoring our individual actions, and how such actions affect the whole is humanity's charge.

We attempt to use time-proven guides in determining behavior but find that our ability to live disciplined lives in accordance with such standards difficult to do.

Kindheartedness, compassion, loyalty, friendship, hard work, fairness . . . these are the characteristics taught to us as right living, taught through example by Jesus and others. Yet, we find that humanity suffers endlessly as our behaviors contrast any good that has transpired.

M. W. – Havens Neck Drive

_____

Mitchell remained in the locked, kneeled position of a man in despair.

The Trinity surrounded Walker, placing their loving hands upon his shoulders, Poama moving directly in front of him. She willed him to come back where the here and now protected him from past evil.

191

Mitchell felt blood moving through him again. Deep within him, he released the long blade he had once held to avenge his wife's murder, feeling the cramp in his hand ease as he did so. His deeply held images and their evil shadows of evil poured into Poama's youthful energy. She absorbed them with her hands upon his chest, crying. Mitchell came to and with a grateful heart thanked her for her compassion.

Mitchell saw the old man, still prone upon the graves of his beloved family.

He took the hand Leo offered him. Leo felt a sudden and heavy pang of grief driven by empathy. Profound understanding welled as tears from an unknown place within.

Gunnar, Rosalie, and Poama surrounded their companions and together respectfully approached the old man who was still unaware of their presence, consumed by grief for his wife and adopted, war-orphaned son.

Respectfully, Mitchell and Leo approached the old man, and asked in unison: "Are you okay, sir?"

The old man blinked his eyes. Tears rolled. He gingerly pushed himself into a sitting position then recognized Walker.

The old man took in Mitchell's eyes. "You've come back," he said.

Mitchell returned the old man's gaze. The words meant more to Mitchell than the simplicity of the statement.

"Yes," Mitchell said, "I've come back. I'm sorry," he said, gesturing to the ground.

"Me too," the old man said. "I'm Charles Hoyt. I don't think we were introduced at the church. I'm not sure why I felt drawn to you and reveal, on such an intimate level, the things that were in my heart at that very moment I saw you.

Mitchell listened to the old man intently. The others were surprised to learn the depth of Mitchell and Hoyt's previous encounter and to learn the old man's last name.

Silent questions began to roll through Mitchell and Leo as the synchronicity of so many moments in the last several days began to coalesce.

"You are Charles Hoyt?" Leo asked, in confirmation of the statement made an instant earlier.

"Yes, I am," Hoyt said, then asked: "Why are you two here? Most of the people in this town cleared out, those who survived anyway, and those who have stayed behind do not come near this place. They don't understand why it still stands. They are afraid of me and of this structure," Hoyt said, taking one hand off the ground and pointing to the tall, blue Victorian home.

"It is odd to see it still standing, Charles," Mitchell said. "And according to my friend Gunnar, this house has now withstood two devastating earthquakes untouched."

At the mention of the name Gunnar, Hoyt looked up sharply, surprised and asked: "Gunnar? Gunnar who?"

They floated directly behind Mitchell: Gunnar, Rosalie, and Poama. He did not answer.

"I knew a man named Gunnar long ago," Hoyt said. "He was my friend, but he went missing many, many years ago. Do you know his last name?" Hoyt asked.

Mitchell turned to Gunnar, wondering if his spirit friend had a last name.

Gunnar rose in the air above Mitchell, looking past him toward Hoyt. Soon a smile appeared on Gunnar's face. He recognized Charles Hoyt as his friend in life.

At once, a name appeared in front of Gunnar in colorful lettering.

"Tell my old friend Charles Hoyt that in life my last name was Johansen," Gunnar said, to Mitchell.

Mitchell offered Hoyt his hand and helped him up from the cold ground where he sat.

"Gunnar says his last name was Johansen."

Charles Hoyt broke into incredulous grin that shown through his tear-soaked cheeks as he remembered his long-lost friend.

He looked around confused. "Where is he?" Hoyt asked.

"He is directly behind me," Mitchell said to Hoyt. He looked in the area immediately behind Mitchell.

"I can't see him," Hoyt said with despair. His gaze returning to the fresh graves near his feet.

"Tell him to try a little harder," Gunnar said.

Mitchell did. Slowly, and with great joy, Hoyt began to see the lightly colored outlines of not only Gunnar but the whole of the Trinity, hovering about him, awash in their joy of fearlessness and love. Everyone watched as Charles Hoyt's expression changed dramatically. He stumbled as he got up. Gunnar and Mitchell caught Hoyt and steadied him on his feet. Hoyt gasped for air at the enormity of what he saw. He laughed and cried at the sight of his old friend Gunnar.

But it was a second face that Charles Hoyt was deeply startled to see. It was a face he knew in every part of his heart. It was Leo.

———

Dearest Red,

    Come back, my own true love. How did you go through such a door of change? How did you bear it?

    I will never stop looking for you. In every blade of grass, in every falling tree, in all the endless rolling changes of time, you shall see my face again. You shall know my love. You are my bridge, my multi-colored sunshine, the night filled light of moon and stars, evolving only as radiance in our instance of hope. Desired and remembered, eternally, gratefully, sadly.

                          Your own true love, your Mitchell

TWENTY-THREE

Apathy kills.

For a moment I consider not journaling. Instead, I might sit in memory of the Internet, that whirling mind-numbing time trench that robs creative flow and life's joy.

I get angry. I want to yell, to drive at one hundred mph, windows down, wind whipping through every sense, waking me from Internet stupor and its mindless banter.

I warn the world about this stupor state, where your right to live in here and now solitude, to be first-born of the world, to know your light, your music, your words in living bookends, to savor time riding your rail, through mountains, valleys, and streams, is forfeit.

M. W. – Morrison Gulch

Mitchell smiled at the scene in front of him witnessing old friends reunite, able to connect across lines of life and death, finding beloved faces.

Hoyt was filled with a familiar joy of friendship and the pain of loss.

He felt Leo's elevated mood as joyful moments encircled him. Hoyt watched Leo and Poama play ring-around-the-rosie, laughing, taking in the sunshine as it sparkled off green grass and trees and from blue sky in every shade.

Their joy brought new meaning to Hoyt.

Leo followed Poama's example, his happy heart dancing in Mother Nature's colors and sounds. Mitchell recalled a song he sang while hiking along the Hassayampa River as a boy. Gunnar remembered music he had written and experienced it again as he fingered wind shapes. Rosalie raised her arms to bliss-filled sunlight knowing all life moved through her. Poama focused on Leo's boyhood joy, allowing surges of blue and yellow light to spark through her.

Hoyt was stunned by the group's arrival at the precise moment he was most in despair. The brown dirt and dried leaves of death's season were no longer relevant.

He thought of his home and its existence and history in the face of so much destruction. He nodded to the names on the grave stones. He turned to all gathered, enthralled by their presence.

"Would all of you like to come into this old home and visit for a while?"

The Talisman group answered that they would like to see it. They had many questions about the house and family who had lived there for the past fourteen decades. Hoyt climbed the stairs and motioned all to come in.

Their spirits lifted as they entered the home. They saw an ancient stained-glass window above the front door entrance with "OZ" emblazoned in blue, a yellow sun rising behind it.

The polished oak flooring was pristine, the craftsmanship honed and earned through living. A stairway led upstairs to lightly colored walls and stained doorways. Heavenly blues ceilings were patched with clouds.

The Hoyt family presence was evident on the walls and hallways of the old home. The kitchen, with few modern amenities, was full of Hoyt's mixing bowls and bread drawers.

One kitchen wall held shelves full of history, science, and math references, including a complete library of composers from all eras. The chalkboard contained quotes from Emerson, Longfellow, and the Bible. Mitchell was struck by the collection's breadth.

They followed Hoyt into a great room containing a bay window with a full view of Main Street.

All were saddened by the town's demolition while marveling that Hoyt's house stood tall amid the disaster.

Hoyt asked his guests to be seated. Mitchell and Leo found two chairs close to the bay window; the Trinity gathered in an adjacent corner.

Hoyt's guests were taken by a mural of the world spread across one wall.

"It is my father's work," Hoyt said. "He was a unique man, with a gift for seeing into the heart of the world better than most. It's a map of the known world at the time my father painted it and is representative of Aqurar, Pomo Indian Chief and my father's dear friend. Chief Aqurar lived until he 151-years-old and is buried in an unmarked grave under that elm tree," Hoyt said, pointing out the bay window.

The Talisman group realized rare information was passed among them by Hoyt, where the immediate past, the tangible present, and the unknown future were merging into a coherent whole.

"The world is paying for seeds sown long ago," Hoyt granted. "Our world has spilled endless blood caused by revenge, greed, and jealously. Humanity has been severed from our God, the Father and Nature, our Mother. The folly of free will is evident and must evolve."

Hoyt moved toward the bay window and gazed out at the destruction on Main Street, now impassible. The devastation included piles of wood and glass rubble that were the home of Louis' friend Amy and her mother Linda, piles that contained his son's invention.

———

To my own true love:

The vibration of your voice echoes in my chest. Your head lay still upon me while you sing your cold mountain songs of winter and of love cradled in candle light.

Your voice, like warm wind whispers, makes my heart a melodic ageless harp. From mortal to legend my heart turns. Yours is the voice of love, of fidelity, of fine things I now know as unique and extraordinary in this terrible world.

I hear your angelic tone that falls from above into my walk upon this wild, cold, blue-green ground.

I thank you for the memory of your song channeling through my heart.

Your own true love, your Mitchell

TWENTY-FOUR

Not artificial:

The start of any creative moment's endeavor—a still dancer, a blank canvas painter's stare, a listening singer, an engineer's toggle or a mother's lights out, when epiphanies flare and truths are caught—is quiet and breathlessness, waiting for experience and intuition to call it into existence.

M. W. – Walker Gulch

Mitchell remembered Hoyt's hands months ago, resting on his cane at the memorial service, saying with reservation: "I think I have something that belongs to you or your family."

Hoyt watched Mitchell pull a box out of his backpack. Seeing it hit Hoyt hard.

"What do you have there?" he asked.

"I think it's a document written by a family member of yours."

Mitchell handed the old parchment to Hoyt. As he read it, Hoyt held back tears. In a moment, he would share that the document was written by his father in 1899. In a moment, he would express the joy and sadness of holding these words in his hands. In a moment, he would speak of his father's life in an intimate way.

Mitchell watched Hoyt's joy and sadness as he held his father's letter. Hoyt felt the years pass and sadness in the tragic deaths of his father, mother, and sister long ago, simply because they left the shelter of their home. He felt his father's graceful life as his own.

Finally he spoke: "My family has safeguarded the secret of a healing cave for over a century as their promise to my father's great Native American friend Aqrar. This promise has bound every generation and, in return, has given us long life. The cave he speaks of is accessed by depressing this symbol on the map." Hoyt walked to the map and pointed at the raised impression of an imperceptible 'X' his father had created.

"When pressed, a trap door opens here," Hoyt said, pointing at the space on the wall under the map. "One can crawl along a tunnel to a circular stairwell that leads down to the cave."

Everyone stared at Hoyt, absorbing his description. Their eyes moved to the space on the wall beneath the mural, picturing an enclosed tunnel and stairwell. Was it lit? Was it safe? Was it still a source of energy as described in his father's document?

"I know you have questions about this cave and our family history. Most of all, you," Hoyt said, looking directly into Leo's eyes noting his face bore a strong resemblance to Louis.

"Why would I have questions about *your* family?" Leo asked, unsettled by Hoyt's stare.

"You look so much like him, young man," Hoyt said to Leo.

"Like whom?"

"My son, Louis."

Leo experienced the same longing and apprehension he'd had earlier that day, when he read the name 'Hoyt' on a toppled church marquee.

"Louis Hoyt was *your* son?" Leo asked slowly, weighing the odds of this unexpected turn.

"He was . . . adopted," Hoyt said. "We went to Illinois right after the war and found him, influenced by news stories that played at my family's movie house." He pointed at a pile of rubble half way down Main Street.

Time slowed for Leo as he remembered arguments between his grandparents.

After some time, he spoke, saying to no one in particular: "there is a family secret that has haunted me since our arrival here in Point Arena this morning."

"As a kid I heard that my great-grandfather was a deaf and blind kid from Jacksonville, Illinois, a WWII war orphan adopted by a California couple" Leo said, looking directly at Hoyt.

Hoyt's mind reeled. *Am I looking at my son's ancestor? How is that possible?*

207

"if this family story is true," Leo said, "then Louis Hoyt, this once-named John Doe No. 24, is not only your adopted son, but he is also my great-grandfather."

Hoyt remembered he and Louis walking the one-mile distance of Kinney Road. It sloped down from Highway 1 to a bare building standing between the end of the road and the roaring five-mile Pacific catch known as Manchester State Beach. Hoyt liked to watch Louis' appreciation of the beautiful natural setting.

Arena Rock, an outcropping that caused a constant rolling white-capped wave, was visible from Kinney Road. Arena Rock was a massive magnetite megalith. Its presence fascinated Louis, given it was the largest single quantity of magnetite known to man. He could feel the rock's magnetic pull. Hoyt would observe his son raise his hands to the whitecapped waves, inspired by thoughts of new worlds. Hoyt felt these were his son's experience of Heaven, its gate, and temples.

"There are immense worlds floating above the rock, Pop," Louis said. "Deep green and intense blue globes rotating around each other. Their beauty makes me cry.

"I feel as if I can extend my hand and touch them, travel into their atmospheres, into their histories and speak to their creators. They have no heavens; they hold no debt spiritual or otherwise. There are no borders or temples to forced idols. There is no hunger or longing, only faith in the day ahead. Goodness reigns. I feel peace there that I can't describe."

Louis kept his hands lifted, palms to the sea, and felt ocean breezes on his face, flowing through his hair. He grasped his father's hand, silently thanking the heavenly bodies and their spirits for the goodness he knew in this man he loved.

Hoyt remembered Louis on the Golden Gate Bridge sensing slight movements in the bridge's suspension, up and down and side to side. He anticipated joy in the familiar hills that would soon be under foot after entering the city.

San Francisco was Hoyt's favorite place to take his son. They had ridden a cable car to the Fairmont Hotel on their first night back from Illinois. It was on that flight home, with his wife and newly adopted son, that Hoyt began to understand how his life choices affected the ones he loved.

On that first day in San Francisco, he noticed Louis' intense awareness of his surroundings, which he seemed to absorb through his fingertips.

The next day, Charles, his wife, and Louis traveled by cable car from one doctor's appointment to the next to evaluate Louis' health. Doctors determined that Louis was extremely intelligent. His mental perceptiveness test results exceeded all benchmarks for disabled children. Being blind and deaf had not affected Louis' curiosity about the world around him.

His senses of smell, taste, touch, and particularly his intuition, were highly developed. By day's end he had learned a new version of Braille and sign language that enhanced his ability to articulate abstract thought. Charles watched his son put thought to paper describing an adaptation of pulleys and the force of gravity to move cable cars easily over hills. Louis wrote about his sensing movement and shift on the Golden Gate Bridge as ocean-born winds moved the superstructure from side to side.

❧

"Are you sure your memory is correct?" Hoyt asked, alarmed. "Your grandfather was a war orphan, adopted after the war, in Jacksonville, Illinois, and his name was Louis?"

"Yes," Leo said. "We weren't sure how my grandmother, Lois Forstater, became pregnant, by this disabled boy."

"Lois Forstater!" Hoyt said surprised. "I can't conceive how this is possible!" He was shaken by the bizarre realization that Leo was his adopted son's biological grandson.

Hoyt could barely comprehend having this encounter in his house at a time of incredible loss. To lose his family only to have another appear, one who was a direct descendent of the boy he loved and lost, was too great a miracle to bear.

———

My own true love,

I hear the voice wail: "Here comes the night!"

I run wildly through the shadows but despair, like a plowman's blade, catches my throat. I clutch at its upward movement, unable to stay its slicing through me.

I fall into the grass, still, wet, hearing cannon thunder from beyond the bounds of my memory.

I touch my neck. I am again free from cold, sharp steel.

And I remember you.

Your own true love, Red

TWENTY-FIVE

Passing thoughts keep pace with the setting sun, strobing through

pine stands. As I head north on Highway

1, the alternating shadows from tree trunks provide contrast.

Paradox

and its role in the evolution of human spirit remains. Can you

look in the mirror, into your own eyes, find the spirit within, and

live with how you spend the day?

Our reflections, in mirrors, in the people we love, in the

community where we live, in our choice of right and wrong, in

our quest for truth, tell all.

Within each reflection is free will's all-encompassing presence.

What will you do today?

M. W. – Hearn Gulch

The stunning realization hung like tapestry magic carpet in the Map Room for several minutes. Each considered minds comprehending time, hearts meeting empathy, spirits in destiny's embrace, understanding how all life is a creation and then a decision.

All but Leo. He was struggling to shift from old life, where symbol-laden math equaled a healthy mind and paycheck. He wanted to feel the time moving through him, free of video game worship and dogma of science run amuck. He wanted to feel the moment and to accept what was before him with unfamiliar faith.

Supernatural phenomena moved toward him, making him toss his head from side to side, eyebrows arched, his strained effort to comprehend obvious to all. The math and science language he knew offered no explanation. With tears in his eyes, he looked at a man not related by blood but by events and actions that impacted Leo far more than any shared DNA.

Leo moved toward Hoyt, comprehending the sacrifices made by this old man. They embraced.

How does a person make such a commitment? Leo thought, with an astonished countenance. He memorized Hoyt's scars, wrinkles, and hands. He saw the large, crooked fingers that had raised his grandfather, and felt the miracle.

For Hoyt, their hug was monumental. The connection reverberated through his senses.

Leo was confused. Hugging a stranger was overwhelming. The hug forced him to acknowledge how a stranger's love changed his grandfather's life. Hoyt now holding Leo as a father holds a son was inexplicable.

The stepped back from the embrace. Longing sparked between them. A vision of Aqurar rose from the ground around the elm. Both Hoyt and Leo sensed Aqurar's love for the world. In the corner of the Map Room Poama and Rosalie cried with joy for Hoyt and Leo's embrace. Gunnar displayed his multi-colored garment and his piano appeared under his fingers and Aeolian winds carried his music into the air. All heard the Mother Spirit. Love moved through the group as orbits of solid, massive, perfect spheres, each holding an infinite number of circles. The day's waning light and the evening's impending darkness came together, revealing destiny and free will in a universal infinite.

Mitchell looked at the Trinity, Leo, then Hoyt. He thought of the earthquake, and of the wooden box in the ground. Leo found his chair. Hoyt stared at the 'X' on the mural. Mitchell took a deep breath, about to make a decision he had put off since meeting Leo near Alder Creek.

"Unfortunately, Leo," Mitchell said. "I have more information about me to share with you before you decide whether to stay with me any longer. All of you should know."

Concerned, Leo looked at Mitchell. "What else could there possibly be?"

"I am Mitchell Walker."

"I know that."

"Do you recall a media event several years ago involving a husband killing a man who killed his wife in Prescott, Arizona?" Mitchell asked him.

"I do."

"I am that man."

"Wait a minute," Leo said. "You're that Mitchell Walker, the one who . . ."

The others looked at Mitchell, unsure of what he and Leo were talking about. Hoyt suddenly remembered the story.

"Well, you are a man with many surprises," Hoyt said to Mitchell. "Presenting my father's long-lost document, bringing a member of my family into my home, and now this news of your revenge killing."

"I am sorry to be the bearer of this news and understand if you don't want me in this sacred home," Mitchell said to Hoyt, accepting whatever might come next.

"I cannot imagine how you lived through such an ordeal," Hoyt said.

"And then to live through that night again and again, as the details were revealed by the media feeding frenzy . . ."

Mitchell felt Hoyt's acceptance of his actions, a forgiveness he'd not yet experienced for the night he lost his wife. He believed he was everything the media had portrayed him to be and felt that portrayal follow him ever since. Everywhere Mitchell went, he carried the stigma his actions. In every diner customers stared, jaws dropped, judging him as evil.

Inside the old Victorian home, he felt none of this. His spirit and human friends welcomed him.

He felt accepted, an incredible feeling for a man unable to feel a part of anything, since his life had been trashed.

216

"I would have reacted the same," Hoyt said, holding Mitchell's gaze.

Mitchell acknowledged his acceptance. As a man alone on the road, this joy was unknown to him. He was now thankful, where once he was bitter. Despite the cost, he was happy, to be on the Mendocino Coast, on Highway 1, at the epicenter of a mighty quake, at the hearth of a good man, among this spiritual trinity, watching his destiny become clear, hearing a distinct call for change.

———

My own true love,

I hear a lightly played piano. This music quiets my disturbed soul and pulls me down the path ahead.

I am drawn to the horizon and have begun my journey towards it. The whipping wind and water induce me to sing with their notes and tones.

I remember us.

Your own true love, Red

TWENTY-SIX

Fate throws hard.

Change is guaranteed.

Find gratitude in all things.

Do what matters.

This is enlightenment.

Chase those you love. Look for long views of the world. Hunger for music and literature that inspires original thought, a page-by-page contribution to your life's book.

M. W. – Ocean View Point

"Well, what's to be done, what should I do?" wailed John Jespa, CEO of Haltronics.

General Orth raised an eyebrow. Here was the wealthiest man in the world, unable to cope with the loss of the world's richest and most complicated company. Orth saw panic in Jespa's eyes.

Orth considered the events that led Jespa to his abyss.

In Jespa he saw all that had gone wrong with humanity, starting in 1914, leading to the assassination of the Archduke Franz Ferdinand of Austria. Unparalleled terror followed the assassination.

Orth believed the recent earth quake was Mother Nature stepping in and clean the slate.

From 1914, Orth reviewed the history of man, back to the Bible's version of original sin, which for Orth, was found in another word: *Debt.*

Debt is the original sin, Orth thought. *Debt is the great regret. Mother Nature was now cashing in. Man's collective choice to take more than he gave had cumulated in Mother Nature crushing every modern infrastructure. Since 1914, debt had followed one generation into the next. Debt's manifestations spanned the absence of courage and honesty when facing hardship to spiritual debts created by gluttony, greed, and power.*

Transformation comes not by the hand of man, but through the will of Nature.

Orth longed for true change. The old general was tired of life in this new, modern world, and looked forward to a simpler way of living. He looked for a new forgiveness of debt, a new kind of courage, of friendship defined by loyalty, of love in deed, of compassion instead of self-service. He was convinced that such a time had come.

He believed that somewhere was a conversation underway about the world and its continued existence without man's addictions and shortsightedness.

Orth knew that his time on this planet was soon to end.

Now he was far more interested in finding the location of this imagined conversation, a collection of souls that understood a new beginning was emerging.

Orth knew that they were out there and he wanted to find them. He wanted to share the experience, strength, and hope that a soldier could bring. He knew what *not* to do and that would contribute to the success of this new understanding.

Orth walked over to Jespa and stated simply; "You are on your own, I quit."

The words did not register with Jespa. For a moment they stood eye-to-eye.

"I don't understand," Jespa said. "You can't quit. You signed a contract to protect and serve the mission statement of my company. I will sue you until the end of time if you walk out!"

"The end of time is here, Jespa," Orth said. "Get a grip; your wealth is gone. Your mission statement is meaningless without the Internet. Mother Nature destroyed it completely three days ago. Don't you get that?"

"I will rebuild it," Jespa cried out in desperation. "There is a fool out there who knows the secrets I own, who can rebuild it for me, and I know he is willing and able to do it. I have possessed his mind. He will serve my mission statement. He will operate under my command and the first thing I intend to do, when I have rebuilt my Internet, is to chase down every person who fucked me today, including your Mother Nature, AND DESTROY THEM ALL!"

Orth looked at his old boss with pity. "It will never be done," he said quietly. "She has stepped in and rearranged all that you think you know. You no longer understand your place in the world, Jespa. From my intel, Kinney Road has been carried out to sea."

The great soldier turned his back, walked through a large backstage door, and out of the shattered Los Angeles Civic Center. A new mission was underway. Mother Nature had called. It was suddenly clear to him that he was to find those *people* and that *place*. *Something* he knew would help restore Her world.

TWENTY-SEVEN

Handless clocks. Needle-less compasses. Faithless inspirations.
Voiceless carolers. Thoughtless writers. Clueless cultures.

Is there something intangible that will move us to act without
references or maps?

Is it belief?

Do we draw our own lines in the sand? Do we command?

Do we silence our constant reaching for what is outside our skin
and quietly listen to the resulting void?

Do we fill our pages, our senses, our time, our destinations with
what moves us from point to point in a day?

Can you imagine a world different, better than today's?

This is hard to do. I long to experience my life as God intended. The
only way to do it is to move.

M. W. – Schooner Gulch

"Does anyone have anything to offer as to why we have all been brought here, to this house, at this point in our lives?" Gunnar asked. "Do any of you feel, as I do, that we are not only on the cusp of a great change but have already stepped into it?"

Gunnar moved to the middle of the Map Room, the Talisman group before him. He hovered above the wooden floor, slowly and thoughtfully.

"As a representative of the next world, I am saddened," he said, in his lyrically wispy voice, by man's lack of character. I determined to rid my world of its presence. There are good people, but their small numbers are unable to reverse the tide of sin rolling through the universe. Each of you will utilize your gifts, your unique perspectives and life experience to implement change.

It is time for us to descend into the cave," Gunnar said.

Gunnar's reference to a cave made Hoyt's heart skip several beats.

Mitchell and Leo, in unison, said aloud: "what cave?"

Charles was consumed by Scott Hoyt's promise to Aqurar. He suddenly felt wildly betrayed by the group, deeply regretting that he had welcomed them into his home. He could not believe that Gunnar knew about the cave and shared this with complete strangers. They were now privy to the secret of the wild and pure world of Aqurar's heart, his sacred knowledge of the universe.

Gunnar had compassion for Hoyt. He wanted Hoyt to understand the cave's crucial role in the changes that had begun, following the quake. Looking into Hoyt's eyes, Gunnar spoke again:

"Charles, please go to the mural your father painted so long ago, find the raised 'X' located below the town of Cape Mendocino, and press it."

Hoyt, incredulous, thought *how is this known by this being?* He suddenly realized that Gunnar, his spiritual companions, and the two men were why his father created the mural so long ago. He knew that his father's life, Aqurar's heart, and his son's insights into this small, beautiful world had created the moment.

Slowly, Hoyt moved over to the wall map, lifted his hand and located the trip mechanism. He closed his eyes and remembered his father's story. He thought of the quiet resting place of Aqurar's body at the base of the family's elm tree. He thought of his odd, good health, long life, and a can-do spirit, despite the growing trouble in the world.

Hoyt gently touched the raised mark, feeling it recess under the mural. He had long wondered what this action would feel like, curious of the sound it would make.

The shift caused by the movement of floor and wall panels gave goose bumps to Mitchell and Leo and brightened the outlines of the spirit trinity.

The wall under the atlas receded, creating a gap along the length of the map where the oak floor met the wall. The hallway floor lifted and attached to the stairway leading upstairs while the wall under the map rotated back and up, connecting at the top of the hallway floor, forming a space humans could crawl through.

Hoyt felt fresh air rush around him. The Map Room filled with the intoxicating atmosphere of the cave far below, lifting the mood from apprehension to love. The cave's air rushed out of the windows and doors of the Oz House into the yard and streets of Point Arena. Rainbow-colored clouds resembled celestial bodies of many sizes orbiting one another, floating over and through the Oz House, turning the Victorian home into the magic of creation.

Gunnar's coat reflected the atmosphere around him, its many colors returning. He disappeared into the crawl space, traveled the length of the secret passage to Aqurar's cave, then back again. He spoke:

"By Scott Hoyt's inspired craft, through his mural of the known world, and because he was Aqurar's friend, a cave deep under this house has been kept secret and sacred from evil. Enter into what I know as the core of existence, and dwelling place of our earth-bound Divinity."

Gunnar gestured everyone toward the secret entrance and underground passage.

"Within lies the great knowledge of intention, the road map for living fully. Enter the core of creation, into the spirit of an evolving world. Become who you were meant to be, without evil, charitable toward your fellow man, spreading good will throughout the universe."

Slowly, Mitchell, Leo, and Hoyt approached the wall opening. Rosalie and Poama glided through the opening behind

Gunnar. Hoyt took Mitchell's hand, knelt, and looked with wonder. He noted the color and texture of his father's handiwork, including wooden gears and pulleys in flawless condition. He marveled at the ingenuity of the secret opening, running his fingers along the handmade joints, cranks, and wooden pressure springs that launched the century-old mechanisms.

Hoyt lay on the oak floor, face-down, sliding his right leg into the opening, letting his knee and foot fall onto the tunnel's flooring. He reached in with his right hand; the flooring was warm to his touch. The air continued to rush through his hair, enveloping his clothing, reminding him of a desert night wind caressing his skin. Joy replaced apprehension. On all fours, he moved toward a landing constructed at the top of a circular stairwell.

Mitchell and Leo joined Hoyt in the tunnel, full of joy and curiosity. Hoyt made it to the landing and stood, using side rails attached to the stairwell walls.

He looked around amazed. Soon his companions were standing with him, amazed by the sound-proofed room. Holding on, they took turns looking over the guard rail into a cavernous well.

The younger men supported the older man. Childlike delight travelled up from the bottom of the well, as the spirits of Gunnar, Rosalie, and Poama encountered the source of its light, sound, and smell.

Picking up the pace, the men descended the stairway to the bottom of the one-hundred-foot shaft. They were about to enter the door leading into Aqurar's cave, when Gunnar appeared at the threshold, joined by Rosalie and Poama.

With solemnity, Gunnar had something to say and waited for the right words to come.

From behind the trinity, deep reverberating echoes roared to life resonating as wind blowing through the tops of trees. Light, bent by the energy flowing from the cave's center, illuminated the group, dazzling them with every shade of color.

Gunnar spoke:

"I will bring into the world a resonance not heard before. It will be the evolution of that which comes from another plane of existence. It will move from the epicenter of this great quake in all directions, covering this pale world with renewed, inspired hope, with fresh vibrations of color and emotion, helping to close this current chapter of the book of life, and usher in the next. Abundance and charity will be in balance."

Gunnar's voice grew, not in volume but in depth. Everyone felt that the declarations he made vibrated behind him. The cave's interior appeared to shift. The bending, strobing light from the cave's center made the walls appear to rotate simultaneously in every direction. Orbiting rondures of colored heavenly bodies spun on three-dimensional axes.

The shifting walls of the cave slowed, and images of the rotating orbs sharpened. Seven large pearl-like stones appeared on the cave's wall. Each began to glow with the color of wisdom: a delicate white.

They were overcome with wonder. There, in the heart of the cave, a universal voice resonated.

Their gazes shifted to the center of the cave's floor where an experience of heaven rose. Light from the delicate white pearl gems drenched the cave, engulfing everyone as unbiased, unchained love in its moment of creation.

From the center of the cave, each heard their name. The ageless voice addressed them through their hearts and imaginations:

Mitchell Walker: bring into the new world your understanding of justice, the kind of justice that sinks teeth into the creators of black sorrow and helps the world to cope with its loss by cascading waves of forgiveness and acceptance. Take with you a white stone. Your future is written upon it.

Leo Brenamann: create and teach a new universal language that will help all to understand the sounds and sights of this lost world. It will be a way of comprehending all that moves out from this point forward. As your science advances, so does God. Louis Hoyt knew how to get there. Find what he left behind and care for the one to whom he entrusted his work. Take with you a white stone. Your future is written upon it.

My spirit friend Rosalie: like the Arc of Noah, take with the Talisman Group my entire natural world and bring back to life that which man destroyed. The debt of man has laid waste to millions of my creations. They shall all live again. Take with you a white stone. Your future is written upon it.

Poama: reinstate the spirit of my children, the great sons and daughters I have sent to this planet in the embodiments of Jesus, Aqurar, Theresa and Ruth, Mohammad and Buddha. Bring forth truth and honesty, hard work and owing the day's living to no man. Your playful spirit and your experience as a grower will allow the new world to understand how to survive, not from life's hardships but from spiritually thriving. Leave now and take with you a white stone. Your future is written upon it.

Charles Hoyt: I thank you for keeping this cave secret, this entrance to my home, my kingdom. It was a burden too great at times. I thank you, your wife, and your son for the character and strength to safeguard its existence within the confines of this home which I have sheltered from all havoc. Leave now and take with you a white stone. Your future is written upon it.

Charles Hoyt felt timeless as each pair of eyes watched him. Mitchell and Leo were in disbelief at the reality of this place. The Trinity became part of the light and sound emanating from the eye in the ground.

"The eye of God," Gunnar said.

"The energy of all earth," cried Rosalie.

"The love of my mother," sang Poama.

Mitchell and Leo heard these words and understood their multiple meanings.

Hoyt was lost in thought. Leo was entranced by Hoyt's face, where tears flowed. His boy was again before him, his heart embracing what the immediate future held for both.

"We are now a part of this new song," Gunnar said, as he glided over to the sixth of the seven pearls of stone and held it in front of him, showing it to his companions. "Become what the forces of God will you to become. Go out into this broken world and mend it."

"How can we do such a thing?" Mitchell asked. "This is like the command Jesus gave to his apostles. Go out into the world and take these new messages to the suffering masses. There must be more to this moment than just repeating past dialogues with God. What can we do differently?"

"For starters, we can eliminate free will." Gunnar held up his stone and within it was the written wisdom that Gunnar had just offered the group. "We can let the world be governed by the changes Mother Nature has brought it. We can leave this miraculous cave with this message—man will no longer get in its own way. We have tried to live differently, with love reigning supreme. The only way that will ever result in a peaceful harmonic world is when free will is abandoned and replaced with abundance, charity, and good will."

≼ઈ৯৯

Gunnar turned away from the group. He stared up, toward that place on the ground's surface where Linda and Amy lay in a pile of rubble.

Charles Hoyt, considering Gunnar's instructions to each member, gasped for air as if punched in the gut. *Find what he has left behind and care for the one to whom he entrusted his work.* "Amy!" He cried out. "Amy! She's been buried alive in that pile. We must help her! She can't move!"

The group made the long climb up the stairs from Aqrar's cave. Charles demonstrated surprising strength as he ascended. Before leaving the cave, Gunnar picked up the seventh and final stone, stashing it in his interior coat pocket.

They flew through the gate and across the street, searching frantically at the edge of the wood pile for Linda and Amy.

Charles cried out: "Amy! Linda Rinton! Can you hear me?!"

Amy heard her name called out repeatedly and choked on a response.

A group of locals, standing on Highway 1, confronted Charles, Mitchell, and Leo, for breaking the town boss' new rule of searching debris piles for earthquake victims.

It had been a while since Mitchell faced-down thugs; he was out of practice. He was surprised by their audacity, attempting to impose their boss' will on others. As he searched for a solution, he remembered that overconfidence is always a weak link in a show of force. He picked up a two by four, cracked it hard on the trunk of a tree, snapping it in half. Recalling the horrific sounds of buildings ripped apart, the locals turned away in shell-shocked retreat.

"We're going to tell the boss what you drifters are up to. We always considered you a stranger, Hoyt, you and that freak son of yours."

Their cutting comment did not daunt Charles. He endured the locals' distrust of the Oz home and its owners his entire life. Mitchell grew angry, recalling the memorial service and Charles honoring the life of his son.

Amy coughed, drawing the men's attention. Charles yelled out for Amy again. She coughed in response, trying to make a sound but could not.

Louis' invention began to glow in the rubble's darkness. The closer Charles got to Amy, the brighter it glowed. He saw the illuminating device deep within the crumbling house and called Mitchell and Leo to help.

They lifted shattered parts of the Linton home and placed them in the gutter on Riverside Drive. As the space cleared, they could see Amy's clothing. They saw another lifeless human shape next to Amy—her mother.

Finally, the men reached Amy. They slowly lifted her limp body, surprised by how easily they were able to remove her. Not a single shard of wood or glass had fallen on her.

Charles picked up Louis' book, placing it on Amy's lap. She instinctively rested her palms on it. The printed email Linda had brought home from work was attached to the bottom of the book, unnoticed.

Mitchell and Leo were awed by the book's glow. Charles placed a massive old hands behind Amy's head, and the other on his Louis' invention, conducting what once was to what would be.

They carried the young girl across the street, through the gate, up the stairs, and into the Oz House, laying her on a sofa in the Map Room. The trap doors were still opened from the Trinity's descent. Air from Aqurar's cave to filled in around Amy.

Slowly she sat up, recognizing where she was. She looked at the strangers. Gunnar, Rosalie, and Poama watched her, realizing she was the seventh and final member of their group.

"Amy," Gunnar said. "We have something to tell you."

Leo and Mitchell rested their hands on Amy's shoulders.

Amy drew sharp, stuttered breaths. In waking from her dreams of stairways, she heard the quiet, distant knells of her mother's life. *Eleanor Rigby* lyrics whispered within her. Her lips quivered. Her hands shook as she touched her mouth to make the quivering stop. She saw her mother's face behind shards of glass. Her mother's name appeared with her father's and knew that time collects all names as its own.

———

My own true love,

I see you struggle with the night. I see the fear from living your life creep into your heart and look for a hold. Roll your head toward me; put my love, my heart, in fear's path.

The music has begun its play. The seas churn as they do and I lovingly remember you.

Your own true love, your Red.

TWENTY-EIGHT

———

Money is the root of all evil.

I have tried to disprove that statement. Perhaps more accurately, it is the soul possessing money that is evil.

I don't know if I believe that any more. I have a small sum of money coming, a pittance to most I'm sure but enough for me to live comfortably for many years, albeit frugally.

There is a chance that it will not come. This chance is unsettling. I have stated to those who love me that without this money I am at risk.

Yet not once have I ever gone hungry. I have never been homeless.

I have never been cold. I have never been without love. I have not become bitter. I am still moved by sunsets and look for my connection to God through Nature. I have never known want, only need, for money.

Good and evil are found between blessing and bane.

M. W. – Bowling Ball Beach

———

John Jespa ran after General Orth. Blinded by anger and fear of losing everything he valued, he yelled, "I will kill you!"

Orth looked over his shoulder and saw the blood rising in Jespa's face. Orth had never known rage. In all his years as a soldier, rage never played a role in discharging his duties. Rage was for amateurs. It cluttered reason and undermined his fulfilling certain responsibilities that were nobody's business but his own.

He pitied Jespa, unsatisfied by his controlling interests in all synthetic things.

"Come back here, right now!" Jespa yelled.

Orth turned toward the downtown LA roads that would lead him to Highway 1. He wanted to see this highway again despite warnings that the road north was under siege.

"You will never get out of LA alive!" Jespa raged on.

Life, Orth thought to himself, *is changing, not by the hand of man, but by Nature's reclamation of it.* At this point, General Orth could not hear Jespa's rage.

"I will hunt you down Orth. I can promise you that," Jespa spat. "You will forever be looking over your shoulder."

Orth turned toward Jespa and pulled out his sidearm. Through his thick black glasses, he pointed it at Jespa's forehead, asking simply, quietly, sincerely: "What?"

Jespa's breath caught, as he tried to repeat his last words to Orth.

"Say it," Orth, demanded.

240

Jespa's mouth closed. His lips pressed together as he focused on the barrel of Orth's pistol, clean and shining in the morning sun.

"Say it again," Orth, repeated. In recent months Jespa's thin face and gray skin made him appear terminally ill. Orth had seen these symptoms before, in men who craved power but had been denied it.

Orth stared at his former employer. He thought of a scene from the 1990's film *Tombstone*. In Jespa's face, Orth saw fear: a weak man struggling for his next breath. Orth's gaze broke Jespa's rage. Jespa collapsed to his knees, not in acceptance of his fate but in bitterness—his life suddenly amounting to a clanking coin in the bottom of a tin cup.

Orth understood that his battlefield life was over. It was time to evolve. Man's understanding of good versus evil was supplanted by Mother Nature's rage against Jespa's machine.

As he headed north on Highway 1, he was becoming a different man, a different human being. He understood the post-industrial age was ending in the depths of the Pacific ocean.

Orth wondered if the magnetic poles would shift. *Would there be currencies in the new world? Would there be love? Would blood no longer spill? Would revenge still appear as the course of free will played itself out? Would greed motivate souls? Will longing fill my heart as an indicator that I have lived?*

He let the questions come and go. He had always tackled any hill with courage and determination. Now he hoped that war and hate mongering with Haltronics would disappear into the ocean.

❦

As evening settled, he was woefully unprepared for his own survival. He had a pistol, a military uniform, and a wallet full of worthless American currency.

As he looked around Highway 1 for a place to shelter for the night, a large black SUV passed him, then slowed down ahead and stopped. A bearded young man with long brown hair stepped out of the front passenger door.

"Are you General Orth?" He asked.

"Who is asking?" Orth responded.

"The driver."

"His name?"

"He said to tell you he is Loki, writhing in pain, causing unheralded earthquakes."

Orth stood for a moment, confused. then smiled. *It couldn't be!* Orth was overjoyed and cautious. *Could it really be Will McKinley, my great, lost friend?*

"Would you like a ride?" the young man asked. "We are headed north too."

Orth moved toward the SUV, hoping to confirm that Loki really might be at the wheel. *Loki,* he thought, *his oldest and dearest friend, who served with him decades ago, fighting alongside him in the oil and terror wars.*

He owed this man his life; Will McKinley had carried Orth on this back to safety during a firefight in a Middle Eastern desert.

Orth loved Will McKinley because of it and had always thanked God for his friendship. They lost touch over the years.

Orth gazed at the man who had single-handedly pounded the enemy with earth-shattering state of the art weaponry, freeing an entire platoon from certain death. It was Will McKinley, an older but wiser Loki, looking tired but happy to see his old friend again.

Jespa lay on the bare, cold convention center floor. He drifted in and out of consciousness, paralyzed by anger then fear resulting from his confrontation with Orth.

Before the quake.

Jespa moved on from Orth. He thought of his custom-made, one-of-a-kind mouses, one for each hand, which used all of his fingers and thumbs, each assigned a different charge manipulating all manner of tasks on his mainframe screens.

Before the quake.

He recalled that he checked his inbox repeatedly. He had sent out an internal email, asking for assistance to find an employee who was missing, offering a reward for information on his whereabouts. The subject line read: "HAVE YOU SEEN THIS MAN?" The attachment, when opened, revealed a photograph of Leo Brenamann.

Anger flashed through, as his recall returned to Orth, who had turned his back to him, ignoring his demands, belittling him.

Before the quake. He couldn't get the phrase out of his mind.

Something before the quake . . .

The floor grew colder. He rolled over onto his stomach, the left side of his face to the dusty floor. Opening one eye, Jespa remembered his video wall where numerous computer screens displayed tasks and applications that carried out Jespa's control of his techno world.

Before the quake.

Closing his eyes, Jespa remembered his chair gliding over the static-resistant flooring in his high-tech office as it pitched during the mega-thrust trembling.

His video wall began to crumble; vital technical data disappeared. At one point Jespa crashed into one of the larger screens. His nose smashed against an enlarged, flashing, pixilated face, a female employee.

His eyes flashed wide open. He remembered. Just before all his data was lost, a face appeared. *The search! It had worked!*

He reached for his phone hoping to find the search results forwarded from his office data center. He touched the bottom right corner and heard the ping from his private facial recognition software. It identified and matched facial features and emotion. His software recognized jealousy, surprise, nervousness, joy, relief, rage, and dozens more, gathering information on Haltronics' enemies and revealing what his employees were thinking and feeling at any given moment.

The ping exposed a conspiracy was now underway. The ping revealed a long-term employee: a technician who had worked for Haltronics for fifteen years in an unremarkable building at the end of a rural road with a beach access known as Kinney Road. Jespa saw surprise and concealment in her face.

It was Linda Rinton in the Haltronics Manchester relay site. She had recognized Leo Brenamann's picture in Jespa's email.

TWENTY-NINE

Good and evil can be sensed.

Any person can see visions of kindness or cruelty if they are willing to let such energy come to them.

The Christmas season promotes goodwill. The Dickens premise that abundance, charity, and goodwill must become the standard principle of our new age, not just at Christmastime. We need to motivate a world of abundance, charity, and goodwill toward men and let humanity be moved to embrace it.

M. W. – Boling Green Beach

Amy sat on the edge of an ancient, wooden chair. She sat with familiar memories of her mother and vague outlines of her father, suddenly realizing that she was an orphan.

She was to live her life without either of them and now Amy was to make her way through the new world.

Kind hands were next to her helping to find her way through the pain. She was comforted by and curious about the book she held. It helped her feel connected to her mother and father.

Leo looked closer at something caught between Louis' book and Amy's lap, the corner of a single sheet of paper, wrinkled and soiled.

Leo bent closer to Amy.

"Amy, may I?" Leo asked.

They recognized each other.

Amy reached up to touch Leo's face. He had tackled the mess in the trunk of her mother's car, not commenting on spilled detergent or scattered tools.

Leo remembered Amy and her mother's kindness toward him, and her caution, her wary presence as he offered to change her tire. Amy was more willing to let Leo help. Linda eventually came around. By the end of their exchange, Linda offered to bring him supplies and bedding for the coming night.

"May I?" Leo asked again, patiently.

Amy looked down at her lap, where Leo's finger pointed.

"Yes, of course," Amy responded. He pulled the paper's corner and nudged it out.

Leo held the damp document up to a beam of sunlight and inhaled sharply. It was his Haltronics company photo.

He was shocked by the subject line of what was obviously the printed email. It offered a reward for any information about his whereabouts, making him appear guilty of something. Guilt was always part of his association with the company. Haltronics life flooded back, his codes, his contract, his friend and confidant—a woman who had used him.

Rosalie saw the faint, vertical pulse, the cursor, blinking in Leo's eyes. She had seen the same disconcerting dash when he spent the night in Manchester State Park. Leo's learned mechanisms, neuropathways that had become dormant in recent days had re-energized. The pathways had been created and indoctrinated by Leo's boss, John Jespa. They stimulated many emotional and mental processes designed to benefit Haltronics. They had been adopted by all Haltronics employees but in Leo especially.

Sheila.

"Sheila," he murmured quietly, showing no emotion.

Rosalie was now in front of Leo, her long hair rose and wrapped around many universal shapes. Planets orbited, dimensions moved through one another, stars brilliantly reflected against the rich black backdrop. Leo considered the natural world surrounding Rosalie, remembering who she was and why she was here.

Sheila.

He reread Jespa's email and detailed his photo, remembering the last project he worked on for Haltronics, an algorithm dedicated to understanding and control of the universe, dubbed the God Code.

Leo showed the email to the others. Amy responded first:

"Why is there a price on your head, Leo?"

Reluctantly, Leo said: "I created code that presents all universal creation in artificial, moldable three-dimensional holograms. Using simple magnetic gloves as manipulative devices, a user could create new digital worlds based on personal likes, feelings, fascinations, including anger, hatred, and revenge scenarios. Its users can create personal universes based on choice rather than chance, eliminating hardship and consequence. Limited only by imagination, the controller could decide how the universe unfolded. He could create life on an infinite scale—and could destroy it just as easily."

"I left Haltronics three days before the earthquake. I made it as far as Alder Creek before the authorities almost caught me. I'm the only one who can recreate the code if it was destroyed. John Jespa, if he is still alive, will be looking for me. My tests were conclusive. The code worked; that is perhaps why such devastating change has taken place. Touching and manipulating the universes' points of creation belong only to the natural world. The code gives unnatural control over the fate of all things. I sense natural order has intervened to end my God code. I also wrote the program Jespa used to monitor and control his employees through emotion tracking software. He can process every feeling that every employee experienced for any minute of any day. All of the information was stored in his massive data warehouses, some spanning acres. This information was used for control. He was awarded contracts to scrutinize thousands of government offices, private companies, and the most notorious of all, joint sessions of Congress, the Supreme Court, and the office of the President of the United States. Jespa analyzed them all."

Mitchell asked Leo if he could take a closer look. The email date was three days prior to the quake. "He must have known the moment you quit, Leo. Amy's mom must have recognized you and brought the email home to show Amy." Mitchell stopped short.

"Yes!" Amy cried. "She did! She was trying to tell me about it right before the quake."

Mitchell passed the message to Charles.

"They may come here, looking for you, Leo."

"That is a real possibility," Leo agreed. "If my software picked up on your mother's recognition of me, of her surprise, and he got to your mother's company profile before the earthquake began, then he has a good lead on where to look."

Two days hence, a gathering took place at the far end of the Hoyt property. Amy took him up on his offer to inter her mother. Linda Rinton was laid to rest. A family was born; at least Charles Hoyt thought so.

Hoyt also erected a memorial to Amy's father next to Linda.

For Linda and Nathan, Amy prayed that the universe would accept them again as husband and wife, that they would find and love each other. She reached into the sky, her hands brushed by leaves from the old immense elm that covered the giant Oz House lot.

"I have something for you Amy, that we believe is intended for you," Gunnar said.

From Aqurar's cave, Gunnar handed Amy the seventh stone upon which was inscribed this phrase: *Heaven is within. Forgiveness is the path. Leave now and take with you this stone, it holds your future.*

Red,

    I dreamt of a three-legged dog walking with a one-armed man through the thinning air toward night. I saw want and need cutting into the dark horizon.

    I am such want, such need.

    Beloved, I look for you, I cry out for you.

                                Your Mitchell

THIRTY

———————

Approximately two out of three people being treated for depression are not getting enough Denytrope.

Learn more about Denytrope.

Call your doctor if your depression worsens or you have unusual changes in mood, behavior, or thoughts of suicide.

Denytrope can increase these thoughts in children, teens, and young adults.

Elderly patients who take Denytrope have an increased risk of death or stroke.

Call your doctor if you get a high fever, stiff muscles, or stomach cramps, as these may be signs of a life-threatening reaction.

Uncontrollable muscle twitching may become permanent.

Increased blood sugar, a side effect of taking Denytrope daily, increases risk of diabetic shock, coma, and death.

Call your doctor if you suffer from dizziness upon standing or sitting. Falling can cause death.

You may suffer seizures, impaired motor skills, and trouble swallowing. We can't have you unable to swallow more Denytrope."

"The haboob of Wall Street and Madison Avenue covers our common sense with its blinding dust.

You do not need a car that can park itself and an estate to leave your children.

M. W. – Saunders Beach

The black SUV roared forward. Will McKinley gripped the steering wheel, staring down the road ahead. He dodged in and out of the smoking rubble along Highway 1, using the SUV's four-wheel drive to maneuver through landscape destruction.

"After the second Oil and Terror war, I went underground. My marriage failed. I lost touch with the kid. Life has become a strange series of circumstances far outside my ability to control it. This was in opposition to my military experience," McKinley said.

Orth looked ahead, sizing up how he might choose to negotiate what was to come, and was saddened by Will's emotional losses.

"I'm not even sure where they are anymore. My ex resumed her maiden name and changed the kid's too. I doubt I'll ever see him again."

Untouched stretches of Highway 1 were a welcome relief. McKinley accelerated above one hundred miles an hour, rapidly breaking to a crawl for breaks in the road.

Landslides were everywhere. Huge alluvial fans of mud and sand now covered two centuries of southern California development.

Orth could hardly imagine how many millions of lives were buried in the sprawling aftermath. Everywhere he looked, he saw the detritus of modern man: chimneys, satellite dishes, two-by-fours, air conditioning units, business marquees, freeway signs, car bumpers, shopping carts, billboards with their advertising disclaimers; the list was endless. Orth identified with every piece, recalling memories from his life. He shook his head, overwhelmed by Mother Nature's reclamation.

"I'm Peter . . . Peter Shroud," the man in the backseat finally said.

McKinley looked in the rearview mirror: "I'm sorry, I forgot your name," then looked at Orth, "I'm giving Peter a lift too."

"I'm Jim Orth." Orth looked over his shoulder into Peter's eyes, sizing up the passenger.

"Are you from the military?" Peter Shroud asked.

Orth wanted to think that Peter's motivation for asking came from a sense of propriety.

The passenger's last name intrigued McKinley and Orth. They recalled the famous Shroud of Turin, burial cloth of Jesus Christ with its x-ray-like quality, and the incredible notion that it was the detailed reflection of the Son of God. It still enchanted Orth's imagination. He always had believed the claims. Now, in the aftermath of epoch change, came a man who had chosen the name *Shroud* as his surname.

McKinley knew what Orth was contemplating. He remembered every story Orth ever shared of the heroes and legends of Greek mythology and Christian lore and listened intently to his stories during the long waits between battles.

"Is it a family surname?" McKinley asked, glancing back at the man.

"No," Shroud said. "I picked it out of a stack of religious literature one night while studying for a test in high school. It's not my real name; it's just what I call myself."

Orth reflected: *How did I know he'd chosen the name? He's on the lam. It's a strange thing to do. A picture of Christ. The apostle and the controversial image of Jesus, all recalled in one name.*

"It's quite the loaded name, Peter," Orth said.

McKinley glanced again at Shroud. "Are you religious?"

"I like the discussions that come from introducing myself as *Peter Shroud*."

"What's your take then, on the *Shroud of Turin*?" McKinley asked.

"I like the idea that it is the burial cloth of Jesus of Nazareth, despite all of the evidence that suggests it couldn't be what they claim it is," Shroud said. "The intrigue for me is about the modesty it displays—the hands covering the groin area. It puts a very specific human emotion on one of the most consummate spiritual deities in all human history."

258

McKinley and Orth lifted an eyebrow as they listened to the stranger. McKinley studied Shroud in the rearview mirror. There was a similar appearance between Jesus and his passenger. Shroud had long brown hair and beard, bushy brown eyebrows, and an ability to organize and communicate his thoughts.

"Why modesty?" Shroud stated rhetorically. "If the Turin shroud is really from Jesus after his crucifixion, then Jesus *was* a man. At least for me, that would explain the modesty, and helps explain Jesus being tempted by human weaknesses.

Another claim: that he had a wife and children also intrigues me. Supposedly millions of descendants or a precise and secretly documented lineage kept hidden and safe by mysterious groups of the faithful. In this *End of Days* play, will his descendants come forward and offer an example to the world of how to live?"

"Another rhetorical question. Sorry, I talk like that. I like the sound of my own voice, I suppose."

"No, I got it," McKinley said. "Good questions. There is hope in the answers."

Suddenly, a brightly dressed man shot out from behind a large pileup of automobiles and diesel trucks. He wore an orange-tinted sac, his neck laden with wooden beads, and his face carried marks of an Indian, from India. Like Shroud, this man had thickly lined eyebrows.

He waved wildly at the SUV. As they passed by, the travelers heard his accented pleas begging them to stop.

They parked about one hundred feet beyond him. Orth and McKinley got out and looked down the highway toward him.

"What's going on?" Orth shouted

The Indian looked confused when he heard Orth's question. He started to walk gingerly toward their vehicle.

"I beg you to take me with you."

"We don't know you or why you are in such a panic," McKinley said.

"What do you mean 'such a panic?'" the strangely dressed man asked. He gestured; "Look around you. Look at what has happened. Of course I am panicked. I am completely cut-off from home, no way to contact anyone I know, I've no way to feed or defend myself . . ."

Orth put his hand up to the stranger, indicating that they got his message but they were more concerned about immediate threats. Orth's hand indicated that the man should walk no closer. The stranger understood.

"No, nothing imminent, but danger seems to be lurking at every turn. I feel that if I could just get into a car that isn't burned and feel protected from the elements and looming stares of other survivors, I would not be in such a state of panic."

"We can take on another passenger," McKinley said, "but we are short of rations. If you come with us, you would have to pull yourself together and follow one simple rule."

"What would that be?" The stranger asked.

"You would have to give to the group more than you take for yourself," McKinley said.

Orth looked over at his old friend.

"This is the only way we are going to survive, if we survive at all."

"Give more than I take," the stranger stated softly. "That's it? You want me to give more than I take and you'll let me ride with you."

McKinley smiled at the stranger's efforts to understand the deal he was making.

At that moment, Shroud got out, noticed the stranger's toying thread between his fingers, and asked: "What's your name friend?"

"I am Santaesh," the dark-complexioned man responded. "Santaesh Parnoon. I promise to give more than I take though I have nothing to give you now." Orth looked at McKinley, appreciating his sincerity.

"This is Jim, he's Will, and I'm Peter."

Parnoon surveyed the motley crew. He tentatively moved toward them as each one returning to their positions in the SUV. He took the driver's side passenger door and sat behind McKinley, looking over the interior and the payload behind him. He was relieved to see the contents: food, water, and other miscellaneous items that would be useful for survival.

He recalled a promise regarding karma in his faith but that promise could not hold up. Parnoon knew many who had not been spared a suffocating death, their lives ended inches away from his position.

He recalled the moment after the terror ended, as he looked up through the length of a trucking trailer, like a chimney, to a calming blue sky. He recognized the feet and sandals of his beloved wife, protruding from under the trailer's walls. The trailer had landed squarely around him, protecting him from the debris-filled sludge but had crushed his wife, ending any chance she had to join him.

He placed his feet carefully on the trailer's ribbing, pulling himself out of the earthly tomb. He took one last look into the trailer and wrapped the laces he had taken from his wife's sandals through his fingers. He then heard the SUV approaching.

THIRTY-ONE

―――――

Let us chase a blood-red moon.

Look to the sky at midnight. The brilliant white light of an untouched full moon will come before you, its light reminiscent of you deep wish for an enlightened life. Your blood-red moon lies between your life and the eternal, your own bone and crimson mass locks you away from your place in the light blue and cascading yellow universe.

If you tired of the same old story, turn some pages.

M. W. – Moat Creek

―――――

Charles recalled Louis' memorial service and his conversation with Mitchell. There was a clue to the Talisman Group's next step somewhere in his memories. The very thing he was to embrace, was just out of reach.

Come out, come forward with you, Charles said to himself. He stared at the horizon, filled with so many of nature's renewing processes. Water, erosion, wind—all rearranging. He put his fingers up to the point where the horizon met his uninterrupted thoughts, and then closed his eyes, willing the two points to melt, to come together, to join as one. Numbers, dates, times, measurements, directions, telephone and page information, sizes, lists, figures, statistics, records, tables, meters of rhyme, facts, figures, musical scores, countdowns, pennies, dollars, whirled in and out of his mind. One became two, and two became four, and the magic of patterns developed, merging into a fine point within him.

In the Map Room, Mitchell and Leo were also introspective. Moments found Mitchell and Charles looking at Leo with more than just passing interest. They sensed the mysteries of life unfold.

Amy looked at the growing energy cascading between the men. She understood this magic and mystery were about her. *Love wanting to live, to breathe. The sky pulls at me. The sun shines through,* Amy thought. *The moment. It is here. Come see.*

She looked at Louis' box. The characters looked at her. Dorothy gazed knowingly into Amy's eyes. The Kansas farm girl smiled and spoke to Amy*: Take your companions with you to the Emerald City.*

"She thinks I am Dorothy," Amy said aloud. "She said that you are my companions, looking for a home and that all of us, collectively, have the smarts, the courage, and the love to find that home. She says it is within us already! What is within? Home? Heaven? Look! She is waving to us to follow her to the Emerald City!"

Everyone joined Amy and watched as the holographic animation in Louis' book came alive. They wanted to join Dorothy as she and her companions began to run toward the gate, toward the keeper, and the gifts they hoped to find.

Amy lost herself in the story. Her physical touch sank into the immersing colors of Louis' invention. She closed her eyes. In her mind, the story began again, like the rewinding of a video, at the point when the yellow brick road appeared.

With her index finger, she traced the road, starting at the first of the yellow bricks. Cut at angles representing a triangle, the brick prompted thoughts of her mother's church and of the three-sided deity. She thought of the mathematical strength found in the triangle-shaped pyramid and of the spiritual energy it generated.

As her finger traveled out in slow circles from the initial brick, she felt the colors and sounds described in Baum's Wizard of Oz. The sensation of touch compelled Amy to comprehend Louis' interpretation of Baum's Oz. The notion of spirit being the ultimate end of any mathematical equation, of any attempt to understand *creation* enlightened her. Her finger circled around again and she sensed acceleration but not wind, light or speed. Like *current. That* was it, her finger in the yellow brick road felt like a current. It lifted her state of being. Tears came as the sensation of lift overwhelmed her ability to process.

Her finger circled around a final time and there before her was the cascading light-blue universe. She looked at the world that encircled her. The yellow brick road did not flow out into poppy fields. There was no distant, beautiful city. A bluntly built mass, the color of blood and bone, obstructed her progress.

She touched the mass, pushed on it, and felt an unusual sensation of pressure in her head.

The mass was slick. She fell face first, into the heavy, ink-like, yellow substance of the road. She stood up, took her fist, and pounded on it, simultaneously feeling a knock in her mind.

Puzzled, she hit the blood and bone mass again and felt the physical sensation she had experienced in her head.

The sensation of spirit lifted her from the trance-like state of standing motionless in the middle of the yellow brick road. Slowly, through the bone mass she moved, experiencing brief vertigo. On the far side of the mass, she entered and became a part of the cascading blue and yellow universe. It was her paradise.

"In paradise, I am." Amy spoke the words as her companions stood around her. Charles immediately understood, for he had heard Louis speak those very same words.

"In paradise, I am." Charles repeated. Amy turned toward him and smiled. She stood and took his hand. Everyone knew that Louis' book led Amy to her insight.

"She crossed through a partition, that part of our physical mind that separates the conscious from its counterpart." Charles stated. "She is in paradise, once mysterious and forbidden, an unaware place, breaking through only in the occasional dream, she is in her part of the universe. She has transcended into paradise by following Dorothy. She has stepped out of the woods and into the light." Charles, Mitchell and Leo stared at Louis' creation.

Amy's eyes reflected the depth-filled color of paradise, lighter and darker, still and wild. She found her way to the edge of the yellow brick road, and there, spoke these words:

"For this is what we know now: a different kind of coo echoes from the dove, it is mixed into distant salty ocean spray, the quiet is magical, blended through whispered chants of other creative extensions, all hanging above my head in silent curiosity.

Here, where Kinney Road ends, it begins again as the spiritual universe. We, who have little but our trust to give, must also release our awe at understanding where we *do* stand in all history.

Our place in the star-filled cosmos is filled with Joy and serenity. We contemplate our stillness and take our home among the blades of Nature, Her aeolian harps.

We play, we sing, we design, in the fulfillment of our own natures, vibrating with each new, dawning moment of life."

To my own true Red:

I stare into firelight rising into the night sky. You are still there. In your beautiful brown eyes, one a shade lighter than the other, I see the whole of my life. I hear the love in your song—you never said 'no.' I taste the truth in your tears. No man has seen a greater fortune than I have known as your husband, your confidant, your heart's desire.

You're still here, your shining, fine skin aglow as passionate memory. Your hair still falling about my face. My heart still beating for you.

Your own true love, your Mitchell

THIRTY-TWO

———

I look for beauty in our world. It is always before us. Today I watched a group of singers, surrounded by a circle of calla lilies, white and new, trumpeting skyward, vocalize in praise of life's progressions. Praise they deserve. Circles and cycles are beautiful to behold. Patterns ground our lives, establishing points of reference in a world turning. The mathematical perfection of nature, full of faultless, chaotic rotation, provides respite for the restlessness of each moment.

M. W. – Point Arena Creek

———

Amy's face was of a newborn baby, sensing nothing and everything at once, simple and silent.

Amy's meditation continued. Light tip-toed across the room, opposite from where she sat.

Charles had moved Amy to a sitting position on the chair and released her hand. She continued her walk along the yellow brick road, with the embodiments of home, intelligence, courage, love and joy.

In a delighted murmur, Charles said to Gunnar, "Speaking of heaven, it looks to be a cold, clear night ahead, perfect for viewing the stars."

Leo overheard Charles' comment on the pending night sky, and was struck by the serendipity with Aqurar's cartograph, discovered by Mitchell in Scott Hoyt's box.

Leo quietly said: "Gentlemen, I believe, if I am reading Aqurar's calculations correctly that tonight we are going to see a blood-red moon."

Gunnar and Charles were puzzled by Leo's statement.

"I think Aqurar's cartograph suggests that time is going to be reset tonight and that it begins with the appearance of a blood-red moon."

Gunnar had not seen the moon in a week and whispered: "I believe we are in a 'new moon' phase. I haven't seen the moon at all recently."

Leo looked at the ancient parchment, focusing and recalculating, then stated: "there will be an appearance of three blue-green planets that will hover over a concentration of magnetite just off the coast. The *Loadingstone,* as Aqurar refers to this, can be seen in the water a quarter of a mile out. Its shallow position causes a constant, long, white-capped wave to surface. You can see it due west on Kinney Road by shifting your view two degrees south. This *Loadingstone* serves as a portal into Aqurar's other worlds. *And,* he says, the *Loadingstone* will be the focal point in the greatest of all the Earth Mother's cycles: a new end, and then an immediate rebirthing of the moment—*a rotation of time*—as Aqurar refers to it.

Aqurar's numerical analysis also suggests that our units of time will no longer apply. The blood-red moon signifies a shift in the earth's magnetic polarity, a polarity that will be overtaken by a stronger magnetic orbit caused by the three new planetary bodies that will appear in tonight's dark sky.

The cartograph warns that a great effort will be made by man to thwart this rotational shift. Aqurar states that this pending rotation makes certain the role of honesty and humility in service to the universe's spiritual world by ensuring a never-ending display of diversity and originality. He warns the world of a great machine that would devours and reduce this variety and innovation to nothing more than a sample of each: where read, it would be the same idea: where heard, it would be the same set of notes or words: where painted, would be the same shape, color, and design, repeated over and over again, ultimately creating a universal fog over all things, from material to spiritual. This reduction will lead to the service of one kind of evil, with its own polarity: itself and its reflection, running unobstructed through the world."

Aqurar's solemn prophesy fed a growing sense of foreboding in everyone.

"The blood red moon symbolizes a renewal," Hoyt added hopefully. "I can see Mother Nature beginning again. Perhaps it signifies a new epoch of nature's ascendance over man. Perhaps it is open to interpretation. There are seven separate shades of a blood red moon, representing waning through to waxing moon. Could each shade represent one of the seven stones that we received from

Aqurar's cave? Could our lesson be that we have not been able to navigate the responsibility of free will—that our choices have soured goodwill? Have we supplanted Nature's harmony with our anger and fear?"

"All good questions my old friend, but there has been, time and time again, fine examples of the beauty of free will creating goodwill," Gunnar said. "Copland's 'Fanfare for the Common Man.' In its achievement we hear the beauty of mankind. It was through free will that such harmony was created. I remember a photograph of Aaron Copland as he conducted an orchestra playing his music. In the movements of his hands and in the garden of his gaze I beheld the nature of God.

Copland's music bought all of us more time. Any creative thought that furthers free will and extends goodwill furthers all of us. I have watched Copland's flawless musical mind unfurl. What I see before me on Amy's lap the same creative force moving the same creative space forward that Copland expressed. Through Copland's music and through Louis' mind and craft, comes the furthering of this free will/goodwill connection.

Louis' invention shows us a way to endure those who would be cruel to us. Through our breaking passed the Wizard's partition, our lives, once an illusion, become real. Forgiveness is the key message on the final stone, which Amy now holds. She will bring us into the light of forgiveness. She knows that the story of forgiveness needs to be told and retold."

Gunnar looked at Louis' invention and its *Wonderful Wizard of Oz* theme. "It is said, all that is happening has happened before. Déjà vu gives us a sense of this, but déjà vu is a sneak peek behind the partition. The foundation of goodwill is the reason for free will."

Gunnar, Charles, and Leo nodded at the collective thoughts expressed, They noticed that Mitchell left the map room, then heard the Oz front door close.

≈≈

Mitchell thought of Red. Her voice rang through him, stilling him. He thought of Zac, the nephew of the man Mitchell killed for murdering Red, and how long ago it was that Zac had left Prescott, Arizona, where Red died.

He thought of his new friendship with Leo, of the parchment he found inside the box Charles now safeguarded, of Louis' mysterious invention, and how life had merged them together in the old Oz house.

Mitchell sat on the front entrance steps and fell asleep. He dreamt of the discoveries in Aqurar's cave and the tenets describing Mother Nature's new ascent, then memories of his father intervened. They came not from his mind but from his neck muscles. His body recalled not only his, his father's, and most likely a long line of ancestors that suffered from the debilitating effects of abuse and addiction.

Red saving him from his past and from his father's fate always followed his recollection of his inability to save Red when she needed him most. He put his face in his hands, feeling old weariness and the horrifying changes in his life.

Amy joined Mitchell on the steps.

She stared across the street, feeling the weight of change, wanting to understand the pile of rubble there.

"Why do things happen the way they do?" she asked in general, and of Mitchell if he was listening.

"There is supposed to be some grand design to it all," he said, as he rubbed the muscles on his neck. "You have asked the wrong guy, Amy. Sorry."

Through tired eyes, he looked across the street with Amy, toward the rubble, and tried for a greater degree of wisdom to her question.

"Wait a minute, Amy, I have another answer. The reason why things happen the way they do is to provide contrast." Amy looked at Mitchell, wanting more.

"Our lives need contrast and that contrast reveals itself in hardship. There is no other way to live. From Aqurar's cave beneath us, contrast shows that heaven *is* found on Earth, but more so, *Heaven is found within*, Amy. *Heaven is found within.*

"May I see your stone, Amy?"

Amy gave it to Mitchell, who placed it next to the stone he was given. Justice and Forgiveness. Mitchell looked for a purpose represented in the pairing of the stones.

Amy and Mitchell softly said together: "Heaven is found within."

At that moment, a black SUV hummed past the house on Highway 1 with five passengers inside.

Red,

I am lulled. I can see but not hear or feel the ocean breeze through the tall spring grass.

I walk a quiet Kinney Road. Every minute, Arena Rock pushes its white caps skyward. Now I hear its roar. The waves are full, large, windswept.

I have long loved my union with nature. Forever it seems, my infinite gaze holds the infinite you, my one true love, singing.

I am lulled into peace flourishing as comprehension. I long for the analog you, the real you. I know this place; this place is love; it knows me.

The symmetry of nature comes into view, not on my terms but on its own.

I hear our love roar. The crumbling fence posts try to interrupt what is perfect on the horizon—my memory of you.

We call out the dead—the past—the looming decay. Nothing swings here save the wind.

This note pad is my computer, this pen my mouse. My thoughts and my luck, they bring me closer to you; they comfort me.

I am glad for Kinney Road. It glimmers for me as spirit, as new. Its still presentation remains unchanged.

And there, upon the road, remains my love, my eternal light, overcoming all shadow. You are my unwavering white light, shining brightly into my shadow form.

Your own true love, your Mitchell

THIRTY-THREE

If we take care of the small and insignificant things over time, they will express who we are. At the end of life, our wake remains.

We hope this wake makes our world a better place. When life ends, like any story, what remains is the blank last page. It absorbs an occasional observer who wonders about our often-mysterious epilogue.

What then becomes of us? The truth of your living lies in your response.

M. W. – A tug from a blue house on Riverside Drive

With Peter Shroud, Santaesh Parnoon, and newcomer Abe Mahud in the back, Orth behind the wheel, and McKinley (Loki) on the passenger's front seat, the dusty brown-black SUV rumbled downhill on a rumpled Highway 1, into the quake-devastated town of Point Arena, California.

The scene reminded the passengers of war, loss and destruction as far as they could see.

"But this was no war," Will said. "It is simply how nature resets."

Gunning the SUV up the hill through town, a tall blue house caught Loki's attention. He saw two figures sitting on a long wooden stairway, deep in conversation, an older man and a younger woman.

The young woman conveyed age and wisdom, the older man hope and imagination.

As the SUV passed the old house, Loki saw two other faces in the home's bay window. Loki's eyes met Charles Hoyt's, then Leo Brenamann's.

With the blue house in the rearview mirror, the SUV rounded a tight corner, coming bumper-to-wheel with a church bell that rested in a perfect, upright position on Highway 1's double yellow line. The bell's church tower had fallen forward from the main body of the structure during the earthquake, now prone on the ground and pointing at the blue house.

"Does it strike you as odd that this steeple no longer rises toward heaven, but lays horizontal and pointing to the house on the corner untouched by the earthquake?" Loki asked.

"Why is that house behind us not destroyed?" Mahud asked.

Shroud added, "When every structure around it has been laid waste?"

"This is chaos at its finest," Parnoon replied. "This is the universe. Why does one life end, while another continues, even as both are subject to the same circumstance? Because chaos reigns. It has always been so," Parnoon said, with a defeated tone.

Orth stopped the truck, noticing the bell's cracked ironwork, thinking of Philadelphia's Liberty Bell and all that had changed in the five days since the earthquake.

"Trying to control chaos is the foundation of all religion," Orth said as he exited the SUV.

"Yet exerting control ultimately creates more chaos," added McKinley, joining Orth at the front of the SUV.

The old bell had many coats of blue lacquer, smoothing out what had once been finer detail in the rope wheel and bell itself.

"And therein lies John Jespa's great error," Orth said, as if continuing a past conversation. "From an early, youthful innocence, he abandoned this simple truth for . . . what?"

"There is a simple truth that is expressed in my faith," Parnoon said, joining Orth and McKinley at the blue bell. "In the midst of the sun, there is light. Amid light, there is truth, and in truth, is the imperishable."

Mahud joined in: "I think this Jespa fellow has fallen prey to the innate human desire to create all light, all truth, and to become imperishable."

Standing beside the SUV, Shroud said, "I think Parnoon and Mahud are right. Jespa is a true product of free will, as both of you have spoken about during our drive." He gestured toward Orth and McKinley. "If goodwill was the basis, entitlement would not have been a factor in Jespa's corporate decisions. Absent goodwill as the foundation for Haltronics, Jespa separated his company and the Internet from natural cause and effect. His soul, along with his company, is missing a system of checks and balances. Based on free will, his soul becomes the universe, destroying the light

Parnoon and Mahud reference, and the natural harmony of Mother Nature, becoming evil."

"But Jespa lost his connection to the universe when he centered on *I, me, my,* and *mine.* He removed *us, we, and our* from the Haltronics manifesto. He was consumed by avarice serving, not the many, but the one. Jespa still hopes to replace God's soul with his own. His evil soul has made Haltronics evil expansion inevitable," concluded Orth. "Depending on the outcome of this earthquake, and his ability to restore order, Jespa has put just hours between himself and control of all original thought."

As they prepared to re-enter the SUV, each suddenly stopped. Cocking their heads sideways, they heard a light, clear call, a melody of sorts from a thousand tiny voices. It was oddly familiar to them. Shroud joined in and began whistling the tune, using his index fingers in the air as miniature conductor's wands. It made the others laugh. "What is that?" Parnoon asked. "I'm not sure," Shroud said, it is coming from the bell."

John Jespa's limousine sped toward the Port of Long Beach. His yacht, the Crimson Ward, was docked in a special slip given to him as part of a trade contract with the City of Los Angeles. The boat was ready to depart as soon as the Haltronics chief arrived.

He'd spent the three previous days inside his mobile office, a stretch military Hummer equipped with a .50 caliber swivel machine gun on the roof and every communications, electronics, and survival. Jespa finally channeled his rage to focus on the profile of Leo Brenamann.

For Jespa, his world came down to one objective; he must find his chief engineer.

Jespa, unsure if Leo was alive or dead, still wondered how Leo might be spending his time. He recalled Leo's intimate presence in his life with strange affection and odd longing from their time together online. As Sheila, Jespa had complete control of the young engineer's life. Jespa enjoyed the young man becoming infatuated, then falling in love with his Internet creation. He liked watching Leo, as his gaming avatar Loker, fall in love with Sheila. Jespa craved Leo's confidences and how he went about it. He liked backing Loker into a corner, emotionally, and watching the thoughts and emotions he shared with Sheila. He captured them on every kind of recording device, from hidden cameras placed in Leo's physical environment to biophysical sensing equipment hidden throughout Leo's Internet connections.

As Sheila, Jespa would sit quietly in his offices: a downtown LA high-rise, Malibu beachfront mansion, and in his mobile office, becoming aroused watching Loker and Sheila having sex. He could not believe how the two avatars entwined, exploding in their lust.

Jespa learned everything he needed to know about his key engineer while watching.

He laughed aloud at Leo's spectacle, alarming his entourage. He checked them for any reaction to his outburst and found none. Snickering softly, he conveyed to everyone in the limo how fortunate they were that he was in a good mood.

Jespa looked through the front windshield of the Hummer and saw a ramp unfolding in front of him from the back of his yacht. The hummer's driver followed prompts from two of his yacht's crew. The mobile office climbed up the ramp, and into the yacht's docking station. Jespa felt the ramp rise and retract into the vessel, then heard the watertight hatch to the docking station seal shut. He got out, eyed everyone in the station before cliimbing topside to the Crimson Ward's bridge.

"Chart a course: 38° 9088′ north by 123° 693′ west," Jespa barked. "We are headed to Point Arena, California."

৵৵

Loki drove the SUV rumbled around the blue bell giving Jim Orth some needed rest from the wheel. Traveling a short distance further up Highway 1 the group saw one of California's tallest lighthouses still standing.

"I am amazed," Orth said. "That lighthouse *cannot* still be standing!"

"And yet, there it is," Parnoon said.

"If everyone agrees, I suggest we head to Manchester State Park on Kinney Road," Will McKinley said. "It's four miles up Highway One."

"Agreed," Shroud said emphatically, worn out from a long three days of riding in the backseat of a hard-driven truck.

"We can get a better look at the lighthouse tomorrow," Orth said, staring at the symbol of hope. "You said Kinney Road, Loki?"

"Yeah, Kinney Road. The campsite is on Kinney Road, why?"

"It can't be the same Kinney Road," Orth said. "Before I left the last words out of Jespa's mouth was an order to find a Leo Brenamann, one of his chief engineers last seen by an employee at his Kinney Road facility. Will, that facility is or was the main North American communication hub for Haltronics."

Orth put his hand on the dashboard of the SUV, to steady his overwhelming sense of serendipity, and the historical implications of the present moment.

My beloved Red

Let us walk together in the grass, always. The grass blown by the winds always transcends. Such peace at road's end. The grass sways and your heart plays, discarding place and time. I know you there on a road marked at its inception by the Pacific Coast Highway, and at its culmination in endless sand and waves where grass harps comprehend and hold dear our love.

Your beloved Mitchell

THIRTY-FOUR

Math and its presence in all natural things intrigue me. Algorithms can be created for everything we sense.

I am interested in an algorithm that unveils two selves, enabling a comparison, representing one's uniqueness mathematically contrasting free will results with goodwill effects. This algorithm has the potential to present a rich ongoing depiction of our unique human choices.

Perhaps if each of us better understood how we tick within both frameworks, we would choose behaviors consistent with goodwill, rather than self-centered free will. As I better understand of the differences between the two, free will reveals as much more self-serving, including the act of defending it against goodwill.

M. W. Saint Aloysius Catholic Cemetery

Leo stood in the middle of the bay window calculating his position relative to angles of glass in his peripheral vision. This math took him back to his young life.

A door opens. His bedroom. His mother. She is humming while she dries her hands on her apron. He notes she is standing in the eight by ten by fourteen-foot box that is his room. She asks:

Honey, what do you have there?

He notes the color of the carpet, height of the door and the light and shadows that pour through a window, too high to see out unless he stands tall on his bed. Assorted lengths of painted wood and connector forms are on the carpeted floor. He lets shapes, designs and angles emerge in his imagination.

Leo's recall was interrupted by a large, black vehicle charging past the bay window.

Honey? Honey, can you hear me?

His mother's voice again . . . asks that question, repeatedly.

He is staring at his hands while he manipulates his *Tinker Toy* set, symbols of the things he made. This process helps him remember how one design differs from the next.

Honey?

Leo looks at his mother absent-mindedly, studies her face and nods *yes.* He can hear her.

Well, what are you making?

"It shifts, then rotates . . . like this," he answers. Leo demonstrates how gravity and tension affect the balance of his *Tinker Toy* models that are lined up in order by the number of spokes, and in a unique pattern around the spot on the carpet where he sits. Leo pushes the arrangement with his finger. His mother is fascinated as each model falls into the next like a circle of dominoes.

She is delighted by the patterns and the way they clink at precise increments, then form a new pattern setting itself up to be pushed again by Leo's finger.

The circumference of the toy patterns spread as wide as the toy parts permit, until Leo's bed, toy bin, or dropped clothing stops them.

Leo, can you do it again?

The impediment of clothing or toy box prompted Leo to sit down on a chair near the bay window. With scrap paper from Charles Hoyt's wastebasket and a pen from Hoyt's desk, he drew the designs he once made as a toddler with his *Tinker Toys*.

He remembered his child's curiosity and the up-down motion of models but struggled to remember how he made these wooden toys tumble forward. Gravity and tension were key but how? As a child he never had to push his mind. His imagination effortlessly reflected stick and connector objects as if looking at an internal mirror.

The objects grew in brilliance and clarity. *Aqurar's drawing* Leo thought. *His cartograph was not a map but an algorithm.* He noted similarities in the diagrams of his *Tinker Toy* shapes and the ancient Native American drawing.

He placed the cartograph next to his childhood designs. The two began to converge in his mind.

Inspired by both, Leo penciled an elaborate equation, first several lines long then several pages, Hoyt handing him sheets of white copy paper. Mitchell and Amy returned and joined the group surrounding Leo.

They watched as Leo's math repeated the last equation. He would start and then complete the same algorithm: a loop. Leo struggled to comprehend why the entire equation was so important to his childhood design and Aqurar's cartograph.

Something flashed: *It is repeating, not as a loop but as a last line of code.*

His *Tinker Toy* regenerated. The cartograph always lead back to its starting point. For Leo, his final line of code matched his understanding of regeneration found in his scientific world: the code was his mathematical notion of renewal. Leo's face fell into his hands. He rubbed his temples.

Leo looked up and said to his friends: "This is the final line of code for Jespa's machine because it will undo every line I have written for Haltronics. If executed, it will release Haltronics' control and domination of this once free information highway, ending Jespa's authority over world-wide connectivity.

If I were to input this into Haltronics' mainframe, and if I were to use this finger to hit 'enter,' the Haltronics' Internet would return to its original purpose."

At that instant, in Leo's beautiful and tortured mind, he answered his mother's question from so many years ago:

"Yes, I can do it again."

"The hope here," Orth said, as the group listened around the fire pit, "is to understand that within each of us is the ability to separate today's circumstances from our strength of character. We must remain unyielding and never let our situations overtake what we know to be true in our souls."

They poked at the fire with lengths of iron or wood and grasped Orth's words. Each Individualizedd their parts in the work Orth alluded to, that their resulting unity and effort could reassure a new and emerging world. Parnoon perceived that good in himself as a doctor, Mahud as a maker of metal, McKinley as a miner, Orth an idealist, and Shroud a sailor in a sea of change. They realized through their joint efforts that they could revitalize, on Kinney Road, man's ingenuity in nurturing this blue green world.

As the campfire's heat and sparks unfurled toward the night, three great hollows formed in the sky above them. A triad collection of grand heavenly bodies, one with red hues and shadows, one with green, and one blue became visible.

Unaware of the heavens changing overhead, Orth continued, "The reason why free will is no longer viable is because there is no such thing as absolute free will. Nothing is free including the will to be free. However, there is such a thing as absolute goodwill, where the act is free of calculated cost or expected return to oneself.

This duality of generosity and selfishness creates inner conflict much like two hands digging a hole and filling it up, cancelling out the results of each. An internal conflict always results when self-seeking abuts altruism."

Referring to a heavily thumbed copy of Thomas Taylor's *The Works of Plato*, Orth said: "listen to Plato's interpretation on this: 'I, therefore, Callicles, am persuaded by these accounts and consider how I may exhibit my soul before the judge in a healthy condition. Wherefore, disregarding the honors that most men value and looking to the truth, I shall endeavor to live as selflessly as I can; and when I die, to die so. And I invite all other men, to the utmost of my power; and you too I in turn invite to this contest, which, I affirm, surpasses all contests here.[3]'

The contest then is this: let each of us stand before the reflection of our lives, the mirror we have fashioned with our hands, and let that reflection be shaped by goodwill toward all persons. Let it motivate our actions, not by choice but by design, by instinct.

As a human family, we can come together—a family broken by tragedy and circumstance, brought together again at this crossroads.

The calculation must be this: *from those, according to their ability, to those, according to their need. Ability notwithstanding need.* This is Ayn Rand's great thesis and her greatest antithesis, depending upon where one starts. However, how could we believe her thesis to be true? Are we to let simple survival continue its grip on the world? The masters of the universe plan to see it through. Men like John Jespa believe that survival is their innate right and theirs alone. If there is only so much survival to go around, then let need be answered by goodwill in the world. How much longer can we ignore the living decay of want? We must do our best to honor all life, not just our own."

Will McKinley followed Orth's words intently and applied their meanings to large chunks of campfire ember rising into the silent night above. One burned larger and brighter, and its glow represented Orth's last thought—that more must be done to honor all life. As a soldier, McKinley found his yearning to make this tenet at odds with his actions. For a better part of two decades, he had served his and his superiors' self-interest. Government *was* big business and big business served only its ownership.

The large ember continued its rise, burning brighter. Lost in thought, McKinley noted the intensity of the ember as it changed from red to green and finally to blue.

He looked at his companions as they sat around the campfire. *How odd that these men are now my peers. It is as if our histories have been reset. I see them as parts of myself.*

McKinley's focus shifted back to the floating ember, now cooling and drifting with the breeze above Manchester State Park. Beyond the ember's trail, odd shapes or waves appeared, foreign to any night sky he'd ever seen.

My love,

The sun casts long afternoon shadows across our afternoon faces. Our breath intermingles with the radiance of our true love, timeless always, through all ages, through all wars, through all peace. We have known each other's breath. You are he, the one I knew in my youthful dreams, as stars passed in the night, as light burned the minutes of each day. I know you in me. I desire above all the things in this shaking world, you next to me.

Your forever love, your Red

The debate between free will versus goodwill shall be free of political and religious bias. Personal understanding through the lens of nature should guide this discussion.

Humans, like all living creatures, should adhere to the laws of nature. We should strive to integrate with everything rather than isolate ourselves from life's hardships and our place in nature. Human suffering stems from being disconnected from reality by relying on conjectures. True virtue and happiness come from understanding and living in the reality of the world.

Free will is flawed. Ignoring man's spiritual beliefs, nature will reset and reclaim its fluid order. This reset will force us to seek truth beyond free will and this search will make us braver and stronger.

Goodwill occurs naturally and part of the universal order and ensures our survival. Free will is a broken Genesis bible story and is vulnerable to man's vices.

Through free will, man has distanced itself from nature's natural order, creating greed and excess then excusing these actions through insincerity and manipulation.

He has found a way to take more than his share by gobbling resources endlessly, creating day in the middle of the night, creating the fat of greed and the full drag of excess.

The concept of free will as an inherit human right has led to cruelty and greed, exasperated by the Internet's rise in 1989, promoting self-interest.

The Internet, sold to the masses as a platform for freedom, is the universal purveyor of free will, selling to the highest bidder.

There will be a massive crack in nature's evolution, but not before humanity has had one more chance to straighten up and fly right, to get out of nature's mixing bowl before she whips human butter into cream.

M. W. Rollerville Cafe

Mitchell considered Leo's plan to destroy the Internet. Finding a seat adjacent to Leo, he remembered that Red's killer used the Internet to find her and end her.

The Internet was evil to Mitchell. Red's murder and Mitchell's revenge was old news but not for him. The Internet, to Mitchell, was the blood-soaked blade that killed both Red and her murderer.

Mitchell shook his head, dispelling the chaotic void that formed at the periphery of his journey. The urge to peer into its depths always left him questioning everything about that night. Again and again, the memories of his fury and desire for vengeance resurfaced plagued him.

It seemed self-serving now, an eye for an eye. Not the biblical reference for justice, but the gratification of *his* accounting ledger, *his* rage, *his* revenge.

ৎৡৼ

Amy took a seat across from Mitchell. "I read a book when I was young that belonged to my father," she said. She could tell he was under a spell and wanted to lighten his load.

"It was a first-hand account of the battle for Iwo Jima during World War II."

Charles Hoyt's ears perked up. Anything that was related to World War II interested him. He asked if he could listen to what she was going to say.

"Of course, Mr. Hoyt."

"Please, call me Charles, Amy. We are equals now given everything you have been through." Charles extended his hand toward the bay window referencing her leveled home.

"Okay, Charles."

"Time and again, the author references supreme acts of charity, twenty-seven in all, where one life is risked saving others. In the margins of this book, my father posed a question: 'How many lives have been saved to date? Hundreds? Thousands? Millions?'

This question stems from my visit to the Emerald City via Louis' invention. Which tenet was the foundation for those twenty-seven separate seconds, when a choice was made for the greater good rather than a single life. Was it free will or goodwill? Which is the better will based on their historical outcomes?

When I stood ankle deep in the flowing Yellow Brick Road and was moved forward through the partition, I went from a life of two-faced posing to humility, gratitude and true splendor all around, as if present in the here and now of everything.

I felt a vibration on the other side of the partition. I can hardly describe it. I wonder, did those men, who gave their lives for the sake of other soldiers feel this same vibration, of losing themselves in the moment, knowing . . . no . . . not knowing, but simply acting so that others around them could go on living. Did they understand that their goodwill would not only save lives in their immediate vicinity but would forever change the lives of thousands, and one day, millions of lives?

'Optimistic Voices,' from the Oz movie soundtrack rang like church bells through me. I recognized its truth, stepping out of the woods and into the light.

Given free will as our starting point, was not our first choice to make the wrong choice and venture further into the woods? It seems strange to say but I feel like I have experienced what nature has long known; that true living regards the goodwill of all life, not the free will of one life."

"Is sacrifice and hardship the way out of the woods?" Mitchell asked Amy.

"I think we can use the stones we carry from Aqurar's cave to find answers," Amy responded.

Amy took out her stone and laid it on the table Leo had worked on. "Lay our stones side by side," Amy said.

Rosalie was the last to add her stone. The pearls formed a slight arcing pattern.

"There are seven stones," Amy said. "We pair one stone to another giving further meaning to each. Each of you randomly choose which two stones might offer an answer to Mitchell's question: *Is the journey out defined by sacrifice and hardship?*"

Simultaneously, each stone's purpose was heard in the mind of its holder:

Justice, said Mitchell, without moving his lips.

A new, universal language, void of innuendo, full of Nature's simple mathematics and rotation, contributed Leo.

All of nature returning to its Eden-like state, thought Rosalie.

Poama reflected: *The spirit of children shall be the simplicity of a day.*

Gunnar's consideration: *Abundance, charity, and goodwill shall reign over the choice not to do so.*

Charles' thoughts echoed through him: *honor and courage shall be the intention of our living again.*

Finally, Amy recalled her truth; *Forgiveness is the yellow brick road. Finding heaven in our own minds and hearts shall be the joy of our living.*

Walker moved toward the pearls, pulling his and another towards him. The message in the pairing spoke clearly to Mitchell: "Justice must be made with a forgiving hand." He moved two others to the forefront and said: "Childlike the heart must remain and speak the peace that a new language would offer."

"Our journeys out of the woods are defined by these purposes," Amy said softly, with finality.

❦

Evening descended upon the blue Oz house. The sapphire arc of evening gave the Talisman group comfort accompanied by a sense of unease.

In the coming night, smoke and ember light climbed high over a campsite in Manchester State Park.

One half of a wake, produced by a yacht washed upon the tilled and jagged central California coastline. Crimson Ward crewmembers could see the ruins of Highway 1, its bridges and old wooden fences, pointing skyward from the surface of the Pacific Ocean.

❦

Above these occasions, great worlds whirled by, issuing spins in their orbiting through the ever-expanding cosmos, by those unknown masters of the universe.

Dearest Mitchell,

When water was your song, when it enveloped you, protected you, and led you quietly to its silent slide over the world, you knew me.

When rocks changed color, when trees blended into bridges, when fear flowed downstream, when time was the long shadows moving through the day, when hunger spurred you, when music entered and stayed on as a part of your soul, you were known as my one beloved.

Your forever love, your Red

THIRTY-SIX

––––––––

We must recognize fundamental truths by humbling ourselves before hardship and the subsequent help from nature and nature's spirit, both tangible and subtle, to find the super-essential quality of a lesson learned.

M. W. Point Arena Lighthouse

––––––––

John Jespa's ship was propelled by the now defunct Northern Pacific flow, formally known as the California Ocean Current. Historically, it brought cold water down from the arctic regions that slowly warmed as it reached southern California, Baja, and the Central America. The Crimson Ward's instrumentation showed that the current was now moving in the opposite direction, taking its warm southern waters north to the Arctic ice cap, speeding the ship's progress along the altered California coast. Since the megathrust, each Pacific Ocean current had begun to flow in a different direction, creating catastrophic global surface temperature and atmospheric changes. *How ironic,* thought Jespa. *All those idiots believing climate change is man's fault . . . typical . . . man thinking he is bigger than the ant he is.*

Jespa was admiring an azure arc in the western horizon. He reflected on his company's efforts to replicate how the mind comprehends such vivid color now present in new technology. He was not comparing technology with the human brain in Haltronics' research and development labs but was seeking a way to connect human senses to his developing technology. He envisioned Haltronics as a massive host, serving and devouring brainpower and energy the same way he used the Internet to feed and consume the collective cognitive power of every computer in existence, and he needed these findings in his R&D labs to establish the connection between Haltronics and the human mind. His smart phones and devices had seduced consumers worldwide. Now it was time to finish the task of creating a dependent race of humans, reliant upon his machines, under his control. The code to arrest and imprison the imaginations and souls of the population rested Leo's mind.

He focused on the profile of Leo Brenamann. His face flushed remembering their virtual sex. He revered his control over Leo's mind, longing for the days when he had him cornered emotionally and physically, unable to function without *Sheila.*

Sheila, Jespa thought.

He looked at a mirror mounted above his head, like a rearview in an SUV, and adjusted it to frame him. In it, Jespa saw his face merging into the high-definition richness that was Sheila's virtual image. His eyes grew large and luminous, lips soft and round in the mirror. He moved his tongue softly over them, and trembled recalling kissing the young man in the many hidden caves, corners, and shadows of bridges in that virtual universe. Jespa's eyes scanned the length of his supple, inviting neck. His fingers ran over the contours of his perfectly shaped profile, feeling lust for the humanoid form that was Sheila. Tiny beads of sweat dotted his forehead. He suddenly remembered he was not alone.

Jespa's intense stare at his own reflection spooked his staff. Uneasy crewmembers nonchalantly viewed the night sky through the ship's instrumentation, which had revealed a gravitational lens. A celestial body had come into focus by bending the light around it. For crew members aboard the Crimson Ward who witnessed Jespa change form in his own mind, the sight of one of the universe's rarest sights provided a strong feeling of paradox, as they motored toward their destination.

Jespa snapped his head away from the mirror and quickly focused on other thoughts.

Jespa wanted the old thoughts, the old ways, to disappear. *Everything comes and goes, my ass,* he thought. "Everything is mine," he said aloud.

"That's right. All of you are mine. Your lives, the food you eat and the air you breathe belongs to me. How many of you 'own' the latest and greatest smart phones and computers? Uhmm? How many? That's what I thought: All of you do. Do you realize how long I have owned your very lives? Since the day each of you submitted your credit report to Haltronics, not only for a job but for the right to possess my technology. All of you are here because I convinced you that working for Haltronics was the next natural shift for humanity. All of you got comfortable being told what was good for you.

You have been bought but *not sold*. I do not release you from your contract with me. You wanted to sample and use my technology. It was an easy sale to convince you to sign your lives over to Haltronics."

While Jespa ranted, an unnoticed crewmember, 1st mate Timothy Villiard, pulled out the ship's sextant. Quietly he positioned it on the earth's horizon, still outlined by the disappearing blue arc. He slid the instrument's sights into position and shot the horizon and the skyward anomaly that emerged in the sky above the disappearing blue sunset. Sixty-six point six degrees.

I have flattened the world, Jespa thought on. *I am pruning, thinning what is knowable in the world, and they have missed the simple signs I could not disguise. Less and less of them lie prone upon the ground, understanding themselves, their natures, especially their boundaries, and have elected to stop the pursuit of a higher existence; the banquet of life's forces: youthfulness, nature, divinity, the heavens, and the comprehension had there— all gone as the feast of living with, and as a part of nature, comes to an end.*

"I'm going to let you all in on a little secret: your credit scores, that thing you've worked on all your lives, devoted all your energy preserving and protecting, and mourning over the decrease of and celebrating the increase of, marks my ownership of your life.

It is the measure of your devotion to me. I am pleased to inform you, the crew of the Crimson Ward and soon the world, that your credit score is your bond to me. In his interview, that son-of-a-bitch coder Leo Brenamann, the man I hired to take Haltronics into the future, showed me an algorithm he wrote that calculated how to average every existing credit score, all of which I own. He figured out that the average credit score will never change. It will forever be six hundred and sixty-six points. 666. He proved to me, that I was the devil. I hired him on the spot."

Villiard, still hidden beyond Jespa's sight shot another reading of the horizon against the sky bound anomaly. Traveling at great speed, the Crimson Ward's position relative to objects in the sky should have changed. Yet it remained unchanged at sixty-six point six degrees.

Villiard lowered the sextant, placed it on the retaining shelf behind him, and returned to his station on the ship's bridge. He looked at his boss. In the past twenty-four hours Jespa had lost all his hair, was thinner in the face than he was when he boarded the yacht. Jespa reminded Villiard of a man's descent into the ever-deepening rings of hell. Villiard closed his eyes and whispered to himself; *Boss, your face has become a living death mask.*

My Beloved,

There, the fall of light upon your forehead and nose outlined what I have known in my life as desire, as love. Did I fall in love with you again today? Yes. I love you even as heaven is now your home. I have loved your mind. I have loved your eyes and the shape of your profile for as long as I have known you. I have loved your broken heart and your will and your fierceness to stay the fates, to fight back, to comprehend the deep purple paradox you and I knew as life.

And there, the color of life takes on every day, when your fierceness became your willingness to be a woman, to sup, to bend, to believe, to offer, to be all things to that which you could lay your physical self upon.

Your senses were my reality. I believe in you still.

Your illuminated profile reveals the world to me and within such an outline is found every hope life can offer.

Your Mitchell

My own true love,

The cold grey walls tumble about me. Dark water trickles by and quench thirst but at a price. It is the cost that a spirit pays to stay. The water comes from above but falls into a hole at the bottom of a broken and upturned bell—a bell made of ancient times—one that has not endured the ages.

I feel as if I slip. I put my fingers out and feel the broken ground slide past me. I drop further, into my memories of steel upon my flesh, of terror in my heart, and of you at a distance unable to guide me through it.

Upon me now is the un-doer. His face is red and cold. My blood is dried upon his hands and now his lips. I cannot fathom it. I am diminishing without you, my love.

Where have I gone?

Your Red

THIRTY-SEVEN

———

Life is a desperate thing.

There are moments in life that can fend off despair but degrees and circumstances suggest that not all sufferers are able to find them. From experience: prayer, nature, touch, acceptance, love, forgiveness, kindness, generosity, laughter and miracles can turn the tide on despair.

I also believe that these things listed above cannot always break through a mind buried in drug use or abuse.

There is one thing I know now about suicide: having felt despair, I judge no one for his or her response to it.

Robin Williams: thank you for putting yourself out there and for making me laugh, saving me, and I bet much of the world, for moments at a time, from our utter desperation."

"And yet, there it is, my unfettered childhood dream:

I know the water-formed shelf of granite, how its heat rises into the beautiful sunlit blue sky. Can this color find its way into my other senses? Can such an instant of perfection exist if it stays for only a moment?

It can.

*I ride the slide of my conscious self into free-bound boyhood
dreams. I feel my short, dishwater-blonde hair, drying once again
as the solar rays bounce
on the rippling Hassayampa River, to dance through my half-open
eyes. Like my hair, I feel the multi-colored granite river rock
drying, as the stream's flow ebbs, changing hue, becoming less
brilliant and quieter as the day drifts through.*

*There in sunlight and shadow, I hear the distant, playful tones of
my boyhood memories.*

Idling.

Breathing.

Idling.

Breathing.

The water glides by my dangling fingers.

*I did not realize it then but each inhale and exhale was my
experience of heaven on earth. Such is the beauty and design of
God.*

*I thank you God, for the water flowing as the Hassayampa River
and as tears in my eyes now, for under that Hassayampa River
summer sky, I knew her love, and knew she was coming.*

Such is my blessed anchor away from despair.

M. W. Stornetta Lands North Entrance

324

Like backlit night clouds, the rainbow-colored shades of heaven, of emeralds, fire opals, and rubies, spilled out into every corner of earth and sky and into the star-filled darkness above Arena Rock.

Such intense color saturated every human sense: auditory and olfactory nerves had interpretated the indescribable visual presentation of other worlds entering the earth's atmosphere.

The Talisman Group headed outside the Oz House prompted by the vibration caused by magnetic fields colliding and merging.

They looked above a row of cypress trees that bordered Charles Hoyt's property and Highway 1. There it was. A magnificently assembled and impossible to imagine cascading imprint of primary colors in every shade. It gave them hope.

Mitchell marveled at the expanding brilliance.

Leo saw the circumference of each sphere line up in a perfect line and plane to the other, their centers intersected by their counterparts. He calculated how pi might intersect itself as the astounding spheres had done over his head. He imagined a fourth sphere appearing inside the heavenly shapes and stared deeply into its core, wanting to avoid calculating, only observing the strength and beauty of an expanding universe. The core of the fourth sphere instructed him to do so. It said:

There is no technological singularity. The quantum mechanics and complex algorithms are, as you stand beneath your earth-bound heaven, no longer

necessary to grasp your unlimited life, it is already
here, without regard to whether you
understand **why** *or* **how.** *Man has pushed the limit*
of numbers, only to find more numbers.
Cease the thrusting and end the incessant reach for
what rests at your feet.

Gunnar leaned forward toward the heavens as if sitting upon a piano seat and began his ritual of striking keys in the air before him. Great progressions of music manifested, pouring forth from his mind's eye. He too stared into Leo's fourth sphere and imagined seeing an angel of inexpressible beauty taking shape within. Notes of music hung from her head like ribbons of blue then green and finally of auburn and ginger. The angel's eyes grew as she watched Gunnar play but in Gunnar's separate observation the angelic figurine did not see Gunnar: but was staring with love and longing at Mitchell. He did not see the spirit in the heavenly shapes above.

Rosalie and Poama put their arms to the heavens and danced. Their movements suggested that there was more kinds of love, of play, of medicine, of courage, of life longing for itself than humankind had understood. Their spirits reached out to the low-hanging satellites and imagined moving within them. They longed to live inside this boundless beauty. They cried for their broken lives, their families, their friends, their memories, and for the heavens above.

Mitchell looked to Hoyt and Amy, who stood together holding one another's hand. He saw Hoyt's unattached hand rise to

326

the sky above him. In Amy's other hand, which held Louis' book, Mitchell saw the Crow, Dorothy, the Tin Man, and the Lion, their attentions turned upward in reverence to the world above them, at the arrival of home, of heaven upon earth.

In his peripheral vision, Mitchell noticed a familiar light burning brightly in the center of the trinity of planets, triggering memories of music and comfort. He saw a bending of light . . . then the bending of love . . . of what he was taught as a child by the river, and as Red's husband, of perfect love. As white light travels through a prism, so did the notion of perfect love travel through Mitchell, where the teachings of man's religions, of a woman's love, of an all-seeing God, of sacrificed sons, of courageous spirits bringing eternal understanding of the history of all humankind and the tenet of free will.

Mitchell comprehended the creative force of all things fell from above. In the detached halls and the divided moments of their lives, humanity understood that their individual creations were not theirs at all but a product of the universe unfolding above and within them.

Inspired by his thoughts, Mitchell broke the communal meditation that had covered the group like a waterfall. His question was a comparative statement of man's supposed *progress,* against the backdrop of the heavens above him.

"Is artificial intelligence no better than artificial sugar?"

Gunnar's response pivoted away from Mitchell's question: "I'm not sure, I've never had artificial sugar, but I must tell you that there is a spirit within those moons, a spirit with cascading red hair that responded spiritually to the music I played, but she looked at you."

⁋ʖ

At the Manchester campfire, the men watched as the fire light changed color from yellow white to a rotating glow of green-white, blue-white, and then red-white. As the colors changed, Will's thoughts of Christmas tree lights sparked: blue striking with poignancy. Flashes of Christmases past surfaced and left.

Will saw the campfire reflected in Orth's thick, black glasses, noting the revolving colors of firelight. Orth felt Will's gaze and returned a questioning look.

Will noted three glowing shapes slowly appearing in the reflection. He looked up and over his shoulder. Orth followed Will's eyes. Looking skyward they beheld the planetary anomaly moving into position above them.

The campfire blew about as a great wind pushed downward, bending them to the ground for cover. Ancient lines of cypress trees were folded toward the earth.

Through squinting eyes, the men saw a commotion in the sea near the lighthouse. Rising from the ocean, Will saw a giant rock rising from the ocean, its mass measured by square miles. Ocean water rapidly filled the resulting cavity creating howling hurricane-force wind. The surface of the great mass of magnetite reflected the colors of the new worlds above. Its elevation into the atmosphere ceased, appearing to stop at the halfway point between the earth and its new moons. Orth and Loki guessed, without the aid of a sextant, that this was about sixty-six degrees above them in the western sky.

When all eyes returned to the horizon, when the ocean water settled into the magnetite crater, when the winds settled in the tops of cypress trees, when the tri-colored campfire continued to reflect the magnificent, brilliant, arrival of Heaven that Will thought he heard a voice ask a question: *Is artificial intelligence no better than artificial sugar?*

"Did you hear that?" Will asked his companions.

"Hear what?" Orth replied.

"The question," Will responded.

"Is artificial intelligence no better than artificial sugar?" Peter spoke in. "Yes, I heard it."

Parnoon and Mahud both nodded affirmatively. They too had heard the question. "Perhaps it was just the wind rushing to the sea, when the earth was lifted toward . . . those," Parnoon said.

"Why are any of you considering what such a question has to do with anything other than this for God's sake?!" Orth shouted, as he raised his hands towards the heavens. "What the hell is going on?!"

"I think the question *is* an appropriate one General," Parnoon said shyly.

"Explain."

"It seems to me that artificial intelligence is static, flattened existence, expanding as a two-dimensional plane, rather than in every direction like a three-dimensional sphere," Parnoon stated. "Where in any dimension of artificial intelligence will one find the presence of calluses?" Parnoon turned his calm attention back to the skies.

"For that matter," Mahud said, "how could artificial intelligence sing? It would need the pumping of blood through a bioorganic mechanism, with moisture producing qualities and more than analytical and mathematical patters of notes and progressions. It would need to *feel* them. It would need to be *inspired* by them. And why am I not afraid of what is taking place above us?"

"Artificial intelligence experiences no hardship," Peter added. "It is hardship that shapes the life in living. How can AI grow without having clarity, say, about the presence of Parnoon's calluses? AI lacks experience of heart and soul. What if AI was to become that advanced, only to learn through its own validation and proof that it is really made up of 'artificial sugar?'" Peter let the new-found otherworld peace circulate around him.

"Again," Jim Orth asked, "why are we having this conversation about artificial intelligence when clearly we need to be addressing that," pointing to the skies above the western horizon.

330

My Beloved,

September is here. It was our favorite time of year. You felt your youth tumble forward, recalling the Jersey Shore moving bathing suits to quiet longing, as every thought of the changing season brought with it visions of your father taken too early in your young life. The shore's rolling surf induced long moments under the canopy of an inlet house, the angle of ocean current, first approached, then departed, like a train in the night.

You remain but changed Red. Let me know you again. I long to touch your face and call your name over the roar of wind and water. We lived intensely. You loved me fully. My heart painted your portrait every day. I reach up toward the changing universe, hoping to see your perfect love.

Your Mitchell

THIRTY-EIGHT

Cones of Silence.

They take on many forms.

Some are visualized as the name implies covering content where the silence falls in, upon itself.

Others are tenets of the heart where again, the silence falls inwardly, layer upon layer, obscuring truths over periods of time.

Cones of silence are secrets:

Children bury their knowledge of abuses.

Retribution motivates neighbors not to call police.

Military organizations hide actions to aid their agendas.

Cones of Silence can also build trust, or at the minimum, prevent misunderstanding between a government and its contented citizenry, who stumble upon dark cars and black uniformed clandestine drivers muscling strange objects through long-closed gates on a remote stretch of Highway 1, in Northern California, while others hold white blinders around the whole scene trying to fend off stares from a contented but now curious citizenry.
Did Sergeant Shultz say it best?—'I hear nothing . . . I see nothing!'

Any silence, given enough time, will speak. I will remain contented but curious.

M. W. Garcia River and Highway 1

John Jespa was the first one to turn and run but with no idea where he would go.

He was consumed by fear looking at the western horizon. He couldn't calculate how three spheres and a shining metallic object floated above the ship's bridge.

The ocean pitched violently, tossing the Crimson Ward, its decks plunged beneath the surface, only to resurface laden with churning water. The ocean surface began to rise. Jespa's crew desperately grabbed anything that would steady them. The ship's engines whined ferociously, compensating for the climb and gravity changes that registered on the ship's instrumentation.

Outside the helm, Jespa was thrown by the ship's downward momentum but cleared stow compartment contents and furniture that had spilled in his path. He slipped toward the ship's single lifeboat, fumbling in his pants pocket for the small boat's remote control. Frantically he felt for the right command button and engaged the dinghy's lowering boom.

The lifeboat started its slide into the rocking Pacific Ocean. Wind whipped past Jespa's face and body forcing him to fight for every step.

Some of his crew looked through the helm's back windows and saw their captain flailing wildly. No one tried to save Jespa from certain death, choosing to stay safely inside the ship's control room. They saw the ocean's surface rising into the night sky toward the new moons. Their ship efficiently negotiated its new course.

Jespa, on his side, slid past the lifeboat's rope ladder, grasping it at the last possible moment. His grip was weak and he felt the rope cut into his skin, ripping chunks of soft flesh from his bony fingers. He screamed in pain. Feeling his feet dangle below him, Jespa grabbed the rope ladder with both hands. He pulled himself up and over a cleat and the Ward's gunwale then let go of the rope falling ten feet down, landing hard on the lifeboat's foredeck.

Getting his bearings, Jespa pressed another button on his lifeboat remote and felt the boom ropes release the grappling hooks.

The lifeboat fell further, its hull slapped by churning ocean swells. The Crimson Ward moved away and isolated him in a way he had never known. With both feet in the hull and both hands gripping the boat's thin gunwales, cold ocean water left Jespa staring at the bareness of his once insulated and lavish life feeling the horror of his situation.

The Ward was well beyond his reach. It disappeared and reappeared moving closer to the overhead irregular spheres and the star-like material that seemed to be linking those anomalies with Earth.

As the lifeboat settled, Jespa's grip lightened. Slowly, the fear that had filled every muscle and nerve in his sallow body turned to anger. Jespa watched incredulously as the earth's atmosphere and water filled in around the magnetite star and moons in the western horizon. To his disbelieving eyes, the Crimson Ward sailed up the giant column of water and air rising into the dark sky. Gravity seemed suspended. The Crimson Ward's crew were standing erect on the boat's decks. The Ward's destination was obvious; it was heaven bound.

His waterlogged clothes revealed nothing but skin and bone—a shell. The boat rocked. He saw subtle hues rotating in lighthouse beacon fashion somewhere up the northern California coastline. Jespa thought of emeralds, fire opals, and rubies, and realized the rotating beams of light reflected the colors emanating above him in the cloudless sky.

Fumbling again for the boat's remote, he started the small engine and fell backward in his seat as the boat lurched forward. He grappled for the boat's tiller, frantic for a second that the steering mechanism had been washed away.

Turning away from the odd column of water and the fact that The Ward motored up it like a boy climbing a beanstalk, he leaned into the direction of the rotating lighthouse lights hoping that his small lifeline would get him to dry land.

Jespa recalled his second in command, General Orth, say to him once that the one thing Jespa's Internet machine, his artificial intelligence would always lack was the ability to produce courage, a key component of a vital, creative, loving culture. Coding it would prove to be impossible to do. He looked down again at his

336

waterlogged clothes, and under them the skin over his bones and knew that not even one infinitesimal unit of courage, was within him. He knew only fear.

ॐॐ

"Look," Amy said.

Rotating at unique intervals and known only during the earlier analog life of the Point Arena Lighthouse, its beam flashed above the Oz House, first as a rich jade hue, then cerulean, then crimson.

"It's the lighthouse," Charles stated, marveling that it survived the earthquake. "That's its Fresnel Lens and it is spinning like it used to as if it were floating on a bath of mercury, as if lighter than air, in a resistance-free environment."

"Isn't the Point Arena Lighthouse adjacent to Arena Rock?" Mitchell asked.

"And isn't that Arena Rock?" Leo was pointing to the star-like land mass floating between the trinity of moons and the Earth. "That is the mass of magnetite that your son Louis talked about, Charles."

"It is Arena Rock. Louis knew it was there and he knew long ago that this rock was a conduit to other worlds. In fact, he would talk to me about his visions while walking on Kinney Road toward the ocean. He described great worlds free of evil where goodness reigned."

Amy repeated: "Look!"

The human members of the Talisman group turned to see their spiritual counterparts glow resembling the lighthouse and the moons above.

Gunnar, Rosalie and Poama began to move toward the moons, each absorbing one of the colors above: Gunnar green, Rosalie red, and Poama blue. They were becoming the intentions of a better natural world, filled with the simple considerations of nature's complexity.

Each spirit turned to face their friends, asking them to find a new start. Music flowed from Gunnar as he spoke to Mitchell: "Find her, find your beloved, she is looking for you."

Poama spoke, saying, "Remember me. Remember my life on the field of play, thoughts, prospects. There are so many new possibilities that have nothing to do with the tumble of ones and zeros. In your imagination rests the true future of humanity.

Rosalie, drifting further up, her face and her magnificent, flowing grey hair surrounding her like a crown, at last spoke: "What is real can be touched by your senses, all else is not to be used by the world anymore. Mother Nature and God have returned to collect what is theirs. Within the notion of goodwill, you will find no more tolerance for free will. The Universe has turned the page.

The four of you must go to the light. Follow the multicolored pulsing to its source. There you will meet both the beginning and the end of many things. We will await you on the other side of the coming dawn."

Like backlit night clouds, the rainbow-colored shades of heaven, of emeralds, fire opals, and rubies, spilled out into every corner of earth and sky and into the star-filled darkness above Arena Rock.

Gathering supplies, Charles, Amy, Mitchell and Leo prepared to follow Rosalie's instructions. They filled backpacks with supplies from Charles' pantry. Leo stowed the two-way radios with those things needed to make the short hike from the Oz House to the Point Arena Lighthouse.

Descending the wide front staircase the group turned right on Riverside Drive then right again onto the ravaged Highway 1 where a once heavily used footpath, a favorite of Aqurar's, would take them to their destination.

My own true love,

What is my heart and soul without your touch, its calloused fingers pressed upon my skin, your sense telling you how precious I am to you? What is my memory without your blood, your pain, your joy within?

I see a weeping dove flying high overhead. I see the sky holding you. I see you in this dim, cold place that runs black with the blood of the world. I know that it is blood for I have tasted it. It is bitter wine to the evil that holds me yet the evil here savors it.

I see it. It is like a dawn cutting above the eastern horizon as the absolute start of many thing and the companion paradox ending many things as well.

My love, do I really see you there, on the ground, standing with friends, near a lighthouse? Am I returning to you?

Please see your precious Red above you.

Your Beloved

———

A friend recently gave to me a written colloquy on Good and *Evil. I posited that it was a consideration of denial; the document stating the existence of one excluded the existence of the other.*

I suggest this: Evil cited man's decision to eat from every tree in the Garden, especially from the Tree of Knowledge. Good voiced no decision at all; only a presence in time that is physically and spiritually boundless. I took note that the four-page document did not address good <u>versus</u> evil. It is often offered that one cannot exist without the other, but I say through paradox that good serves the wellbeing of the universe, while evil serves the tenet, and the cause/effect rational of free will.

M. W. Mountain View Road and Highway 1

———

John Jespa lay prone in his shallow world. Time passed. A day and a night had passed in his once well-stocked lifeboat. Huge tumbling waves had reduced it to battered wreckage. Many times in the previous twenty-four hours Jespa had lurched over the side, heaving up nothing from his insides in a constant state of nausea.

Sea cliffs and rocks remained part of the changing coastline, made more so by the reversal of eras-old ocean currents, the unseen continuous rotation of magnetic poles, and an altered horizon in constant flux.

Jespa's head rose sharply, then landed hard on the boat's bottom. The raft had run into a jutting pier foundation. The jolt woke him from a fitful dream where he was buried alive by money and gold pieces. Jespa pushed aside the suffocating reality of the nightmare and sat up. Shaking with fear and anger, he inhaled deeply, breathing in seawater and coughing wildly.

He saw a line of tattered buildings on top of a precipice. The scene made him think of a hand around the throat of a stranger, a shapeless face in the fog of his skewed mind, a face banded red, then grey, then red again. Jespa lashed out at the figure hanging like a phantom in front of him. Slowly the figure took form. He gasped. Before him in a churning backdrop of transformation was the face and shape of Sheila. She appeared trapped under concrete and steel shredded by the explosions of a war. Electronic paraphernalia spilled out of her body. Her eyes opened, then her mouth, and out came the original hand-written code of his new Internet. Ones and zeros ran from her in chaotic and progressive sequences. Jespa recognized the pattern: it was Leo's work.

Jespa's boat struck another pier post rising from the seabed. Sheila's memory was knocked from his senses as a new terror took shape in front of him. Along the beach, just yards from his position, Jespa saw hundreds of bodies strewn about, human and otherwise. Scavengers had set in, human and otherwise, pulling and ripping before him. Jespa recognized within his own rapacious notions of survival.

344

His vision blurred. Sheila and the Internet form of Leo returned. Visions blended in with a childhood melody at the edge of his memory. A joyful, wanting, earthly voice called for home and love: *If you return me, to my home, I will kiss you, Mother Earth, take me back now, take me back now, to the port of my birth.*[7] The poetic verse picked up momentum as a hum coming from between his lips.

He was pulled back to the scene on the beach. Glass broke in the distance. Cries of anguish crushed him as he struggled to hold tightly to the hope of his childhood memory.

How could he have known then that it would end this way? Somewhere within, he looked for character-driven qualities that would have left him a home to enter, and people in his life that would search for him, even now, as he waited for his end to arrive.

The tide moved him closer to the carnage on the rocky beach.

Bright torches threw warring shadows across the sea cliffs. A cry from one group drew the attention of every scavenger to Jespa's boat. He knew that he was about to be eaten by wild packs of living things. He realized that he might survive the initial attack on his flesh, feeling teeth sinking into him, ripping way what had covered him as a boy.

Jespa lost consciousness again. He woke to the sound of waves washing in and out of rock jetties. He heard seagulls and seals in deep tide pools. The sun was coming up. The boat was motionless which distressed him. His mouth was parched, his lips crusted with sea salt.

Startled, Jespa saw a white, towering spire: *a lighthouse.*

He stood on the boat, his body listing, and threw out his arms in hopes of stilling himself and failing, sat back down. His weary mind and body stared helplessly at the singularly tall edifice.

Human shapes appeared around the lighthouse. One shouted at the others and Jespa could see the group assembling at the edge of the cliff. One man called out to him, and he feared scavengers had followed him but he recognized the voice.

The Talisman group had arrived at their destination as the sun rose behind them. High water marks were everywhere. Roads and footpaths disappeared into the fresh wash of tidal waves. In the immediate distance the sea had recently washed ashore, noting nature's reclamations were already at work.

As the group moved closer to the newly formed coastal features, Leo spotted a life raft wedged into the jagged sea shelf formations surrounded by seals and seagulls. Life had resumed its normal course, yet there, in the middle of the stark scene, the battered remains of a human life struggled to survive.

The group moved to the cliff's edge and looked down at Jespa's boat. "There is someone inside," Leo stated.

Charles put his hand on Mitchell's shoulder to steady his own gaze.

"Hello! Are you okay?" Leo yelled.

The mostly naked body shuddered at the sound. The group was sure the man was near death.

"He needs our help," Leo said, and began to scale the cliff that fell out of sight between the group and the boat. "Wait," Mitchell said. "I don't have a great feeling about this."

"Nor I," agreed Charles. "There is something about him that alarms me."

"We must see if we can help him," Leo said. "We can move closer and be cautious."

"Can you see a way down?" Hoyt asked.

"Possibly," Leo responded.

Leo handed one of the two-way radios to Mitchell. Positioning his pack over both shoulders and finding a foothold, he began to descend.

Charles was frustrated at not thinking of rope in advance.

"Be careful, son," he said, surprised by the concern in his voice.

Leo looked up at the old man, also surprised. He hung precariously on the face of the shifting rock and soil, stepping as carefully.

Minutes passed. The group watched Leo's head get smaller.

The man in the boat had not moved, but Charles was sure the survivor had at least one eye watching them.

Looking up Leo pulled out his two-way and spoke to Mitchell.

"Mitchell, can you hear me?"

"Loud and clear. We lost sight of you. We're relieved that you made it safely. Be careful. Charles thinks he is feigning his condition."

Leo thought the man *was* vaguely familiar. Tide pools were everywhere. He watched the ocean waves hurdle over roughly hewn geologic features, cut at ninety-degree angles to the ocean's surface. Great sea lions, four times the size of their female mates, tossed their enormous tusks at Leo, barking at him in challenge and protest of his presence in their territory.

Leo cautiously moved toward the lifeboat.

My Beloved,

I lie quietly at night considering your place in the universe, your place in my life. I let not one moment pass without such a reflection giving it life, my life. Your place, the space between every breath, every pulse of my still beating heart is in step with every thought falling through the moments of each day. Your kindness was the good you willed through my fears. Your faith, it was in your hands, they labored your faith's shape. You worked the old ways, the demonstration of hearth and bed. Your faith laid bare the truth of the world and showed me how character influences fate.

I sit here on the road of life and at times cannot bear the emptiness of it. You have become, not the road, but its plane on each side. You are the earth to me. You are the natural processes of the world I see before me. You are the kindness of each step, and the faith of each foot print I leave behind.

Your Mitchell

FORTY

Change.

I see it on my skin. I feel it in my bones. I am in the autumn of my life; DNA has dictated my fate.

I am fine with this. I am both hope and have love. I have the songs of the past, and regardless of their origin, I am overwhelmed by the memories they invoke.

Care must be taken in each passing instance to not let old nonsense invade every waking moment. If not careful, one will find oneself engulfed with ten endless thoughts, all clamoring for center stage, all needless attempts to reconcile irreconcilable transgressions, all ending in despair, with no way out. Old nonsense has had its way.

Find your heaven in song and in books and in the eyes of true love and in quiet contemplation. Find your heaven in possibility, create your own parallel to eternity, your soulful mark on time. Realizing these marks will take your breath away. Fly above the petty and mundane, into the mist-filled morning sun. No need to ask the universe 'why?' Know what this good world is. Fly away always, leaving the sorrow of life in your wake as it becomes the salt within the sand.

The misty morning sun. That is your point of reference, your foothold, a hand falling from above, from overhead, from sources not known beneath your feet.

Your breath claims the heaven born air. Your life—filled with far-off sights of hope, your reflection seen in the seas far below, holding within your own true love.

Change is relative. DNA holds the reins of the meat package your soul was assuaged to occupy, by what force, I am not sure, but within the grateful senses of faith, of joy, of charity, one finds, while on this earth at least, one friend who loves you as you are, and at least one moment in this life that makes from here to there worthwhile.

M.W. Manchester, CA on Highway 1

———

The sun rose over Manchester State Park. Sea air filled the gaps between the extended morning shadows cascading through long lines of cypress.

Will raised his head out of his sleeping bag and saw a massive heard of deer grazing slowly through the park's borders. He saw the black tip of the lighthouse poised above the fogbank, its crown of metal and glass beckoning him fin the bright morning sun.

He took a deep salt-scented breath. He felt rested and oddly settled in his brave new world and, like the deer, accepting the new age where realms would, like nature, find balance. Deeply held revenge would be countered by peace, and swords would be laid down.

Songs from childhood coasted by in memory following the fog bank's pattern. He remembered his father and thought it strange that life had taken both his father and son from him. It seemed improbable but his father's music had become his own. Familiarity with it made him feel closer to the man who had taken him in, giving him new life even as his real father's life was destroyed.

Destroyed. So much is destroyed, he thought, as the recent days suddenly flooded in. He thought of the day he said goodbye to the man that became his dad, not knowing that he would never see him again. It was not that he owed the man anything; it was that man's choice to take him in and that man's choice to let him go.

Will McKinley was not angry with those days as a boy. *Shit happens. However, that man was good to me.*

A radio scratched to life. Buried in the SUV cargo hold, the sound it emitted was not immediately recognized.

McKinley heard it first and found the alternating crackle and chirp a warning and gratifying sound.

"Did you hear that?"

"I did," Jim Orth responded. "You have a radio in your gear?"

"I had forgotten about it. In this modern world, two-ways are not often used. That radio, if it is the one I am thinking it is, is as old as our friendship Jim. I didn't know it still worked."

Will headed for the rear door of the giant SUV. With the push of a button on the SUV's remote key system, he watched the hatch rise.

He rummaged through the tightly packed cargo hold hearing again the crackle and chirp. Setting gear on the ground, he found the pack that held the radio and pulled on its strap.

The pack was given to him by the man who had occupied his thoughts. With Orth and the others gathered around him, Will arranged its contents on the cargo shelf in front of him. It was an odd assortment of memorabilia from his teenaged years.

He found a small silver baby cup first, placing it above his head, trying to remember of why he had it. *That's right, it belonged to my father's father, the man who adopted me.*

Orth never pictured his warrior friend with such an item. Will looked at him and the others and said, "it belonged to one of my ancestors." He passed it off to Orth, who felt its weight in his hand.

An unrecognizable tin was filled with old pennies, collected by the same man Will had once known. He put the container up to his nose and inhaled, smelling the old coins through a slit that was cut into the lid. He remembered the man's hands and face, which in memory, were now younger than his own.

Will handed the cocoa tin to Orth, who was interest its contents.

354

"May I?" Orth asked Will, who nodded *yes.*

As Will turned back to the pack containing icons of his life, Orth marveled at the quantity of coins. Under the first layer of wheat pennies, Orth saw a second layer of Indian heads, and under those were layers of half cents, and large cents. *A fine, layered history of this country on a penny,* Orth thought.

A baby food jar contained an assortment of nuts, bolts, and screws. Will remembered: "A man can never have too much hardware." The jar's lid had a hole where it was once screwed to the underside of a shelf, along with dozens of others. Will remembered his adoptive father pulling down a jar thumbing through the contents, finding what he was looking for, and returning the jar, with a twist of his wrist, back into position above his workbench.

He grabbed the chrome handle of a toolbox, and there inside the container, Will found an old finish hammer, hand-held wood drill, wood rasp, and assorted screwdrivers, and the radio. It crackled and chirped again. Will picked it up remembering the voice of the man who had taken him in and cared for him as a young teenaged boy.

Tears rolled down the soldier's face remembering why this man had taken him in, washing away not only the banks of fog surrounding the lighthouse, as well as the fog surrounding those days in his life lived in the woods south of Prescott, Arizona.

He pushed the talk button and said, "Yes, I can hear you."

My Beloved,

It is as if you are in the next room. I hear your purposeful hands at work, your feet brisk across the kitchen floor, your thoughts convey your wish to be grateful, for it is Thanksgiving Day.

I watched you do this day for decades. Even as life dwindled down to just the two of us, you still made several pies, honoring the womanhood that define you.

I remember the distinct smell of freshly cut rosemary from a bush that grew right outside our backdoor, laid on the cold skin of an uncooked turkey, and the smell that filled the house as it cooked.

Mostly it is your thoughts I miss. You are as you were . . . I remember thinking. You had been the same person you had always been—a character-bound girl, in a woman's body, still believing in true love yet wary of the shadows around you.

You live still, in my memory, as the songs I hear you sing, as the bread I smell wafting in from every kitchen we lived in, as the girl covered in flour, making me believe in family and tradition. You are the place where I hung my every heart-filled hat. Red, you were what I was grateful for. You are still. I love and long for you.

Your Mitchell

FORTY-ONE

———

Murmuration of thought—

—the Internet's process of controlling the mind of humankind.

Anyone who is paying minimal attention can see how the Internet dulls the awareness of humanity by compressing its ever-flattening lack of story.

The Internet escalates unfounded fears of endless line items by its promotion of if/then rationalistic binary observations of everything, without question from its users, accepting all as tenets to live by.

Murmuration of thought—

—the Internet's process of controlling the if/then narrative of humankind mimics the unquestioning movement of starlings around a lighthouse.

We disconnect from our individual experience and blindly follow precise, predicted patterns. We know only what the if/then world knows. Where the Internet points, we follow. When the Internet skews left, we head left. When the Internet fires right, we capitulate.

We weave. We become the pattern of the moment. We no longer make our own choices because we have forgotten our own story, only living how the Internet instructs.

Soon the 'top ten' list will become a 'top three' list, followed by a
single solitary choice that has suddenly and sadly, been made for
us, as each of us as starlings, moves in concert with those around
us.

M.W. Kinney Road and Highway 1

As Leo stared at Jespa, his facial features rooted deeply into the coder's memory files.

A giant swell flooded the tide pools below Leo and Jespa, shooting white capped ocean water twenty-five feet into the air, stealing Leo's breath. The magnificence of Mother Nature engulfed him. Seals scrambled to maintain their hold on the rock shelves. Sea gulls squawked while flying over each new spray of sea foam.

Jespa's boat pitched, then moved forward, riding one of the great swells toward the rock jetty where Leo fought for a foothold. The Talisman group watched in terror as the mighty waves and the craft holding the dying, emaciated man rushed by Leo.

Jespa tried to grab Leo. Mitchell gasped. Gunnar, Rosalie, and Poama swirled toward Leo, protecting him.

The raft was no longer visible from above. Mitchell fumbled for the two-way and said: "Leo, that man is bad news. He tried to pull you into his boat. Can you see him? Stay clear of him, Leo. Do you read me?"

Leo waved at Charles and Mitchell, turning toward the beach in time to see the skeletal man step and stumble on the slick, moss-covered rock tide pool rock.

Jespa balanced precariously. He gazed at Leo clinging tightly to the cliff above the ocean, an arms-length away from his tortured mind and grasping hands. Both were still out of sight from the party above.

He grinned at Leo, sending a chilled electrical current through Leo's body. Jespa's presence recalled depraved events buried deep in Leo's memory, scattering the information over Leo's conscious mind like so many lengths of driftwood that dotted Manchester State Beach.

Leo felt the presence of his spirit friends, relieved, finding calm and reassurance from their energy.

Jespa's face transformed from grey death to rich color, from foggy shades of ill omen to a hammered and chiseled reality. The skull shape of the bleached man pulled at Leo's heart, from the blessing in his newly found circle of friends, to the sex and depravity in a false world.

Standing before Leo, on the shores of Manchester State Park under the white spire of the Point Arena Lighthouse, was his great love, his Sheila.

∽◅◅

The four men with Will gave him a moment alone, wondering why the two-way radio haunted Will. They watched him dial through the twenty-one two-way radio channels. He put the unit's speaker to his ear listening to each channel. Finally, he stopped on channel eleven and clicked the talk button twice. Orth saw time stand still in his old friend's countenance. He could tell his friend was under a spell.

He never talks about his life before being assigned to my division, Orth thought. *I too have endless regrets and sadness in my life as a soldier. I could not expect it to turn out any other way. But this tenderness in a man made so resolute, so rough by the ravages of war is almost more than I can bear. He mentioned losing touch with family. Maybe the two-way is just a symbol of his past, his way of remembering the sounds of voices that no longer speak to him. Like me, perhaps Will McKinley wants to know love again. Battle plans, hand-to-hand combat techniques, and memorizing the protocols of war can no longer sustain him. His tears say to me that he is missing his heart. Perhaps he is reaching out, longing for a trusted companion.*

Tell me son, tell me. I will listen to your thoughts and give you kindness that I know, like you, has been stowed them away. I can reach out to you, my old warring friend. We have put each other's lives in each other's hands. Being so long in the trenches of hell, it will take effort to support one another.

Will, I have long been your commander, but I beg you to see me now as your friend. Let us walk through our remaining days honoring and respecting our lives. I love you, son, like my own. I am proud of you. You have inspired me to be courageous in the face of hell that still exists in this changing world.

But, as this stairway to heaven suggests, war no longer reigns, Dante's Divine Comedy has played itself out. The tenet of free will is broken. Let us be friends in what may very well be a new age of peace. Perhaps man, through this great intervention of Mother Nature and by our Father in Heaven, has terminated self-styled personal gain for general good, letting general good be defined by gratitude for ability, not entitlement through need.

Orth looked at his friend and noted the streaming tears had quieted their presence on the soldier's face. He stepped toward him.

"That has to be nearby," Orth said, referring to the voices on the two-way in Will's hand. "Unless it's a very powerful two-way, that signal is coming from a location nearby."

Orth saw the lighthouse spire jutting above diminishing fog banks. Beyond it, a column of ocean water connected the Earth to three new orbs. Marine traffic increased on the water column's surface: craft of every size migrated up and up, disappearing into new worlds. Whales, dolphins, osprey, migrating geese, sea gulls, and birds of every kind ascended. Innumerable schools of fish, seen as the morning sun illuminated the interior of the column, stunned Orth and Will as they joined their faith-filled comrades in observation of the new world above them.

Peter Shroud, Santaesh Parnoon, and Abraham Mahud gathered in a circle just outside their fellow SUV's two-way radio conversation. They talked of religious consequences that new orbiting planets will impose on world's great faiths.

Orth and Will agreed that nothing in any of their faiths could have prepared them for what was above them. Seeing boats, from makeshift log rafts to yachts, all streaming toward and ascending the column was an act of supreme faith.

Shroud said, "I feel relieved. I am grateful for a second chance, a second life, a second opportunity to live hand-to-hand in this heaven known as Earth."

Parnoon said, "I have hope. I am hopeful I will truly find the nature of wind, water, spirit, and sky running through humanity."

Mahud said, "I am ready. I want what they are seeking," pointing toward the water column, ships streaming toward the magic above. "I find the notion of living in a truly spiritual world, one without agenda or religious fanaticism a calming one. It is no longer a question of survival, but a question of forgiveness and unconditional acceptance of Mother Nature, God's love, and God's peace."

My own true love,

I see you there. You are still out of reach, still beyond the touch of my wakeful, wanting eyes. I see you still, as I left you long ago, walking yet not living, your heart becoming ash, as Presley let me fall softly near our oak.

I see you there still. I see your breath move out before you, which becomes my very essence. I envelop each exhale and my soul stills in its warmth. I smell what I knew on your lips. Each breath moves behind you as you walk down on Kinney Road. I gather them as a child gathers stones, and I keep them in my breast pocket, holding them close, knowing in my soul that I will know your lips again. I weep for my own true love.

Please see your precious Red above you.

365

———

I interpret the first part of Dante's Divine Comedy, 'Inferno,' as a depiction of humanity's abuse of the principle of free will. This abuse leads to and is likened to Lucifer's act of devouring the worst sinners, drawing a parallel to one of the gravest choices modern man can make: allowing his soul to be consumed by Transhumanism.

The Earth is Heaven. Earth is God's dwelling place. How could it be anything else but Heaven? What could you imagine would be more beautiful?

Man's invention of organized religion erected barriers to God by granting access only through man's invented dogmas and rituals. Invented barriers of bitterness, greed, and treachery abound as well. Religions present choice as a right of man. If one so chooses, one has the right to bitterness, greed, and treachery.

In all constructed religions, God, as a nurturing father, has entrusted humanity with the great gift of free will. However, this free will has evolved into a self that often overshadows the soul, distorting the essential paradox of good and evil that is crucial for spiritual growth.

Today, technology undermines faith and trust, translated through living and dying, played out as we live our lives. Technology, our new religion, offers no paradox at all, just the promise of living forever as digital code in a Freon-cooled hard drive known as Transhumanism.

Today's free will promotes this migration of the self from organic and analog to a flattened and senseless digital experience. The organic is replaced with ones and zeros. A life time of memories and experience become one file and zero consequences.

Dante's Inferno is representative of this. In Transhumanism's sterile culture there lies the notion that one possesses an innate free will to choose attachment to the indefinite force of 'forever.' This is Dante's self-treachery, self-absorption, and self-lust.

Imagine the digital skulls of infinite numbers set side-by-side in storage capacitors, held in place by floating gates designed to trap your spot on the copper or tin plate where your mind's eye realizes too late that you have chosen a living death.

Do not believe for a moment that Transhumanism will be yours without checking the Terms of Service *box. That will be your final conscious act of free will. Checking the box and clicking* Accept *will end your participation in God's Garden, where life with Mother Nature is short, but sweet.*

This is the gift . . .

. . . that Man has destroyed; the knowledge that every moment counts.

Don't give up being imperfectly human, where all beauty, all chance, all creativity, and all wisdom are found to be, if for only a moment, unique to you.

Will McKinley adjusted the radio in his hand. He put it to his side, then lifted it again, unsure if he wanted to speak into it. He popped the talk button, the radio *cackled and chirped*.

Parnoon, Shroud, and Mahud heard Will push the talk button and speak, "Yes, I can read you." Will stared aimlessly into his past.

There was no response from the two-way.

The unit cackled and chirped again, without Will's push of the talk button. He looked at it, sensing someone out there was reluctant to speak.

"Can you read me?" Will said urgently.

Nothing. "Do you
read me?"

Nothing.

Then suddenly, "Yes, we can," blasted over the radio. The SUV group was shocked to hear the voice of a young girl.

"Who is this?" Will said, snapping out of his momentary shock.

Orth and Will stared at one another. For years as soldiers, they lived with battle and survival. A child's voice was totally foreign to them.

"We can hear you. What is your location?" Will said.

The radio was silent. Will looked at Orth with unspoken questions. In unison, the five men turned toward the lighthouse now in full view from their campsite. The sea column, further out but lining up to the right of the lighthouse held an El Capitan-sized chunk of metallic, shining earth. It continued to accept the living in whatever manner used to make the trip: wing, fin, or piston engine.

"Do you think the radio transmission is coming from the lighthouse?" Will asked, pointing to the white spire standing tall over an ever-brightening day. "I feel . . . drawn to it."

"I do." Orth said. Using powerful binoculars, he surveyed the landscape around the spire. He saw ocean borne mists billow up, around, then down again to cover the entire land mass that held the long-vacant Coast Guard outbuildings, offices, and dormitories.

Orth knew the rock jetty where the lighthouse stood was the closest point from North America to the center of the Pacific Ocean. This site was significant to the Military-Internet Complex. The lighthouse would throw its magnificent nineteen-mile-long Fresnel beam into the heart of the glorious, luminous water column, causing the magnetite rock hanging above the ocean's surface to glitter like jewels.

The men moved through a stretch of brush that served as a boundary between the state park and Kinney Road.

Orth thought it was a serene and charmed stretch of pavement. He pointed toward a non-descript building at Kinney Road's end, thinking it's placement peculiar. He motioned to a water tower, saying, "The amount of conduit running under and into that water tank is odd, don't you think?"

"Like the water tower holds more than water, if at all," Will said.

"The building is decimated from the quake," said Shroud. "Maybe we should check it for survivors."

"Maybe, but this place is familiar," Orth said, absorbing details of the water tower and nearby building. "This place is important to my old boss, John Jespa. Haltronics owns this post, gentlemen. And, like Will says, that water tower is no water tower at all; it houses Jespa's sophisticated communications antennae. That building *was* the central nervous system for his Internet domain."

The building sunk into the sand. Ocean surf surrounded and pounded its foundation. The SUV group could see the worthless electronic wizardry that had enabled Jespa to force his will and power upon the world. All of it was in utter ruin.

Two images of man appeared from the ruin. Ghost-like and luminescent as a full moon, they glided closer to the group and turned out their hands in greeting Their smiles calmed everyone.

"You know us as the apostles Peter and Paul. Often referred to as saints, we acknowledge that no man is truly a saint." Peter and Paul then exchanged a glance before gesturing toward the dilapidated water tower and building. Peter continued, "We symbolize the world of debt, having frequently borrowed from one another to settle our obligations. With a sense of great relief and finality, Paul and I are here to dismantle the presence of debt on God's green Earth.

Inside those walls lies electronic wizardry symbolizing an accounting ledger that has cursed humanity's existence, reminiscent of Dante's descent into what he described as hell. This ledger snaked out under the sea and through the air, enslaving all by recording every transaction between humanity. Every individual was assigned a code, a score that linked each soul to a universal average of 666, binding the world to an ancient curse of avarice and duplicity.

But now, it is gone. Paul and I have obliterated all traces of that ledger, once owned by a wicked man facing his own treacherous end. From now on, each life will be recognized by what has been done for the goodwill of all."

Gesturing toward the group to follow them, the Apostles Peter and Paul walked together toward the grind of ocean, churning against the legs of the water tower and Jespa's electronic machine. As Peter and Paul stopped at the surf's edge, which floated back and forth over Kinney Road's paved dead end, the group watched them gesture again toward the sea column. It was an invitation to the men to accompany them across the water and rise into what they would soon understand was their ascension to God's Heaven, now visibly attached to the Earth.

At that moment the men knew their numbers were about to change. Peter Shroud, Rajesh Parnoon, and Abe Mahud looked at one another, recognizing the saints' invitation as their continuation of spiritual roads, finding there, at the end of Kinney Road, the service of their souls on Earth concluding, and the joy of living, beginning. They walked forward, then turned to say goodbye to Will McKinley and Jim Orth, each thanking the soldiers for giving them a ride to a new and glorious existence. They joined hands with the ancient saints of legendary goodwill, and at once were surrounded by a spirit unknown to them. She swirled around their feet, giving them lift, and the entire group began to laugh and shake hands, and smile at all they beheld. It was Rosalie, known to the local flora, fauna, and wildlife. Every color of the rainbow appeared in each strand of her hair; in her eyes, the endless universe expanded; sunlight flowed out from the palms of her hands, showering all with calm, wisdom, and charity.

The saints and the religious then joined together in a dance across the sea, to the rise home, a watery stairway up, to rest in the sky, to a final bridge in an old walk of life, of faith, of believing in miracles, of the goodness of man.

Tears appeared in the soldier's eyes. Their hearts could barely contain what they witnessed: the Earth was a beautiful world, and Man's history, driven endlessly by avarice, had now passed.

The two-way in Will's hand cackled and chirped, pulling the soldier's attention from the rise of spirits toward Heaven.

The radio sounded a second time and a third. Will fiddled with the squelch dial and checked the channel: still on eleven.

They heard channel eleven cackle open but not chirp shut. Will pulled the radio closer and both men heard the ocean's surf pounding from the radio speaker.

They heard a man's questioning voice. It had a young quality, but innocence was not part of it. Each question was separated by shallow breathing as if the words represented more of a hope, than the expectation of a response.

With questions of their own, the old friends stared into each other's eyes, searching for an answer to the young man's inquiry.

He asked, and then asked again, insisting on a response.

"Dad, is that you?"

My Beloved,

I am called to close my eyes and look up, toward heaven. There I will see my own true love. I will see you. I imagine your hair falling around your face, covering us from the world's madness. I walk on. Your tone and inflection surround us as you sing your grace notes one more time for the world to hear. Your voice rolls over the grass taking every unclaimed portion of nature for its own. My heart sings your name.

Yet something is changed. It is no longer just memory, of scent, of tone, of taste. It is like you are before me, and that I might be able to touch you again. Can I? My Love? Touch you again?

Your Mitchell

FORTY-THREE

———

A sign appears on a corner of an intersection in a town on the Northern California coast.

On several occasions I have found myself absorbed, lost, staring.

Normally, such a contrast of reflective red and white conjures alarm but of late, this sign, at this intersection, feels like an invitation. Delicately, it blurs.

The pressure of the morning stalls.

The sign's octagonal corners soften.

A rounded gaze rolls past and then stops, looking intently through me. Large sky-flaked blue eyes and brilliant blond hair gently recall a melodic piano heard often over the years.

Time passes, becoming air, and I, disbelieving, go with her.

M.W. Kinney Road.

———

Leo was agitated. The engrossing and exposed shape of his Sheila stood before him, in the flesh. She *was* his debilitating madness and addiction to the inhuman hide of Internet skin replication code. Her secret intimacy, streamed and flattened, became crystallized high-definition stimulation. She was the image he loved and trusted, yet here, as the ocean roared about him, her bone suit bruised and sickly, true intent appeared in her eyes. Leo saw a decayed and starved stick figure reach out to him in despair. Sorrow overcame Leo. Pity for Sheila's wounded body filled him.

Jespa licked the salt water off his lips as he struggled for balance on the shifting sand and beach rock. Rogue waves pounded the sea cliffs behind him, blowing back, knocking him about. He could no longer see Leo's party. From above, cautiously monitored Leo's struggle to climb safely back to them.

Jespa looked down at his own waterlogged clothing, examining through threadbare sleeves his bone-thin arms encased in pale-white skin. Jespa felt his facial features and realized what he had become to the eyes of a natural world, and to Leo; he was waste.

His life was dedicated to mastering digital code so that he could conquer the world, only to realize that he could never dominate organic code—his own skin, blood, and bones.

Twenty-five short feet away was one man that could dominate organic code and allow Jespa to transcend from mortal blood and bone to ones and zeros in a prolonged so-called life, as hard drive-bound lifeless memory.

Jespa's stare toward Leo, who gazed oddly at a two-way radio, held not a longing for life but an addiction for power. He bitterly wanted yesterday to return, where treachery, greed, and the spoils of war money fed his ambition to rule over the inert worlds of binary code. He was consumed by an insatiable desire for supremacy.

At precisely the moment his thoughts of Leo faded, his feet had shifted in the sand beneath him. To his horror, soft, pale skin around his toes and ankles began to peel. Jespa saw no blood. He was melting into the rocky shoals beneath him.

He remembered that the tall spire, now out of sight from where corrosion skinned life from him, filled the backgrounds of security camera views trained on the walls of his non-descript binary empire fortress.

Ignoring the burn of his torn flesh, John Jespa took a step toward Leo, savoring the idea of re-absorbing the mind he had dominated long ago. He moved toward what he desired and loved: the mind and soul of young Leo.

Leo watched incredulously as the earth opened under Jespa, catching his leading foot in a jaw-shaped hole rimmed with razor thin, tooth-shaped formations. Ocean water spilled into the opening and steam billowed, removing Jespa from Leo's view.

Jespa fell forward, his skeleton-like leg falling into a rock mouth, up to his hip. In disgust, he watched as the rock jaw clamped down on his leg, severing it from his torso. The mouth opened in time for Jespa to watch his leg fall into the conflagration below.

The throat of the rock beast was filled with fire. Sulfur filled Jespa's eyes, mouth, and nose. With his hands, he pushed against the hard, wet edge of the opening to no avail. The chomping motion continued and Jespa watched his wretched body become a feast for the demon sent to devour him.

Jespa suddenly realized he was *watching* his flesh and bones disappear in pieces into a mouth from hell. What was left of him, his body, his skull and eyes looked at Jespa, now a malevolent mist blended with salted sea air, betrayal written across its countenance, revealing a head and body abandoned by its soul. It cried out for Jespa but he backed away into the sea mist. Hopeless, his human form fell into the inferno below.

Jespa looked on without calling out. There was no scream for mercy. What he was fell in pieces into the cauldron far below. With no regret, Jespa realized he was shapeless, shadowless, a pure evil conscience that malevolently desired human souls.

He observed the slippery sand and rock shelf on the beach where he had stood just moments before. There, hovering over the wet, rocky beach surface as ghost, he beheld the form of his desire, his Leo.

෴

Amy's daring response into the Talisman Group's two-way radio shocked them.

When Leo heard Amy's transmission, her voice pulled him back from the terribly cornered and trapped imagery of his treacherous Sheila. He asked himself; *how could the world allow such evil to exist?*

380

Amy's response into the radio—*Yes, we can*—recalled other distant memories for Leo. Wildly random thoughts washed through him as ocean water ran from his clinging clothes. He pulled the two-way out of his waterlogged backpack, looked at it then up to the Talisman Group. He watched as they demanded that Amy not use it again to establish contact with strangers.

Memories of his father rose in Leo. The same memories he had minutes before the earthquake had struck, when resting ankle-deep in Alder Creek just days before.

Amy's statement "Yes, we can" resonated with Leo. He continued to stare at his two-way radio. The channel dial was set at eleven. He realized that he had not touched the dial since he was a kid with his father on their camping trips.

Clinging to rock and resisting the cold, ocean water rushing through him, he was consumed by memories of his father's voice over the two-way.

He was a rugged person, Leo thought. *He was hard on me when he was around but mostly, he was gone. Mom never talked about him. He was a soldier. He would talk to me about getting along with nature. He loved playing music—I remember his thumbs bouncing rhythmically on the steering wheel in time with the beat when he drove.*

Leo looked toward the sea cliffs and saw two things: Jespa disappear into a hole made of water and rock, and he his friends staring incredulous at Jespa's demise.

He felt for the talk button on his radio, pressed it, and spoke. "Dad, is that you?"

❧❦

The hole that ate Jespa disappeared. Charles had gone in search of rope returned with a long stretch of nylon line. The group worked together to retrieve Leo. He made his way safely back to the top of the sea cliffs surrounding the lighthouse.

In a circle, the Talisman group faced one another. Each viewed the world changing. Each faced the four winds of transformation. Heaven was now on Earth. Freewill was gone; goodwill prevailed. The circle of life would forever remain in the realm of organic cause and effect.

As the spirits Rosalie, Poama, and Gunnar moved over the terrain, into the callings each perceived, the remaining four humans, Charles, Mitchell, Leo, and Amy made a tight circle, hugging one another as goodwill asked them to do. Through their tears of wonder, they watched as the radios used moments ago, or was it hours before, dropped at their feet.

They gazed into the units. At the other end was another voice of survival and change.

Who is it?

Where did the call come from?

Are they friend or foe?

Dad?

Each question appeared on each face in the circle. Each pair of eyes sought answers.

The lighthouse.

The waterway to Heaven.

The evil in the world.

The love.

The random contact puzzled Mitchell. He looked at Leo, then thought better of asking him what the odds were that the units would be on the same channel used by a third party.

"Can I try again?" Leo asked.

Slowly Amy bent down to pick one up and handed it to Leo.

She said, "Ask, Leo, ask again."

From the edge of the sea cliff rose the non-descript mist of John Jespa—now known by another name—*Sheila*—peering into the circle. He rose up from the edge, far above the lighthouse, toward a line on the horizon known as Kinney Road.

My own true love,

You have always given myself back to me. It has always been your love that brought me through my life's sadness. Your love gave me life. And while my body is gone, my love and belief in you is not.

I see you make your way. I see you scramble for a foothold, for a way through this haze of change. I am your way. I am your heart. Find me, my dear Mitchell. I am here. Reach for me, my love. Reach for me the way you once did, when we first met, a cold cup of coffee between our fingers as we touched its handle, moving it back and forth in gentle engage. Play with me Mitchell. I am here for you to fall in love with again. I am above, and in love with you.

Please see your precious Red.

FORTY-FOUR

Technology has dismantled our souls, shucking them like oysters,
removing us from the roar of a king tide on a long sandy
catch—into a flat and inconsequential sound file.

Technology has numbed us. We forget what adversity teaches us.
We understand only what is easy.

We no longer care if we are immoral and have lost the courage to
mend or live by certain tenets that once gave us purpose.

We have allowed technology to sever contact with our natural
selves. We no longer embrace our unique ebb and flow,
relinquishing responsibility for our general wellbeing over to the
drone of algorithms and machines.

It is called viral *for a reason.*

Technology lures us, tempts us, relieving us of our frailties,
hardships, and our ability to comprehend the moral imperatives
driving our lives. We forget our scabs-on-skin processes, but we
will remember.

I know that the natural beauty of our world is within the covers of
this book. Accessible to us is an organic measured directional,
one that will unwind our flattened sense of self. It is from Mother
Nature, found in Her analog code, about the state of our existence
as human beings on this, God's Earth.

For you, searchers of such code: continue your quest.

———————

"Dad, is that you?"

Will stared at the unit in his hand. It had sparked to life, asking a question that flapped in the air like a clotheslined bed sheet.

Where did the signal come from? He thought.

He spun and looked sharply through the cypress trees and tall grass surrounding the park.

The spinning continued through the soldier's mind. He saw himself as a boy in Prescott, Arizona. He spun again, this time looking above him, toward the sun, now shining brightly at a late-morning angle. He recalled a thermal that lifted the hair from his neck, cooling him in the mile-high alpine sun. In memory, he continued to watch his playful spin as a boy in the waters of the Hassayampa River, a short waterfall or two above a waterhole—its surface glistening, reflecting the big, blue sky.

McKinley watched the spinning of a young imagination, the drinking of cool water, the truth and beauty of a boyhood blessed with solitude. The boy fell under the shallow water and took in the colors of the rainbow found in water-polished granite stone.

Such joy and wonder—such sorrow-less and shameless innocence found in time cutting through rock and light—such rhythm in the play of water and gravity. Look, he cares not for anything but the cool water and the fill of rainbow rock marking his day. He sees only what nature presents in its subtle grace of interchanging color and flashing light. Mirrors abound. He perceives that he is a part of a natural progression, finding security in natural cracks of erosion and renewal.

The boy spun again and turned his head to the shining sun. He put his hand up to his brow to shade his gaze. At once Will McKinley recognized his eyes. They were his own. In his memory, as he stood on Kinney Road, he looked up, remembering the boy he once was. Innocence and experience were locked in his gaze through time.

As the images ended, McKinley watched his youth turn away and look upstream, toward movement in the shrubs above the gentle, rolling of the Hassayampa River. He asked: "Dad, is that you?"

McKinley cried out in pain. He looked upstream to see the man who had taken him in and cared for him when he was a boy lost in the mayhem of an adult world cut and diced by evil.

In painful emotion and recall, he looked away from the memory of his adopted father. Downstream, on another river, McKinley saw his own son turn toward him, look directly into his daydream, into his heart's eye, and ask in the same careful calling: "Dad, is that you?"

Jim Orth saw McKinley's fingers tremble as they often did in battle after a long firefight. *Adrenalin*, Orth thought.

"What's going on Will?"

"That voice . . ." McKinley responded. "That voice. I've asked and heard that question often in my life, as a boy, as a man, as a father. I have a boy, now a man out there Jim. This person," McKinley said, holding the unit, "whoever he is, has sparked these memories and visions and I want to respond. I want to say, 'Yes, it's Dad'."

The boy Mitchell had known as Zac Walker, who had become Will McKinley the soldier and dad, was beginning to understand that the voice on the radio belonged to his son.

Orth weighed the implication of McKinley responding into the two-way. *What ifs* flashed. Who was this stranger that knew to ask such a poignant question of his dear friend. Who was the person speaking? Is it a trick or are they genuine in their curiosity. Orth wanted to help Will find his compassion—to be the man war had never let him be. Service to higher ideals, used as camouflage to blind the masses, hiding profiteering and power mongering—an ever-reoccurring theme in the history of Man—did not diminish their honor as soldiers, but it did put family second. Families suffered endlessly.

Hairs on the back of Orth's neck rose. He felt an ice-cold chill cruise through him. Flaring thoughts of his ex-boss, on the day he quit Haltronics, distorted his senses.

"Then do it Will," Orth said, shaking off the momentary distraction. "You must find out why this is touching your heart.

Maybe this is your boy. Stranger things are happening, all around us. I want to say something to you Will. I want to say that I am proud of you. Everything you are, as a soldier and a man, I would want to see in my own son. Could it possibly be your son? It is a question worth answering. What'd you say his name was again?"

"Leo."

From above the soldiers, who slowly walked west on Kinney Road, Sheila stared incredulously at Will McKinley. She looked menacingly into Will's eyes and to her astonishment saw distinct similarities between this Will McKinley and his beloved Leo Brenamann.

So! This is the man my Leo never knew. This is the one who left, who carved a hole in my Leo's heart, where I know I still live. I will have my Leo. This man will not stop me but I must bring them together to separate them. They must see one another and then Leo must see me. I will find his secret, his restorative code that will restore life back into the frozen light of electronically charged graphene and silicone. I will own my Leo and my universe again and will control the world from inside my network of computers and servers. I will move through his mind and his heart, giving him only my treachery as love. I know what moves this child and you, soldier boy, you have failed to see him through. Now Leo only knows the love I can give him. I own him, and his every thought.

Sheila floated with Orth and McKinley as they moved closer to the Haltronics station at the end of Kinney Road. With evil intent, she tried knocking Will McKinley over by moving through him. Sheila's hatred grew, and her rage worked to overpower the grace that nature presented all around him.

The soldiers looked toward the lighthouse and stopped walking. Will McKinley, without further thought, spoke into his ancient hand-held radio. He clicked the talk button and answered clearly, "Yes, son, it's Dad."

To my own true Red:

I dreamed of you. You were hitch-hiking on this very highway. I stopped and picked you up in our old truck. In my dream, I discovered you all over again: your kindness—willingness—beauty—your voice—your faith in me.

I am on the highway again, right now looking to see you standing on the side of the road around every bend.

Your own true love, your Mitchell

FORTY-FIVE

The Earth rotates and orbits, setting the example for living.
She is consequential to our wellbeing and remains our greatest
mystery even while we know far too much about our own self-
interests. Her experience enriches us wholly tranquil and imparts
her analog rhythm as the format for our living book.
We knew tall grass as a bed and pillow. Let us know it again. We
knew our solemn selves as insignificant yet unique in Life's
revolving path, finding balance. Come home to your leaves of
grass, to your naturally abundant, imperfect selves. Your unique
skew leaves a whirl in the scheme and furthers the innate
rhythm of our natural world.
Breathe its air; drink its water; sense for yourself a manifest of
time, position, temperature, and visibility. Say for yourself what
such a sprig . . . a jolt . . . a slice . . . a moment, would mean to you.
                                                    M.W. Kinney Road

---

Leo tossed the two-way radio from his hand. The shock was
evident on his face as he abruptly recognized a voice he had not
heard in a very long time. It shot through him, as did fitful
memories of his father's face and his own innocent sense of
longing. He remembered an outline in the carpet of his mother's
room, where his father's dresser once stood, flowing out from
locked memories within him.

Leo's face turned ashen as the radio fell to the ground.

"Leo, what is it?" Amy asked, alarmed.

Leo responded with an empty stare. He looked through her as his mind filtered old memories. Amy noticed his lips moving in silence. She had seen Leo do this the day before at the table in Charles Hoyt's bay window. She was moved by his intense expression.

Leo was counting. Digits spewed forth in his mind like sparks on whetstones. The numeric sequences strung out in front of him and connected to a hundred different kite-like shapes—then a thousand—then billions. Each kite was a different shape and color, moving out in all directions; all a part of an ever-widening array of algorithms. Numbers engulfed Leo's mind, looping repeatedly. Wrapping together, the lines of numbers formed a tether that strapped his heart. He cried out as he struggled to make sense of his father's long-lost voice emerging from the radio.

The vision continued to engulf him, as lines of numbers unfurled out over the ocean and up the water column, into the three-part heaven above him. He abruptly understood that the lines of numbers characterized souls. He observed that each was a prime number. He connected the two thoughts and realized that his soul, connected to God, and to the universe, to the mathematical calm of nature, was the equivalent of an exceptional and beautiful integer, attached to the line of a single prime number. His prime number.

This observation immediately served as proof to him of his simple, unadorned uniqueness in the universe.

His vision of all prime numbers continued. By focusing he reduced the multiple lines of prime numbers to just two. These two primes were long, beyond his ability to transcribe, but familiar. His earlier memories sitting in an outline of carpet as a toddler roused him. He said: "These are his prime number, and mine. They mark our souls and are separated by one."

"What do you mean," Amy asked. "Separated by one? Whose numbers?"

He walked hurriedly away from Amy into the tall grasses that spread from the lighthouse. The grass filtered the heavy sea mist, camouflaging crags in the ground at Leo's feet. The ocean appeared below him.

He stopped and turned toward his brethren. He gazed at Mitchell. Mitchell was suffering from the pull of some unreconciled deliberation. Leo was sad to see his new friend become almost transparent before him, and suspected that Mitchell was thinking about the wife he had lost. Leo was certain that Hoyt was lost in thought about his son, Louis. Amy seemed to be the only one that remained present.

Amy recognized that each of her friends was struggling. Leo's countenance pulled her toward him. She bent over and retrieved the two-way Leo had dropped.

Amy repeated her question as she walked swiftly toward Leo: "What numbers are his and yours, Leo? Who is *he*?" She emphasized her questions by shaking the old radio in the air.

Leo paused for a moment and then said, "My dad."

"The voice on the two-way is your dad?" Amy asked.

"Yes, it's my dad."

Not able to fully absorb Leo's answer, Amy repeated her question again.

"What numbers are you talking about?"

"There," Leo said. He pointed toward the water column then to the triangle of moons in the morning sky. "Souls are defined by prime numbers Amy, each unique yet just a number. Sometimes prime numbers are paired; they are separated by the value of one. I see right now, right here, that my prime number is joined with another, which reaches toward that contour on the horizon." Leo pointed at a stretch of road running through the grass-laden fields north of where they stood. "I believe, with all of my ability, that the prime number I see that is bound to mine, is my dad's. My dad and I are twin primes, separated by one. And he is, based on the voice I just heard on that two-way, on that road, on the horizon."

Amy looked out to the water column. She too, with the help of Leo's description, could see the endless tethers, lines made of infinite prime numbers, running up the length of the column, reaching into the beauty that awaited them. "Those lines are really souls that are represented by prime numbers." Amy repeated, making sure she understood his claim.

"Yes," Leo said. "They are proof of the intelligence of a divine nature. We are coded into a heavenly, eternal existence by way of a prime number, assigned to you at your moment of awakening—a number that is divisible only by itself and one, one being the first prime, or God. You are a singular prime number Amy, and previously a part of eternity by design. We are already a part of a singularity. We don't need technology to make that transfer for us. We are endless by nature's blueprint. Isn't it a wonderful thought?"

Amy's youthful exuberance ignited, coupled with her marveling at the universe because of Leo's take on their new world. She made his description of her soul as a prime number her own, infinite and perfect as the purpose of a divine nature. She hugged Leo around his neck, kissing his forehead with sincerity and gratitude.

Amy pulled away from Leo, putting him at arm's length. She took in his childish face, only now growing into a young man's angles and features. For the first time she noted his eyes and how beautifully their blue-grey irises reflected the ocean and water column behind her. She put her hands on his face and pulled his eyes closer to her, examining them. She noted a peculiar line in both of his pupils. It was extremely thin and it pulsed at regular intervals, like the cursor on a computer screen.

Leo looked sadly back into Amy's eyes. He could tell by her expression that she saw how a lifetime of long hours in front of a computer screen affected his retinal display.

"Leo, what is flashing in the pupils of your eyes?"

"It is the mark of our technological age, Amy. Since I was seven years old, the last fifteen years immersed in the array of high-definition computer screens. My retinal memory has been marked by the computer screen's cursor. It's a mark shared by computer coders, especially Haltronics employees. I can't seem to get rid of it. I am hoping in time, it will diminish."

Leo was not fully forthright about everything he knew of the pulsing dashes in his pupils.

Amy stood as tall as she could and lightly kissed Leo on his mouth. He reddened. The focus of physical, real, female affection touched Leo for the first time. He gazed at Amy's lips, slightly open, and light in color. Imagined intimacy, never known, became tangible to him at that moment, stunning him. He inhaled deeply, taking Amy into his lungs, feeling her presence shoot through him. He put his hands on Amy's shoulders, realizing how demure and perfectly feminine she was, and returned her kiss, a tad longer than their first.

Feeling self-conscience, Amy and Leo flushed, saying and not saying what they were thinking, and looking as if they had blindly bumped into each other in a grocery store.

The intimacy was short-lived. Leo solemnly remembered the moment he accepted John Jespa's offer. As a Haltronics employee, the benefit package included a space in the Haltronics system that housed Jespa's transhumanism effort. Jespa promised Leo that he would live forever. Leo bought it and signed his eternity over to Jespa upon Leo's death. He was consumed by great regret as he remembered how and when Jespa marked Leo. All employees who agreed to the benefit package were injected with the dash into their retinal memory. It was Jespa's tracking device—how he kept tabs on employees willing to commit their souls to him.

Amy could see the pulsing dash in Leo's eyes suddenly glow brighter. Leo's face became ashen again, losing its shine and luster in reaction to Amy's kiss.

"Amy, there is more to the pulsing dash than I have told you."

Amy looked carefully at her newfound object of affection. She cocked her and with her eyes, asked Leo to continue his thoughts.

"It's a mark, put there as proof of my acceptance of employment terms with Haltronics. Jespa promised that I could live forever if I signed my soul over to him. I foolishly believed I *wanted* to live forever. I signed his terms of service and accepted a place in the Haltronics servers where supposedly I would exist perpetually. It is binding Amy, and unless I do something to reverse Haltronics' plan to devour the world's souls, I can still be taken by Jespa and his system."

Amy deep into Leo's eyes and knew beyond any doubt that everything hinged on getting Leo to Kinney Road, to the campground where she and her mother had spent the night before the quake, to where her precious mother worked—to the Haltronics lab inside the nondescript building at the end of Kinney Road.

She grabbed Leo's arm, running into the fields of grass east of the lighthouse. She moved toward the horizon of farm fields and cypress trees. Amy knew where Leo had to go to find the voice he heard on the two-way.

"You are right, Leo. He is there," Amy agreed. "That voice you say is your father, he is there, on that road in the horizon. And so is the way out of your contract Haltronics. There is a lab at the end of that road. Maybe there is a terminal that still works inside that building."

"How do you know this?"

"Remember the stones we were given in the cave," Amy said, as they ran. "I was told to find heaven in my own mind. You are to find the universal language for this new world. turning, and I believe both will happen there, on that road in the horizon. Come on Leo, come on. Let's run as fast as we can and meet our coming futures, our heavens behind our mind's partitions, our unique prime numbers as our true singularities, our true reality. If this voice is your destiny and if we can reverse the Haltronics contract, we will

402

find both there. My mom worked for Haltronics. She once told me that the building she worked in was the nerve center for the company. Look, it's still there."

Amy pointed to the end of the road line found on the horizon. She put her hand in Leo's and picked up the pace, encouraging Leo to follow her lead. They ran as fast as they could north through the fields.

Mitchell and Charles ran after Amy and Leo. Bounding through the tall grass, their motion lifted their hearts. A picture, with Amy as Dorothy, Leo, the Tin Man, Mitchell, the Lion, and himself as the Scarecrow, made Charles Hoyt laugh out loud. He longed to see his Louis again, feeling for his son's box secured safely in his backpack.

Gunnar, too, saw the scene below him, and began to sing *The Wizard of Oz* tune *Optimistic Voices*, laughing through the lyrics as they engulfed his friends below.

❧

Sheila shot straight above McKinley and Orth, noticing movement in the fields south of Kinney Road, enraged and lustful at what he saw there.

It was his Leo, arm in hand with the girl in the group from the lighthouse, bounding through the fields, laughing. This was odd for Sheila. He could not remember ever seeing Leo laugh. Leo was happy.

As the four fools moved north, Sheila moved toward them, only to be rebuffed by three very powerful spirits he would soon learn were Leo's trinity of protectors. They charged at Sheila, forcing him back to hovering over the soldiers on Kinney Road.

He gave up on Leo. The spirits were too much for his newly found ability to move through air as a ghoulish mist.

Sheila also faced the ever-growing, multicolored beam from the lighthouse, rotating brightly like an umbrella. Even in daylight, the beam pierced through him like a laser, challenging his malevolence with the light of a new age—one where goodwill would surpass the self-fulfilling prophecy of free will. To Sheila, the lighthouse was a beacon of a new world emanating from an ancient, symbolic tower.

Abandoning the effort to intimidate his foes, Sheila directed his unnerving gaze at the nondescript building, battered by the ocean and cracked by earthquakes, eager to uncover what remained of his digital world.

My own true love,

You often said through our life together that it was the small things I did that were the inspiration for our love. I loved preparing your meals, making your bed, believing in you, laughing with you, touching and craving only you.

Now you must remember these small gestures for us. I beg you to not let us become vapor. Remember to see what is right in front of you. Remember my touching your skin, tasting my breakfasts and dinners, the smell of clean sheets on our bed, and the shoring of your soul against the treachery of an unfair world. Remember who you were with me. I need this now, more than ever.

Mitchell, in all of my heart, spread in thin layers over memory and emptiness, in all of my yearning and weariness, please touch me again. Look to the sea and you shall find me.

Please see your precious Red.

FORTY-SIX

————

The tall, glass front door opened slowly, reflecting passing cars and pedestrians in front of her salon. She watched with some trepidation as a stranger entered. Although there were no immediate indicators—he seemed clean enough—he had the air of want about him. She took a deep breath, squared her shoulders and faced him. He shut the door.

"It's my wife's birthday," he began. "We've been struggling since I got sick last year."

She held his gaze, conveying her ability to detect bullshit.

Her eyes told him that she was not dismissing him outright; she would listen to the short version of his long, sad story.

He continued: "It has been sometime since she's had her hair done. We used to set it up every six weeks or so, when her roots would start to show. It is hard for her to look into a mirror these days. We see the hard times in her hair. I was wondering if you would accept a trade of some kind. It doesn't have to be today; it could be another time. I've got DVDs. We kept our favorites, brought them with us. You could have all of them." He laid them out and stopped talking.

She continued to stare into his eyes—appraising his soul. It was the longest of moments . . . for both.

Dreadful.

Embarrassing.

Finally, she spoke.

"Okay. Can you bring her by tomorrow morning at ten?"

He left, hope renewed. She watched him walk out to an old pick-up truck. He told his wife. She wrapped her arms around his neck.

The stylist closed her eyes to the tenderness; her faith in humanity rose one degree, maybe two.

Goodwill is revealed as grace in living.

M.W. Kinney Road

———

Will noted the damage to the nondescript building at road's end. A particularly large, gapping crack had appeared in the bunker-like construction. Foot-thick concrete slabs formed its walls. High voltage energy popped and sparked from all sides. Will's gaze followed the fallen power lines that fed the structure hanging from treetops along the northern border of the state park.

Meanwhile, Jim surveyed the open fields south of their position. Huge cypress trees planted long ago by farmers as windbreaks spread out from horizon to horizon. Catastrophic earthquake damage was everywhere he looked. Dark, wet earth, having never seen the light of day, began to gray in the high noon sun. Sheep and cattle grazed, unaware that the world had changed under them. Tractors and combines were upturned, buried, or carried halfway out to sea.

Through the feathered grass, four moving heads of hair appeared. Jim put his hand on Will's shoulder and squatted, taking Will with him.

"We've got company, coming fast, directly south of us. Might be the young man you talked with earlier. It looks like they are coming from the lighthouse," he said looking directly into Will's eyes, remembering the words he spoke into the two-way, moments before.

Will peered through the brush seeing four people headed straight for them, galloping fast: a girl, hand-in-arm with a young man, and two older men.

"Well?" Jim asked. "Is it your son?"

Moments passed as they watched the approaching party, playful and laughing.

"I'm not sure, Jim. It's been a long time since I've seen him."

Overhead, the lighthouse beam absorbed the sky colors behind it, rotating throughout the full horizon in every direction, blending blue and white.

"Will. I don't think we have anything left in this world to defend or any reason to fight. It is obvious this group is not our enemy."

Will paused before responding: "Nothing left to fight for? Could that be right?"

Jim saw his silhouette reflected in Will's hazel eyes. The two soldiers let go of what they had known for the entirety of their adult lives: the hounding of war. They stood slowly and faced the approaching group, their faces resolute, their uniforms patched, laden with straps and weapons.

Jim and Will heard the two older men shout: "Amy! Leo! Stop!"

The girl and young man stopped, letting the older men catch up. They pointed at Jim and Will, expressing concern. The younger ones nodded in agreement to what their elders had said.

"Are you the people we made contact with this morning?" Will asked, into the two-way radio.

Amy reached into Leo's pack and pulled out their unit.

"Yes, we made contact with you this morning," Amy responded. She looked at Leo. He was not upset that Amy spoke to the strangers. Leo stared at the two men.

"Miss, could you hand your unit over to the man standing next to you?"

Amy did so carefully. The Talisman group watched as Will pressed his talk button again.

"Are you Leo?"

"Who's asking?" Leo shot back, now recognizing the older man standing next to the one speaking into the unit. "I know that man next to you. He's from Haltronics, their head of security. I quit

410

Haltronics. I'm never going back! I'd rather die than work for that asshole ever again!"

The recognition was mutual. Startled, Jim spoke up. "It's him Will. It's the employee John Jespa is after. He's the guy who built the code for Haltronics and is the only one Jespa feels can rebuild it. He's wanted Will. Jespa is after him."

Will's expression was pained.

Jim referenced Leo with his hand and said: "You picked me up on Highway One not two hours after I quit Haltronics, just after he did. That young man is quite talented."

Will remained quiet. Jim could tell Will was growing increasingly upset.

"Don't worry. I know Jespa put a price on his head but I will have nothing to do with turning him in."

Jim realized Will was in some kind of trouble—something was affecting him. His eyes were glazing over.

"In fact, Will, *this* is what we have to fight for. We Will protect Leo from Jespa! What do you say!"

Will was lost in thought, back to a time when he did not know who he was or what would become of him. He had left his adopted home at a young age, changing his name for a fresh start in a new town, wanting a future that had nothing do to with his troubled past he left behind.

The two groups kept their distance. The silence of the two-way radios grew in volume and was reflected in the severity of light emanating from the high noon sun. The silence was palpable.

The next seconds were filled with darting glances. Charles and Mitchell were fixed on Will. Leo and Jim, remembering their times at Haltronics, watched one another's expressions.

Will extended his hand toward the strangers. He slowly traced an outline of the young man in the air . . . considering him.

Leo mirrored Will's movement, doing the same kind of tracing with his fingers, recalling ancient memories. He silently counted the prime numbers he had interpreted earlier, as belonging to himself and his dad.

Leo was seven years old when they said goodbye his father. He had come over unannounced. Leo's mother called him from his tinker toys and the models of self-propulsion and gravity that he built on his bedroom floor. He was in uniform. Leo liked seeing him like that. He could tell that his father was sad. His father bent over, picked Leo up and hugged him, saying "I am going away for a while. One day, I will come home For now I am headed to distant shores. I promise to write and call."

Leo couldn't bear it. He lunged for his father's leg. He wailed and cried while his mother pulled him off. Through layers of tears, Leo watched the back of his father get smaller—his feet moving swiftly away from him—disappearing into a black SUV with dark windows that sped away into the white of a bright, clear day.

∾

Will could not come to terms with his new orders. He was again being sent into the madness of the Oil Wars, unfolding in different theaters throughout the world. He was now a lieutenant in the Marine Corps, ordered back to the Middle East.

It was going to be hard this time to say goodbye to his son. He was seven years old now and they were close. He walked quietly up the walkway to the front door of Leo's mother's home and knocked.

He bent over and picked up the little boy. Tears were already present in the boy's eyes. Will's eyes reddened while he memorized his son's size, weight, hazel eyes, and the smell in his white-blonde hair. He put him down, turned to go but was almost knocked down by his son's lunge at his legs. He looked down to see Leo's small face buried in the pant leg of his uniform. Leo's mother rushed over and pulled Leo off Will. He could not bear the pain on Leo's face any longer.

Will felt, in that singular second of time, as if the love in his heart for Leo was being put to sleep by the contents of a syringe and a needle—its beating soon to be stilled on the cold steel slab of a veterinary doctor's table. In Will's mind, his heart turned white, without color, then grey, then to dust.

By the time he returned to his base, his boy was gone—his experience with war ushering in the dead calm of a heart turned to swamp.

Slowly, Will and Leo lowered their fingers and began to walk toward one another. They were both afraid the moment was not real. Just as quickly the miles and years since their last meeting disappeared. Light and color grew from one set of hazel eyes to another. Their feet picked up the cadence of mending a broken love between a boy and his father.

They cleared the grass with swift steps. Their leaping easily maneuvered over rocks and barbed wire. Using powerful arms and young legs, their breathing increased, their heart rates elevated, and the dreadful moments of saying goodbye long ago evaporated with a father's hand on his boy's face bolstered by a boy's longing for his father's touch.

Leo and Will embraced, neither letting go. They stumbled into the feathered grasses laughing, then disbelieving the moment, then laughing again.

Yet the reunion of hearts and minds was not over. Out of the blue sky a shadow was cast across the faces of father and son. Through his joyful tears, Will looked up to see the face of another familiar stranger.

The odds of meeting him here, with his son, on this day, at this hour, were too great to comprehend, yet there he was. There, in the broad light of day, as his eyes adjusted to the shadow that fell across his face, was the countenance of his adopted father Mitchell, smiling down upon him once again.

My beloved,

I have read it yet again. This poem by Robert Service that
somehow helps me feel closer to you:

PREMONITION

T'was a year ago and the moon was bright
(Oh, I remember so well, so well);
I walked with my love in a sea of light,
And the voice of my sweet was a silver bell.

And sudden the moon grew strangely dull,
And sudden my love had taken wing;
I looked on the face of a grinning skull,
I strained to my heart a ghastly thing.

T'was but fantasy, for my love lay still
In my arms, with her tender eyes aglow,

And she wondered Why my lips were chill,
Why I was silent and kissed her so.

A year has gone and the moon is bright,
A gibbous moon, like a ghost of woe;
I sit by a new-made grave to-night,
And my heart is broken,
it's strange, you know.

Dry your eyes. I feel them for you. Your warmth. Your salt. They are my only reason to carry forth into each hopeless sunrise. Let me see your precious eyes again, let me behold them, gaze with awe at those two windows into an angel's soul. Through everything, you still have my love, all my awareness, all my senses, all my ache, all my hope, you are a single thing to me. I need you now. I need you now. Find me Red. Reach for me. Hand me your heaven's touch. Every season of life was found in your touch. Let me feel your fingers again. Your tiny, precious hands, warm to the touch, salty to the taste. I am a stranger to my own life, because you were all I knew. You were my every waking thought, and every idle dream.

I know one thing, I have never felt alone. All these years, I have been lonely, but I have never felt as if I were without your life. You were the one I was to find and to love forevermore. You are, still.

Your Mitchell

FORTY-SEVEN

Service.

I've said nearly all I can on this topic. It's time to match my words with action and dedication.

This journal entry captures our era's voice—a voice of clarity, common sense, and unwavering love.

No one here is running for office. We are all simply running out of time. Hearts must be aligned before the inevitable quake, flood, or reckoning occurs.

Our envy of the universe has undone us. Our choice is to want it all. Be it knowledge, possessions, or souls, we have drained the freewill tenet of its unique intent. This is our original sin—squandering the gift that Nature extended to humanity so long ago—the short and sweet breath of life.

In this digital age, the further we travel from our understanding of how things work, the less control we have of the life we have been given. We are diverted and slip further away from those things that traditionally anchored us.

Now, unprecedented in the history of man, we need the examples that ocean tides provide us. We need to know the four winds. We must remember the paradoxical light and burn of fire. We must lay prone to the Earth in the dark night, and as the stars pass, remember who we were intended to be.

M.W. Kinney Road

Gunnar soared into the open sky, drawn by the currents of an ever-expanding universe. He understood the creative spark that had ignited every original thought in human history, now renewed by the timeless familial love flourishing on the grasses south of Kinney Road.

Surveying all that the curve of the Earth would allow, he wept at the sight of heaven before him. Gunnar gazed at the bright, continuous star-filled burst of a single spirit entity, her divine hair flowing around her. Her eyes revealed the impression of longing, of searching. Her feet glided motionless above the surf, skimming over foam and sand.

Inspired by her apparitional loveliness, Gunnar positioned his fingers over a keyboard made of passing wind. Whispering cantatas, chants, and melodies in every octave flowed out to sea around the lighthouse and up the water column into the heaven-bound orbs floating miles above the Earth's surface. He noted that their existence enchanted this spirit woman.

She placed her arms around waves the of music emanating from Gunnar, her hands moving toward the new worlds. Sea mist flowed through her snowy silk garments. From distant shores, the spirit heard her once-living voice from her isolated and shredded past. Moving her fingers to her throat, the spirit recalled not only the horror of her death but the love she had for another, a man, her husband. She cried out. Her wailing echoed off the white-tipped waters, rising to Gunnar who heard not wailing but the angelic voice of heaven.

Rosalie and Poama joined Gunnar in the sky. For a moment, he paused playing the winds to hear the spirit's perfect replication of cathedral bells, of stones dropping into wishing wells, of joyful sounds resonating eternal love. She drew her hands across the horizons regarding the heavens above, now crowned by her voice and her longing.

From her broken heart, lyrics echoed in a sacred melody of pure and unwavering love, a song she had sung often in her afterlife for the one she still loved:

Life has left me still and alone,
My breath stolen, my fears overthrown,
Heaven is above, yet you are near,
I am unable to endure being here.

You are my home,
I wait for thee,
Oh shores of forever,
Oh eternity.

Perfection embodied in all that you are,
Our souls, like windows, stretching far.
To dwell in flawless love once more,
With hands entwined, forevermore.

You, my cherished husband,

And I, your humble wife,

Together we walk in reborn sand,

Timeless in this shifting land.

She looked down at the beach below. Shards of memories caught in her voice. Her love song faltered as her loneliness and despair grew.

Gunnar noted her bright presence had diminished. He increased the intensity of his playing, inspired by her musical light. He yearned to hear that light repeated. He sent his music to strengthen her against the darkness that pursued her.

Having ended her song, the perceptive spirit looked through the sea mist, through a broken water tower and a devastated cement bunkhouse, toward the orchestral music she heard. It was emanating from a morning sky she had often moved under in her gray existence, searching for her love, hoping he would find her.

She rose above the sands Manchester beach. Her hair and garments billowed around her. She moved toward Gunnar, joining him. His overcoat became every color of the rainbow. With his fine fingers as Aeolian harps, he directed the spirit's gaze toward the party of six humans below.

Tears flowed from the spirit, turning to rain as they fell upon the face and hands of the one she knew.

As drops streaked his tired soiled face, Mitchell looked up to see his Red filtering the bright sunshine of this strange and beautiful day. Guilt buckled his knees. Holding her bloodied, lifeless body in his hands, his despair turned him away from her and pushed him onto the tall grasses. He buried his face into the ground next to Leo and Will.

Mitchell couldn't comprehend what he was seeing. His thoughts and emotions spun between the reality and proximity of a boy he once adopted named Zac and the beloved essence of his wife as sunlight above, the warmth and memory of their ritualistic evening fire filling him.

Somewhere in his remote heart their love connection remained heaven-sent, respectful, loyal, humble, and everlasting.

Mitchell remembered his true love and the warmth of their shared affection. Red began to sing again the song she sung to the heavens moments before.

Mitchell rolled over. The rain had stopped falling but a voice cascaded down in its place. It was his Red, her unmistakable voice a miracle, her love reaching through his mind, time suspended. Gunnar joined Red and turned the winds into timeless orchestras.

Mitchell mouthed the words he heard:

You are my home,
I wait for thee,
Oh, shores of forever,

Oh eternity.

Red moved toward Mitchell. Gunnar's wind movements inspired one small reunion of love. Another rain of tears poured down on Mitchell's face as Red realized her reason for staying on a cold realm of afterlife along the northern California coastline. Two layers of longing meshed as one. Two realms became one love again.

Red's angel outline settled into the outstretched arms of her widowed husband. She sensed he was remembering what it felt like to hold her. He recalled how big his love was for her, how he adored her, delighted in her, planned for and romanced her. All that she was to him was evident on his face.

All the afterlife despair in a lifeless slide down cold walls and broken stones was now worth every agonizing moment: she found her joy in a field of grass, her Mitchell far, far removed from her last earth-bound minutes.

Here, in his arms, Red was held by Mitchell as his spirit wife, filled with starlight, her eyes richly brown, her ginger-colored curls a picture of youth. Her heart filled with a kaleidoscope of transparent pearls sparking galactic light from within, her shredded hope renewed, her memory of the minutes before she died wiped clean.

❧❧

Slowly, Mitchell turned to his side and saw two similar faces. One he knew: Will. The other, not: Leo. Both were looking back at him, and at Red, grinning. Two sets of hazel eyes and identically lined wide-brimmed smiles forced Mitchell to reach out and put his hand on Will's head. He touched his adopted son's grey hair.

Mitchell felt joy and pain. He remembered meeting Will for the first time long ago and the longer odds that he was once related by a previous marriage to his beloved Red. She rested on Mitchell now as water might rest upon rock. He saw in her eyes memories of Will as a boy, navigating lonely days and long nights as the nephew of the man who would eventually kill her.

Mitchell recalled tall stands of American elms that lined the walkways of the Yavapai County Courthouse in Prescott, Arizona. They were the backdrop to that untimely meeting. Will glared at Mitchell from the top of wide courthouse steps. Mitchell was accustomed to being stared at but *this* set of hazel eyes was different from the rest of the townsfolk. This set was not fearful or wary, but fierce, full of hate and full of questions.

"Who do you think you are?!"—the first words his adopted son ever spoke to him. Will was less than six inches from Mitchell's face then, and here, today, the same distance lay between them.

"I am the man who adopted you," Mitchell said aloud, in response to the question asked in memory. "And this, Will, is my wife, the woman you may remember as Red."

Now it was Will's turn to crash through the ugliness of evil in Prescott, Arizona. He recalled Mitchell chasing after him the first time they had met, at the conclusion of Mitchell's murder trial, when Mitchell was acquitted of killing Will's uncle. He hated Mitchell and wanted to destroy him in whatever way a fourteen-year-old could.

Mitchell was unrelenting, coming into town every day to look for and talk to Will. Mitchell was determined to turn the tide that had taken so much from Will, determined to help him shed the evil in his past.

Will remembered when Mitchell invited him to move into his cabin south of Prescott near the Hassayampa River knowing his prospects as the nephew of a killer in a small town were slim. Will cautiously accepted the proposal and the rules Mitchell demanded he live by.

He remembered the day and the reason he left Mitchell's home. The darkness he felt toward Mitchell was ever-present. Will did respond to Mitchell's leadership, allowing it to loosen the noose that family legacies bind their members to. But he could no longer bear the weight of what his uncle had done to Red, and by what Mitchell had done in revenge to his uncle.

With Mitchell's blessing, Will left Prescott in the quiet of night to join the Marine Corps. He remembered the long last ride to town in Mitchell's old, red pickup truck, almost missing the bus that would take him to Los Angeles. But what Mitchell did not know was that Zac Walker, the boy he adopted, became Will McKinley upon check-in at Camp Pendleton in southern California using a doctored birth certificate and Social Security card, ensuring a life not trampled on by a scandalous murder and revenge killing.

Will never contacted Mitchell again, believing it best to leave Mitchell alone, never again to remind him of what had happened to his wife.

Will felt Mitchell reach out and cradle his head with his hand, saying "you are Zac, the boy I adopted in Prescott, Arizona."

Will rolled over on his back in the grass. He looked at Red with tears in his eyes. She knew his reason for breaking. She remembered horror and a blade and for a moment, she considered that darkness again. But she let the night in question go, once and for always, never to burden her again. She had found her own true love.

Her eyes sought Will's. She offered reprieve from the torture of carrying her death within him. Will felt her brush of forgiveness touch him. He reached up and with the tenderness only a soldier could muster, held her hand and smiled at her for the first time in his long years as a boy and a man.

Amy, Jim Orth, and Charles Hoyt watched with intense curiosity. Will looked at Mitchell, holding his Red, and said, "for these last many years I have been known to the world as Will McKinley. This is *my* son, Leo Brenamann . . . and you are his grandparents."

Our Love,

We will unmake our premonition, and remember no more, our chilled lips and stoic hearts, shining darkly in the gibbous moonlight. Let us hold our lives in whatever form they come, true in thoughtful recall, in hopeful reach toward our rising sun. You are my own true love.

We were told to let one another go. We will never leave one another again. Heaven is here, in our embrace, on our Kinney Road, where heaven and earth are renewed, where richness of spirit is enough to sustain us. We will persevere. We will be happy.

Our Life

———

Goodwill is the rain for which our world thirsts. This has been the collective chorus of Emerson, Whitman, and Longfellow sounding their yawps over the world's rooftops. They call us to recount. Their authority resonates just as sleep overcomes us, and our eyes are startled wide at the intensity and clarity of their written works, their evidence, word by word, is the timeless spiritual path of our collectively lost souls.

The cyclic cliché: Insanity is described as . . .

Repetitive humanity, how foolish you are. Upon you is the consequence of knowing and feeling the weight of every decision throughout your existence on the entirety of the universe. Diminished or renewed, in direct proportion to your output, so goes all life.

Yet nature forgives this indentured race and immediately seeks balance with humanity's presence upon Her soil.

M.W. Kinney Road

———

Discontent, John Jespa existed only for the moment when he could manipulate and exercise his cruelty upon employees, heads of state, and the collective soul of the world. He existed to exact his freewill as divine, to control the code of thought and imagination in the world. He did not grasp that his enterprise would naturally end.

As the digitally altered specter Sheila—still lurid, still delusional, still craving vengeance and dominance—he gazed out of a crack in his bunkhouse, eyeing the arrival of several indentured followers aboard the Crimson Ward. They were soldiers of fortune who swore allegiance to the villainous chief of Haltronics.

He had paid the men in gold and promised future positions in his digital empire. They accepted his terms, received his mission coordinates, and committed to meet him at his North American Internet hub, the dead end of an obscure coastal road in Mendocino County, California.

Sheila watched the men, eight in all, drift quietly toward his crumbling bunkhouse on rubber rafts and paddles, the surf nudging them onto the beach. They were out of sight from Kinney Road.

They rushed from their rafts to the shore. Their shoulders were laden with guns and ammunition, and they each handled crates filled with associated warfare gear. The soldiers eyed the crack where Sheila gazed at them.

They heard him hiss demands of obedience and silence. Muted in fear, their spirits and footfalls answered him as quietly as the mist that surrounded him.

He spilled out of the large gap in the bunkhouse wall. Seawater shifted in and out of the same crack, mixing with shadows of gray that silhouetted his movement. He created vaporlike tails as he stirred. The indentured gathered in a huddle on the beach, peering at the creature who was now their leader. Some felt superstition and premonition. The cold ocean water chilled exposed skin and senses. Wiping eyes and blowing noses, each fighter resumed their loads and the trek toward the bunkhouse, prompted by a cue from the shadow-smoked phantom.

They approached a rusted door on the ocean side of the structure, its hinges corroded. It swung open, startling the men, breaking off and falling silently into the new sand built up by the recent chaotic shift of ocean tides.

The shapeless entity Sheila hovered in the frame of the door silhouetted by darkness. He endeavored to take the form he knew in his previous existence. The mercenaries paled as they watched the bones of his old life assemble into a hapless skeletal pattern, then disassemble, over and under-shooting the proper fitting of one joint of bone into another, missing connections. The apparition flexed and heaved. Blood vessels appeared but failed to attach and red liquid spilled from the ends, gurgling like water from a hose. Arteries, veins, and capillaries pumped, first filling with liquid then deflating, all to the beating of a faintly outlined blackish heart.

Sheila was enraged at his inability to assume his old appearance. Mercenaries looked on as he struggled to take shape. He hissed at his embarrassing predicament.

She failed to transform into his once living body, abandoning the effort in a fit of rage. He recognized scorn in one of his soldier's eyes. For a moment Sheila felt belittled and his embarrassment became hatred. The fighter's scorn made Sheila feel disgust for who he was and contempt for the world from which he came.

She lunged at the transgressor, forcing his potent mist into the mouth and down the throat of the scorn-filled man. The fighter dropped to his knees, grabbing his throat, turning first red, then ashen, as he realized his life was ending. Sheila enjoyed the spectacle from his view inside the man's lungs, observing his victim flailing wildly about without making a sound.

The seven remaining fighters watched with revulsion as Sheila exited from the mouth of the dead man. He rose above the corpse and paused for a moment, looking down at the body as it floated in the shifting surf. Sheila became aware that his rage had reduced his fighting power significantly. An idea came to him: *If I cannot assume the form of my previous self, could I use this body to serve my purpose?*

Immediately Sheila dropped back into the body of the dead mercenary. Once inside, Sheila focused his considerable rage upon the man's heart, capable of manipulating its muscles with his hatred. The corpse hacked and coughed up ocean water that had seeped into his lungs. With bloodshot eyes and a snarl of hot, glowing iron, the dead mercenary slowly stood, and with both of his fists pummeled the nearest member of his fighting unit just to see if he could do it.

With his newfound freedom, Sheila jumped about, kicking, splashing, and yelling wildly, showing his deep-seated madness. His men indicated that he needed to quiet down, pointing to the dead-end road on the other side of the bunkhouse.

Jim Orth left the happy reunion on the grass and sat on the SUV's tailgate. He was happy for Will. He marveled at how three generations of men found one another in this crosshair of time and space.

He recognized his connection to nature while journeying through the mythical crossroads of humanity. Before him was Heaven on Earth—a concept he had long studied in history and mythology. It appeared in unexpected ways, just as he had suspected it would during his military career's discussions and debates.

Out of the corner of his eye, Jim saw movement beyond the Haltronics bunker at the end of the road. Dark humanoid forms moved in unison and Jim recognized the military precision. This group of eight was laden with weaponry and hardware.

Alarmed, Jim stood up abruptly, catching Will's attention. Will stood erect, gazing into Jim Orth's distant eyes.

Orth faced Will, moving his eyes sharply to the west, signaling of imminent danger.

Will's sudden movements alarmed Leo and Mitchell. "What's wrong Zac . . . I mean Will?" Mitchell asked.

"Jim has signaled that an enemy is inbound," Will said in a hushed tone.

"He said all that by just standing up?" Charles Hoyt asked, observing Jim's location about one hundred feet north of the party's position.

Will noticed Hoyt's presence but set the distraction aside to pick up further directions from Jim. "He and I go way back. I'm Will McKinley. You obviously know my dad and my son. What a small world this is."

"We've just met since the quake, and we've all arrived right here as if it were written in the wind to do so."

Hoyt wasn't sure if he should keep talking to Will. He didn't want to distract him from Jim but wanted to finish the reunion that started on the steps of his Oz home. Will drew Hoyt's attention, resembling Louis' physical character.

"There is something about you Will, which I can't quite put my finger on, like I know you somehow . . . like we are connected." Charles was thoroughly entranced by the nature of their meeting. He then turned to turned to look at the water column and the heaven above it.

Hoyt said expectantly: "If you three were destined for this meeting, as grandfather, father, and son, then why am I here? What do I have to do with this?" He hoped his questions would stir Will's curiosity.

Charles pulled out Louis' invention from his backpack. The box glowed brightly, warming Hoyt's knotted hands. He joined the group of men and Amy hunching in the grass.

"My son made this," Hoyt said to Will. Will took a moment to admire its beauty while keeping eye contact with Jim. Will was taken by the technical wizardry displayed by the device and its connection to the Oz House.

"Louis said that the knowledge to create this box came to him as proof of divine thought in the human mind. Through his goodwill and intention to make his world a better place the technology for the message this device contains became a reality."

"It was the reason why he was killed," Hoyt said sadly. Mitchell painfully recalled the memorial service he had walked into in Point Arena, just days earlier. He realized that Hoyt had not shared with him *how* Louis died.

"He was walking down Main Street with it in one hand and his cane in the other, smiling brightly. Holding the device brought him joy. One of the locals spied the images that appeared like apparitions around Louis' hand and got spooked. He tried to knock the box away but hit Louis instead, pushing him into the street. He was hit by a passing logging truck and killed."

They heard the wind filtered by knee high grass. Amy's eyes welled at the memory of Louis' fear-filled accidental death. She recalled her bedroom window's view of both Louis's bedroom window and the front door of Point Arena's post office where he was headed on that fateful day. Hoyt spoke again:

"He said that by holding it, anyone including the deaf and blind could experience a sensory journey through the Oz story. The story presents our individual journeys through life as we work through our unique trials and challenges by passing through the partition in our mind to find heaven in our hearts. God imagines the world and the world exists. He has imagined each of us and we exist. In living our lives, we travel through our infernos toward the light of heaven if we have the perseverance and imagination to see the Emerald City within."

The box then changed the shapes and faces of the Oz characters. Dorothy and her companions took on the appearances of Amy, Mitchell, Will, and Leo.

Hoyt continued talking to Will. "Louis told me that his soul was made of love, courage, intelligence, and home. Here I see the four of you, each representing these four parts of who he was. I believe Louis wanted us to remember our good human nature. He chose the Oz story to convey that at our best, we resemble one another. You are family and in the fictional Oz tale now come to life on this device. Is this the reason why I never left my Oz home? Have I lived there for over a century waiting for all of you? Am I the wizard? Am I a member of this family?" Hoyt referred to the group around him and the holograms moving effortlessly through his hands.

440

Will regarded the old man with kindness, looking thoughtfully at the device, then at the group. He turned his attention to Jim Orth. Using familiar eye and hand signals, Orth told Will to stay low in the grass. Behind the blown-out bunker stood eight enemy soldiers on foot, most likely headed into the bunker from the ocean side.

Hoyt asked Will: "Are we in danger?"

"Yes. All of you, keep your heads down and out of sight from any point along the perimeter of the bunkhouse."

Will looked into Hoyt's eyes. Charles spoke. "I feel like I am looking at Louis when I look at you." Hoyt stared into the matching sets of hazel eyes in the faces of Will and Leo.

"Wait . . . Louis?" Will responded to Hoyt's statement, still paying attention to Orth's urgent signals, but confused by Hoyt's story of his son.

"My son Louis, he invented this . . . box . . . book . . . device. We never knew what to call it."

"Your son's name is Louis, and you say he was deaf and blind?" Will asked.

Everyone focused on Will's face countenance. They watched Will's skill in reading his commander's body language and hand signals and for what he was about to learn about his ancestry.

"Yes," Hoyt said.

"Did you adopt Louis?" Will asked.

"Yes."

"From Jacksonville, Mississippi, at the end of World War II?"

Hoyt nodded touching Will's face with his knotted hands. "He was injured, losing his sight and hearing during the London Blitz. He was orphaned in a subsequent bombing that same year. You are his legacy, his descendants, his faith, his knowledge that his love would change the world for the better."

Will's eyes began to water, as horror contrasted beauty in a short, fifteen-second conversation.

"How is this even possible?" Will asked, unable to control himself.

Leo and Hoyt moved within arms' length of Will, ready to steady their soldier if needed.

Red stirred. She lay upon her Mitchell's warmth, finding him intact, still able to recognize her through her changing form, from woman-wife to spirit filled being. Her love and her longing washed away her lingering shock and quieted the ceaseless ring of her death knell. She could see his love for her in his eyes. She understood fully that Mitchell was going to be with her always and that her life was not a waste. She loved him and he her, come what may.

Mitchell turned to Red when Hoyt asked his question, communicating to her that whatever was about to be revealed when the question was answered, was going to concern them, and their life together in the woods south of Prescott, Arizona—that they should brace themselves, as Will was about to speak.

FORTY-NINE

———

"Life is difficult."

No truer words have been written. We address this by staying true to our human purpose and recognizing that the path forward is through enduring struggles. We understand what has broken our hearts, and those experiences should restore our faith in life. The essence of humanity lies in embracing simple truths. Although heartbreak persists, we can choose to lessen its impact.

Historically, we've often failed to understand our darker instincts. This has led to a metaphorical 'night of technological barbarism.' We must recognize and resist technology's overwhelming influence on our souls.

Our narrative serves to warn and guide us away from relying on freewill in excess. Instead, we should embrace goodwill and sacrifice for the well-being of others. It's time to reclaim our humanity and reject a future devoid of depth. Let traditional values guide us, allowing us to appreciate life's small joys, boundless as love.

This understanding should lead our actions for the greater good, maintaining our place within the vibrant world we inhabit. Our foundations must be grounded in tried-and-true principles, shaped by experience, so we remember who we are.

Let's remember that our soul's greatest strength is endurance. Our commitment to goodwill was meant to foster abundance and generosity. Are you truly abundant and charitable? I know I fall short.

My faith wavers, even though I've seen life as it truly is—relying on the kindness of others and experiencing the hardship of living day-to-day. Yet, I recognize the spirit's value in such a life—one of great faith in God and the nurturing power of Mother Nature to grow and thrive.

M.W. Kinney Road.

———————

Amy urgent to whisper into his ear tugged at Hoyt, diverting his attention from his grandson's face.

"Show Will the email my mother printed the day before the quake." Amy reached into her back pocket and pulled it out, giving it to Hoyt.

"Will, I know this is a lot to digest. I'm still trying to understand what it all means but you must look at this. We know who the enemy is that your friend has alerted you to."

Will opened the document slowly and was perplexed by seeing a picture of his son.

"Haltronics?" Will asked Leo. "You work for Haltronics?"

"I did. I quit about a week before the quake."

"Why is this John Jespa looking for you?"

Leo looked at his father. His face revealed shame and pride as Leo remembered the regretful meetings with Sheila under a virtual bridge and the lengthy algorithms he had developed to further Jespa's agenda for world dominion through the Internet. Developing code was his life and source for seeking approval from his boss and Sheila. He shook his head slowly from side to side, reflecting on hard life lessons.

"I know what he needs to restore order to his quake-devastated Internet empire. I know the code. It's in here." Leo pointed to his temple.

"You mean, without you he can't reboot the network?" Will asked.

"That's it in a nutshell, Dad."

"And you have seen him here? You think he's part of the mercenary group at that washed-out bunkhouse?"

"We know he is there. We've seen him in the rocky tide pools off the lighthouse. He was shipwrecked. We tried to help him but he literally disappeared," Leo said. "He is up to no good. I know that man. He is evil personified. And he stalks me. He hunts me."

At that instant, gunfire whistled over their heads, hitting nearby cypress. Will pushed everyone to the ground, pulling out his sidearm.

"All of you need to follow me to the SUV. We need to crawl on the ground. Let's go."

447

Everyone fell in line behind Will. They moved over the grass on their bellies, propelled by adrenalin, elbows, and feet, toward Jim Orth who was crouched behind the SUV preparing a stash of weapons.

Bullets continued to whistle over their heads. Amy started to cry but still pushed herself along. "Why is he shooting at us, Leo? If you're dead, what does he gain?"

"He's trying to scare us, Amy." Leo stopped for a moment to look at Amy behind him. Her eyes and cheeks were wet with tears. He reached down for Amy and pulled her close to him, hugging her, whispering a promise to not let anything happen to her, into her ear. She clung to him, feeling her heart grow for this wonderful, strange man-child.

Will reached the edge of Kinney Road, where their grass cover abruptly ended. He and Orth signaled a plan to get everyone across the road and safely behind the SUV.

"Okay, Jim and I will provide cover. One at a time, I want you to sprint over to the SUV. "On my cue . . .""

"Wait," Mitchell said. "Let me run with Hoyt. We will be faster if we run together." Mitchell met Will's eyes. Will remembered standing in front of Mitchell as a confused kid on the lawns of the Prescott County Courthouse. Will remembered Mitchell seeing good in him and how Mitchell protected him from the town's vile gossip after Mitchell's murder trial. *Now he wants to protect the old man,* Will thought.

"Okay, on my signal Jim and I will provide cover while you two get across. Ready? Go!"

Machine gun fire erupted from the SUV, pelting openings in the bunkhouse's east-facing wall. It was effective enough to get Hoyt and Mitchell across safely.

Jim turned to Will and saw him make the same deal with Leo as he had with Mitchell—to run with Amy, flanking her from any incoming fire. Will knew the moment well; quick decision carried dire consequences. He had just reunited with his son and the risk of losing him again sharpened his determination to get him and Amy across the road in one piece.

"On my mark, run like hell, and dive behind the SUV . . . got it?"

Will studied the man before him—no longer an inwardly possessed boy, but someone brave fully formed. He noticed the growing affection in the girl's eyes for his son. Their physical ages differed, but their spirits and minds aligned. In Will's eyes they were made for one another.

Will stood, drawing fire. Jim followed immediately. Amy and Leo lunged onto the road. They too drew fire. Bullets skipped off the blacktop, buzzed overhead, and tore into fence posts and blackberry brambles.

Then Leo's lead foot snapped sideways. Will watched in horror – Leo was hit. He cried out and crashed hard onto the blacktop, a shot tearing through the base of his leg. Amy dropped on top of him, shielding Leo and screaming for Will.

Hoyt and Mitchell took aim and fired. Jim and Will rushed forward, dragging Leo off the exposed stretch of Kinney Road. Jim pulled Amy away and pushed her toward the SUV, then grabbed Leo's collar. Will lifted Leo's legs, and together they hauled him to cover.

Behind the SUV, Will worked fast, wrapping cotton cloth under Leo's knee. The bullet passed through the calf, missing bone. *He's going to be okay.* Will turned to face the enemy's brazen assault on his newfound family.

For the moment, everyone was safe behind the SUV. Will and Jim spoke quietly, mapping their next move. Jim turned toward the bunkhouse, its position set against a column of water and a sky filled with heavenly bodies.

Jim nodded – all clear.

Will broke north of the SUV toward a stretch of redwood drift laid out by the park service to block vehicles from entering the protected wilderness around Manchester State Park. From there, he traced a route along a line of cypress trees stretching from the camp host site to the dunes that ran the coastline from Point Arena Lighthouse to Irish Beach five miles north. The thick overgrowth offered excellent cover. Wind-twisted branches and knotted trunks would conceal toward the bunkhouses northern side.

450

Will signaled his intent to advance. Earlier, they had agreed – he would strike from the bunkhouse's blind side. Laden with guns and grenades, he slipped into the latticed shade, thinking about his dad and Red.

∞

The shadows and light of ancient cypress trees pressed in around him. Light and dark – good and evil – mirrored the forces he had carried since Mitchell entered his life. Memories of his uncle's cruelty flickered against memories of the love Mitchell had shared with Red. For years, Will believed he would inherit his uncle's darkness – that he would harm others and take pleasure in it. As details of his uncle's terror on a woman living in a cabin south of Prescott, Arizona, were revealed, the notion of sharing familial blood filled him with dread. He tested himself in small cruelties – tormenting widows from a nearby convalescent home: throwing garbage, mocking their age, their canes, their missing teeth, their loneliness.

One day, Mitchell Walker saw Will at work. Mitchell charged. Will and his lout friends scattered off the courthouse lawns into an alley, never again daring such public behavior again.

Will remembered the last time Mitchell approached him as a stranger. – and how that meeting turned. Mitchell offered him a home, a place to be accountable, a place to become a man.

Mitchell always claimed that his spirit wife had planted the idea during his murder trial. She had visited him then, bringing peace as lawyers laid out their cases.

Will remembered the day Red finally departed. He and Mitchell had been passing time at the waterhole when she appeared on the Hassayampa River, drifting toward him. The current carried her close.

She spoke of release, of letting go of pain, of losing her life. The flowing river carried those burdens away. She rejoiced that Mitchell could still know her, even as a transparent spirit.

Then the current pulled her past him. Joy turned to fear. She fought to return, to reach the riverbank, but the current held her. As it swept her away, she told Mitchell she did not wabt to go. Mitchell saw her struggle. Her desire to stay become the blood in his beathing heart.

Their eyes locked. Their hands reached across a widening void. The river pulled her into another world, tearing husband from wife.

In the months that followed Mitchell's darkness deepened. His premonition proved true: Red had not gone on. After Will began his military career, Mitchell sold everything and set out on foot across North America, searching for her.

That day never left Will. Now, he too could see her. *How odd it was, yet how wonderful, for Mitchell to have found her after twenty-five years of searching. How unusual for this peculiar family to reunite in such beautiful and strange circumstances,* he thought.

Will felt grateful that his uncle's evil had not taken root in him. Mitchell's influence, his life south of Prescott, had changed that path.

Will rounded the last cypress. From between two knotted branches, he studied the bunkhouse's northeast corner. Voices leaked through broken windows and cracks in the structure.

He sprinted forward, dropping beneath a shattered sill to listen.

Someone inside, likely the leader, hissed orders. Faint blue flashes pulsed within. Repairs perhaps.

Will pulled a small mirror from his belt, wedged it into a twig, and raised it just above the sill. He angled it carefully and looked inside.

What he saw shocked him.

I have had too many moments that travel off the scale of beautiful. Endlessly exquisite were the days I spent with you. This life was so richly colored and scented, backdropped by your song, matching the greatness of God's angels in earthly form. All are found in the loveliness, the tenderness, the perfection in memory that is you, from my youngest yearnings as a boy to my hard-won and honest assessments of what constitutes living as a man. I constantly question the fates: how was it that I was the one chosen by such a divine figure as you?

I know now, it was not I who lived on. Your generosity moved outward from its center as goodwill intends. I see now that freewill thwarted my place in the universe and has kept me from perceiving your presence in the sand before me. The light of goodwill is in you, my Red, as the heart of God.

FIFTY

————

Fate's Beautiful Necessity

*A perfectly formed spider web spanned the view of my upstairs
bedroom window. It was nearly three feet in diameter, hidden
from daylight but seen well with the soft shade of a table lamp at
dusk. Beautiful to behold, this magnificent creation represents
flawless artwork and a symbolic sign of caution and danger. The
web's maker hung veiled in plain sight at the center of its net full
in body, striking in its grey and black veneer. I leaned forward
into the glass pane that separated my skin from its bite. I
examined the spider while it examined me. It moved two steps to
the left then four to the right, assuming postures its nature
intended, affecting the web's design as it swayed in the bedroom
window. All this played out in my mind's eye, as I perceived both
sides of fate—control and chaos—as a glass pane.*

*What do I on one side of fate and a spider on the other do with
the time we are given? Are we the unwieldy monsters of fate to
which Emerson so often refers? Does fate follow defined action?
Shall I follow the spider's example and spin a like web that I
might survive this harsh world? Shall the spider follow me and
ruthlessly suspect the world of monstrous self-serving works? The
fly? The pine needle? All suspect?*

*'The book of nature is the book of fate. She turns the gigantic
pages leaf after leaf, never returning one. Fate is built upon*

experience. One cannot exist without the other. What we know is what we see, hear, taste, smell, and remember. Such memories last lifetimes. Such memories become our freewill. We, like the spider, commit our nature to confine our movements within the three feet of silk we have claimed as our own. We create our mental and spiritual mindsets that in no time possess us upon a shelf containing large mason jars that hold the various muds that make up the character of the species man.

Fate spoons from each jar randomly ordered recipes, and from those concoctions come the chaos of man, heated by freewill.

———

Will pressed his fingers to his eyes and rubbed, exhaustion pressing in. Smoke poured from the mouth of a fallen mercenary and gathered itself into an apparition – formless in color, with charcoal-dark, shadowed eyes that radiated wrath At what, Will could not discern.

The apparition whipped through the bunkhouse, hissing as it moved from shattered computer terminals to the doorway cracked by the quake. It peered outside. Whatever it saw enraged it further.

But Will sensed more – hunger, and lust.

He understood.

The demon wanted Leo.

The apparition turned and looked directly into Will's mirror.

Will met its gaze. It had seen him.

Cold flooded his blood. He dropped the mirror into his belt and stilled himself, waiting for instinct to guide him.

458

A chill rolled over his head. Goosebumps climbed his neck. He lifted his hand and felt a cold mass spilling from the window above him.

He looked up.

Two malicious eyes locked onto him.

Lips formed from vapor hissed something vile—something he felt more than heard.

Fear rose, but Will cut through it. He saw the thing for what it was: temporary, constructed, raging, obsessed with control.

He smiled.

Will remembered the hunger in the apparition as it stared outside. A deeper fear followed—one born not of battle, but of fatherhood. He thought of Leo... of what Leo had said about his Haltronics boss.

Sheila.

The entity faltered, confused by Will's lack of fear. It ricocheted wildly, striking unseen barriers like a deflating balloon.

Will didn't wait.

He sprinted, full speed, back to the cypress tree where he had taken cover earlier. He tore across dried grass and low dunes, putting distance between himself and the bunkhouse before sliding behind the trunk.

He turned toward the cul-de-sac at the end of Kinney Road.

Voices.

Leo. Amy.

Will's stomach dropped.

Leo stood in the center of the dead end, shouting at a security camera fixed atop a fence post. Amy leapt onto his back, dragging him down. Both cried out.

Blood soaked Leo's pant leg.

Inside, Sheila refocused, locking onto Leo and Amy's voices. It suppressed its rage just long enough to move, slipping through the same window Will had used, vanishing into the bunkhouse.

Will watched it move toward them.

Resolve ignited.

His body changed.

Sound vanished. Touch disappeared. Breath stilled. His mouth narrowed. His vision sharpened, his balance, his direction, his awareness of every limb in space. Proprioception surged.

Time stretched.

Seconds slowed into minutes. Each moment unfolded like a storyboard. Details revealed deeper details.

This was where instinct lived.

Through that slowed time, Will's vision passed through a perfect spider web—symmetrical, umbrella-wide. The strands caught the light and magnified everything beyond.

Leo stared toward the bunkhouse entrance.

The web revealed more.

The specter's hunger still lingered, growing.

Will recognized it.

He had faced this before—in battle, in fire, in the collapse of worlds.

Pure evil.

And now it would fall on his son.

Within that stretched second, Will remembered being a boy—standing face-to-face with a spider suspended before him. Young Zac stared into its eyes. They adjusted their distance from one another, each sensing threat.

Those same eyes now stared at Leo.

Will stepped from cover.

He fired.

Bullets tore into the cracks around the bunkhouse entrance—each shot true. Metal sparked. Rounds ricocheted inside, shredding what remained of the structure.

Leo climbed.

He grabbed the chain-link fence and pulled himself upward, moving on all fours toward the camera and the razor wire above.

Amy clung to him—begging, pleading, anchoring him—trying to pull him back from whatever held him.

Will fired again—harder, faster—searching for any weapon aimed at Leo.

Then he ran.

He pushed toward the line of refuse containers near the entrance, drawn by Amy's voice.

The others joined him—armed, ready.

From behind the bins, Sheila appeared hovering above Leo.

"I see you've come back to me… my prized Leo," it hissed.

"Do you have what I need? Will you return what belongs to me—your thoughts… your desires?"

Sheila saw it in Leo's eyes.

The pulse.

The dash.

Connection.

Control.

Leo was hers again.

The four men unleashed everything they had.

Gunfire. Force. Precision.

Nothing touched it.

Sheila stood beyond it all – untouched by bullets, immune to courage, untethered from the physical world.

Binary.

Unbound.

They could only watch.

Leo moved closer.

Closer.

Closer, toward the evil reaching for his soul.

From Mitchell's journal to Red:

I have rested here on this side road for years.

Upon a chair, next to a side table, with wind intimately echoing through the ancient cypress, with white caps in relentless pursuit of the shore, I have placed my senses to the moments. And they unfold.

For here, as I mingle the resonance of your song with our friend's piano and toss into the mix a thought or two from Ralph Waldo Emerson, I know I am inside this moment of living. I am within the craft of God's hand.

Here under the intense light of the sun, I know a moment of peace. Here I gather each note as they turn from creation to blessing and I pen a thought or two of my own, no greater than the notion of a raven choosing a motionless glide, suspended in air, content to be the wind passing through it.

Here is a space where I know life as it is: perfection. Found on a chair, next to a side table, blessed by the timbre of your voice, and our friend playing his piano.

FIFTY-ONE

———

A simple human existence is not enough for the techno-industrial pundits. They state the Earth is no longer able to sustain us on any plane of existence. As humans, we must put our evolution in their hands.

Their electronic products and futuristic services from engineered food stuffs to colonizing of the moon and Mars are our only viable options for the future of humankind.

Their propaganda is insulting.

The new money pundits live on the same planet as the rest of us; a super-heated, twirling

ball of gas and fire covered by a thin skin of dirt and water. It's like the

Earth never existed before these narcissistic asses were born. Geologic history clearly shows the Earth repeatedly cleansing itself for a fresh start.

"Trust me money pundits, you are gluttonous dinosaurs and you are not going to realize your iEarth ambitions. Humanity will not migrate from its short, stunning, tragic, and glorious existence to a nonhuman presence on a computer chip, just to proxy votes for further designs in profit centers on Mars colonies. Is there anywhere in your new frozen world of code, your flattened existence for sacrifice? For hardship, fundamental building blocks of the soul?"

Money pundits want you to view these necessary steps to evolution and character as unimportant. They want you to purchase their insulation, their insurance and live a chance and fate-free life. Organized and timed down to the second, they want you to taste your next pizza through their block of binary code and make love to your new virtual fling on the ultra-brilliant and money pundit monitored flat screen. Does 'flat screen' monitor scream at you? At all?

If you could see this uniquely beautiful blue green ball from low Earth orbit you might find that the only thing that matters is not what you say or do, that you succeed or fail.

It matters only that you love and are loved in return.

————————

Desperation shown in the faces of the group, each one counting the seconds, drawn by their love for the boy who could now reach out and touch the misty, maniacal presence of Sheila.

Leo's Sheila had given him so much of herself, feeding his aspirations as a coder for the dominant tech firm in the world. He believed that she loved him, changed him, respected him, giving him everything that a woman could.

Sheila registered the admiring eyes and longing beaming from Leo, as he hung desperately to the top of the chain-link fence, wanting Sheila to touch him. Sheila could tell he was still beautiful to Leo. Leo's eyes told him that he still saw Sheila as a hungry, beautiful, lustful woman who would give anything to him, if he could share his life and his work with her.

In a deepening trance, Leo began to recite to Sheila the code she wanted from deeper recesses of his mind, the code that would enable Haltronics utilities to patch and repair its broken infrastructure. Sheila signaled one of his men to record and capture what Leo was reciting.

～✧

A mercenary appeared at the crack in the bunkhouse entrance, placing a recorder near Leo. Will took aim and blew up the mercenary's arm and the recording device.

Sheila's concentration on Leo's pulsing eyes wavered. Leo nervously looked around at a loss as to why he hung to the top of the fence, his palms and fingers bleeding. Sheila, enraged by this so-called *father* of Leo, rushed for the group of four men who had taken cover behind the refuse containers.

Will charged out into the cul-de-sac to meet Sheila. It was time to do something he should have done while hunkered under the windowsill ten minutes earlier. He unleashed his weapons on Sheila, to break her focus on Leo.

It worked. Sheila's rage intensified as he focused on Will. Mitchell signaled for Amy to get Leo down off the fence and move him to safer ground.

Gunfire erupted from the bunkhouse. In slow-motion, Will saw the bullets racing for his chest and legs. He had only an instant to view the boy he loved. And he did. He beheld his son, and at that gracious moment between knowing life is going to end and the end arriving, Will felt the intense pureness of a father's love for his son.

Will fell to his knees. Blood and love poured from him. Leo saw his father fall. He released his grip of the fence, falling helplessly to the ground, his own hands bloodied by razor wire. With Amy's aid, Leo rushed to his dad, covering him with his body, grasping Will's red hands with his own.

Will's breath was labored. Charles, Jim, and Mitchell continued to fire upon the bunkhouse, simultaneously moving over to the red reunion on the blacktop, providing cover for the wounded man, his boy, and the girl who loved him. In a second, the group moved behind the giant steel refuse containers, protected.

It was evident to everyone that Will was gone. His body convulsed. Leo pleaded for the blood on their hands to move back into his dad's heart, for his father to please stay with him at the end of Kinney Road. Amy cried, holding Leo's head in her hands. Mitchell remembered past bloodshed with sadness. Jim Orth put his hand on Will's heart and said a warrior's prayer to the three-part heaven above, asking for the miracle he knew Will deserved. Charles' gaze held a vision of Aqurar, standing tall on the green Earth in harmony with the nature of the world.

Will's last breath shuddered through his body. Each inhaled a portion of life leaving their friend. That breath created a vision of a single last soldier, alive but defeated, on his knees, accepting a fate he knew would come but never fully understood.

There was another above the group who also inhaled the life of Will McKinley. It was Red. The presence of a human breath within startled her. Will's dying breath triggered waves of memory and emotion. She remembered the child she once was, the child she conceived, and how a murderous, evil death found both. A single psychopath, related to each person below her had shattered them all.

This same terrible providence and grief had brought them together to face one last evil turning time forward, beyond the avarice and freewill of the age to the sweetness of breath and the precious senses of the soul.

Red remembered her baby girl, kidnapped and killed by the same man who eventually did her in. *Sian.* With that single thought, Red's young spirit child joined the vision of the broken souls below. Red could feel her child share her sight, her sense of right and wrong, and a life of love and joy with a husband who loved her but found her too late. Too late to serve the premonition, too late to save her life.

Red saw the evil in Sheila, who danced a celebration of death around Leo's father, filled with the wicked bliss only the truly demented knew.

Filled with blood lust and avarice for pain, Sheila started to regain his living form, first bone, then skin began to wrap around her essence. She brought her hands up to her forming face, not believing that she would return to her previous existence. By a thin thread, her body was functioning enough to register the incredible pain that she should have felt on that morning, two days past, when the Pacific Ocean opened and shredded John Jespa to pieces.

In sudden and complete righteous rage, Red became those razor-sharp joints of justice. She slammed the fully formed John Jespa hard against the steel refuse containers, knocking one over, holding Jespa down while she waited for her next signal from the Mother Nature and Heaven.

It came. The San Andreas Fault roared to life again, opening a crack in the earth that ran the length of Manchester State Park Beach from the Alder Creek inlet to the Point Arena Lighthouse. It swallowed portions of the bunkhouse and the remaining mercenaries.

A crevice opened under Jespa's head and he slipped into the abyss. Weak beyond measure, he looked up at the strange and beautiful spirit holding him in place, her long red hair flowing in the ocean breeze. She seemed luminescent. Massively bright and golden yellow, a pair of angel's wings spread behind her in a wide arc, blinding Jespa and the others. They did not comprehend that Red had moved from her earth-bound journey into an immortal life. Mother Nature had summoned the eternal Aqurar to bring Red into her new existence and to address the disturbing evil presence at the end of Kinney Road.

Wings and all, Red fell with Jespa into the opening black earth, gushing with ocean water, smothering anything that the gaping ground took with it. Initially, Red pushed John Jespa, but then she no longer had to. Sheila was pulled, falling away from Red's reach. Red understood that Jespa was slipping into the court of *time*, an immediate and swift serving of justice, known simply in the world of math, as an equal and opposite reaction to his wicked life. Jespa, and his world of fiber optics and satellite impulses was absorbed into the rushing advance of time and space. He spun into it and Red thought his spinning would never stop.

She found her way back to the breathless, disoriented group, lamenting their loss of son and comrade, suffering under the roll of a second intense earthquake.

Leo stood, tears engulfing his face and falling forward into Amy's hair. Each member of the Talisman group looked at one another, feeling their collective grief over Will's passing.

A collective of angels appeared at their sides, who they knew but did not immediately recognize. Standing beside them they saw: Peter Shroud, Santaesh Parnoon, and Abe Mahud, messengers of goodwill, come to ease their pain by absorbing their tears.

Leo faced the crevice and remnants of the Haltronics bunker and eyed the strangest of sights: one computer terminal remained behind. Somehow, a portion of the bunkhouse, sufficient to hold one terminal was standing on the sand near the edge of the filled, miles-long, earthquake gap.

It glowed. Waves of blue light moved through it – a last surviving Jespa-created terminal, containing within it his latest hardware and software technology. *St. Elmo's Fire* Leo thought, as he walked over to the terminal, against the advice and protests of his fellow Talisman members.

Upon first inspection, Leo determined that the terminal, unconnected to any cables, communications or power lines, was functioning.

Leo put his palm and fingers on the terminal's visual screen. Instantly, the machine read it and identified: *Brenamann, Leo*, flashed in bright neon red. A stern warning from John Jespa appeared stating that any employee knowing the whereabouts of his coder and withholding this information would be detained by company security.

Leo looked around at the contrast of this last desperate breath of Haltronics Corp, this lone terminal, pulsing electronic breath and blue-white light, representing an empire sinking,

472

trapped in quicksand. Did the terminal recognize its impending demise? Leo believed it did, positing that the terminal easily identified him because an aspect of John Jespa had transitioned into the static existence of the singularity. Leo considered that a duplicated version of Jespa resided within this machine.

At that moment, Sheila's synthetic yet appealing visage appeared before Leo, presenting a smile. He required input, needing code to function within his silicone and graphene hard drive.

With swift, mesmerizing precision, Leo filled Sheila's crystalline features with line after line of code, drawing the gathered onlookers into the spectacle. In his mind, he recalled a special Tinker Toy contraption he had built on the carpet of his childhood bedroom. The model had rolled forward on its own, gradually expanding its orbit until halted by a door or bedpost. At the Oz House table just nights ago, he had called this the "return code" – a formula designed to reverse the forward momentum of the Internet, silencing the voices of evil, greed, and every form of predatory advance. It aimed to restore the universe to a state where only paradox, imagination, spirit, time, and the awe-inspiring cycles of suns and stars existed. To comprehend how the universe's momentum expands was one thing; to claim ownership of it was another entirely. Such vast power belonged solely to God. To think otherwise – to even attempt such control – was perversion of freewill, sinking into its lowest depths. In that moment, Leo knew the truth: the Garden's experiment had failed.

Sheila understood what Leo typed across the features of her virtual face. His eyes followed the cursor from behind the screen until it traveled across Leo's expression. Sheila's despair became apparent to Leo when Sheila no longer saw a cursor in Leo's irises, just its pulse on the screen flashing an instant ahead of Leo's thought processes reflected in the computer's coding dialogue box.

Sheila realized that Leo had just stopped the forward motion of code vital for an ever-expanding Internet world, and he cowered at the courage Leo showed in doing so. However, Leo's next act was the truly terrifying one: his hand had slowly moved off the terminal's keyboard. It disappeared over the side, out of view of the screen. Sheila's eyes flashed from Leo's cursor-less gaze to the unseen hand, then back to Leo's face. Suddenly Sheila screamed as he realized what Leo was about to do. Sheila's appearance and survival were being shredded, piece by piece, like a bladed pendulum swinging ever closer to blood and skin and life, sinking in one millimeter at a time, swishing and swiping through Sheila's virtual world.

With one last glimpse into the world where Leo and the Talisman group stood, Sheila saw the wrist and arm muscles of Leo's left-hand twitch. Sheila thought he heard the tipping of a switch, accompanied by a microsecond of horror, followed by nothingness. Sheila was gone.

The Talisman group lunged at the computer terminal and with great effort pushed it into the ocean-filled abyss. They

474

watched it sink down into the water, until blackness and distance made the block of metal come to a point, then disappear.

Mitchell and Red, sodales anima, sat in the embrace of
a new dawn fire, warmth radiating from their hearts
and minds, already gazing into their shared future –
an everyday life rooted in the gentle reign of nature's
laws, the sacred rhythm of seasons, currents, wind,
rain, and the sun in silence upon their faces.

In their hands lays Louis' creation, alive with
vibrations and hums of luminous colors – an opening
door to the Emerald City, slowly unfolding before
them. The scene ascended along Kinney Road, now
paved with golden bricks, stretching over fields of
grain and oceans vast, spiraling upward toward a
newly born heaven – an incarnate heaven mad visible,
a place where the collective spirit of man joins with
the multi-faceted, multi-dimensional Spirit of the
universe, all held in harmony by the forces of wind,
fire, earth and water.

The exchanged knowing glances, passing Louis'
wondrous device to Leo and Amy, their hand entwined
in silent strength. Their faces met, still, in the glow of
eternal stars above – an unspoken vow, shared in the
quiet language of the soul:

For eternity, come what may.

Epilogue: From Will McKinley's interment service in Manchester, California:

Loki was my friend, a soldier of a time untouched, fighting battles beyond the reach of his era's grasp. A heart out of sync with the age he walked, yet one blessed with the gift of lifting souls, transporting them to planes of hope and joy, where light and love cast shadows of doubt away. His courage, a hymn of nobler dreams, inspiring us to glimpse a better way of being. Within his mystical skill lay a door, an entrance to heaven's quiet voice, a promise that the great stories of eternity were within reach, plausible in deed and dream. He led each of us, silent, steady, through our partitions that fear constructs, across our private gates, our own golden thresholds, to the roots of life, to what it means to truly live, a journey carved from the courage and love he bore, a beacon in the darkness, still shining bright.

-General James Orth

———

THE END

Afterword

Woven through Mitchell's path are the lives of others—some broken, some searching, some lost to forces they barely understand: a young man consumed by the digital world he helped create. A mother and daughter standing at the edge of change. Voices from beyond the visible world that remind us of something older, deeper, and more enduring than the systems we have built. These lives intersect not by coincidence, but by a kind of gravity the novel suggests is always at work: destiny shaped not by spectacle, but by choice, by hardship, and by the quiet courage to continue.

Kinney Road is also a meditation on the tension between two worlds—the natural and the constructed. It asks what we have traded for speed, convenience, and control, and whether the cost has been our connection to one another, to the earth, and to ourselves. In its most powerful moments, the novel reminds us that nature does not argue or persuade; it simply endures, waiting for us to return.

Kinney Road character map:

```
Aqurar
    └─ protects the sacred cave beneath the
                        Hoyt/Oz House

Scott Hoyt + Ava
    ├─ Murella Hoyt
    └─ Charles Hoyt + Mary
            └─ adopt John Doe No. 24, naming him
                            Louis Hoyt
                └─ Louis + Lois
                    └─ Leo's maternal family
                            line
                        └─ Leo Brenamann

Mitchell Walker
    └─ adopts Zac Walker
            └─ Zac becomes Will McKinley / Loki
                └─ father of Leo Brenamann

Nathan Rinton + Linda Rinton
    └─ Amy Rinton
            └─ becomes keeper of Louis' book and
                            partner to Leo

The Talisman Group:
    Mitchell, Charles, Leo, Amy, Rosalie, Gunnar,
                        and Poama

The Threat:
    Haltronics → John Jespa → Sheila → mercenaries
                        / digital control
```

Acknowledgements:

Mary Lynn Preiss
Christina Wernette
Sam Parsons
Lily McFarland
Laura Jane Dallison

Special thanks:

Julia Allen

If this story moved you, please consider leaving a review and
search Amazon.com for more
Thomas Preiss books:

<u>*Children's stories:*</u>
The Boat Under the Boat
The Other Side of the Window

<u>*Pictorial Essay:*</u>
Everything Comes and Goes

<u>*Novel:*</u>
The Hassayampa King

<u>*Reflective workbooks on grief and gratitude:*</u>

One Bow — An After-Ever Gratitude Journey — For Monday's Compass
Part of **The Bow Series**

ABOUT THE AUTHOR

Thomas Preiss is a cyclist, writer, and student of endurance, gratitude, and the open road. His work often explores grief, resilience, nature, and the unseen forces that shape human lives. He writes with a deep appreciation for landscape, memory, and the courage required to begin again.

ABOUT YOU

You have read this book for a reason. Perhaps it is time for you to take your own walk, to write your epigraphs based on analog experience. Perhaps it is time for you to go and do. Your intent will be found there and then.